An Irish Solution

Cormac Millar lives in Dublin, where, as Cormac
Ó Cuilleanáin, he teaches Italian at Trinity College.

An Irish Solution

CORMAC MILLAR

PENGUIN
IRELAND

PENGUIN IRELAND

Published by the Penguin Group
Penguin Ireland Ltd, 25 St Stephen's Green, Dublin 2, Ireland
Penguin Books Ltd, 80 Strand, London WC2R ORL, England
Penguin Putnam Inc., 375 Hudson Street, New York, New York 10014, USA
Penguin Books Australia Ltd, 250 Camberwell Road, Camberwell, Victoria 3124, Australia
Penguin Books Canada Ltd, 10 Alcorn Avenue, Toronto, Ontario, Canada M4V 3B2
Penguin Books India (P) Ltd, 11 Community Centre, Panchsheel Park, New Delhi – 110 017, India
Penguin Books (NZ) Ltd, Cnr Rosedale and Airborne Roads, Albany, Auckland, New Zealand
Penguin Books (South Africa) (Pty) Ltd, 24 Sturdee Avenue, Rosebank 2196, South Africa

Penguin Books Ltd, Registered Offices: 80 Strand, London WC2R ORL, England

www.penguin.com

First published 2004
1

Set in 13.5/16 pt PostScript Monotype Garamond
Typeset by Rowland Phototypesetting Ltd, Bury St Edmunds, Suffolk
Printed in Great Britain by Clays Ltd, St Ives plc

A CIP catalogue record for this book is available from the British Library

ISBN 1–844–88025–7

In memory of Arthur Lockett

The house goes quiet. Leo sprints up the staircase.

Traffic echoes from the street. Sirens weep in the distance.

'Billy?'

Nothing.

'Billy-boy?'

Faint scraping from the room. A pigeon at a chimney breast?

Leo nudges the door with his left hand. Grey light from a tall window. The child, hiding behind a broken chair. Slouched against the wall, the remains of Fozzy Maher. Red sprays the wall like autumn fern.

'You there? Billy?'

'I not Billy,' whispers the child.

'I know that.' Leo tries to smile.

Fozzy's father, felled like a tree.

The front room still in darkness.

'Billy-boy?'

Leo peers into the gloom, takes one step.

'Billy?'

Hearing the slightest of sounds, he stops, turns, trips into a wilderness of light.

An Irish Solution

Part One

Five minutes to midnight, and Gloria was there at last, sitting at a table on her own. Paul Blake, *patron* of Blackwood's, slipped into the holy of holies to apply a spot of L'Occitane to the chops, only to find the Robin ensconced at the table, fugging the air with cigarillos.

'Robin!' Blake beamed. 'A thousand pardons. We've been absolutely! Let me fix you! Burgundy? Snack?'

The Robin cleared his throat: 'You told Pat he was gone.' Eyes opaque, his voice filtered through what sounded like a permanent head-cold.

Blake chuckled: 'Pat exaggerates, as usual. Heat of the moment, I assure you.'

'Cause he's not.'

'Of course not! Worth his weight. Absolutely! Top-notch. A bar manager in a million. My sole concern remains that he should not bring the club into disrepute. And our new décor?'

The private suite had been lined with dark-green striped wallpaper, chosen by Blake to set off his new collection of Victorian caricatures. A mirror, leaning at an angle against the wall, reflected the two men: Blake broad and courtly; his interlocutor rat-like, skinny. Blake smoothed his auburn forelocks. And yet, he was not as he had been. Failing eyesight, for one thing. The tragedy of creeping decline.

Behind him, the Robin persisted: 'You bawled Pat out in front of the guests.'

'He was indulging in an inappropriate relationship with a cheap tart. Peroxide to the gills. In my bedroom.'

'Not your room.' The Robin was seriously vexed.

'In which I reside, since my eviction by –'

'Not your gaff,' the Robin said. 'And you don't talk that way to Pat. Pat doesn't work for you.'

'Not for me, for Blackwood's. Forgive me for being proprietorial. Others may own the physical accoutrements, but the name is mine, the ambience, the look and feel. To say nothing of my bearing the costs of dry rot treatment, following the evaporation of my partners.'

'If Pat hadn't of brung me in, you were gone.'

A diffident knock and Pat O'Hara himself scuttled in, grinning. Sandy-haired, wiry, head hunched as if to ward off well-deserved blows, Pat was the humanoid equivalent of a crab. 'Sorry, gents, but one of them bankers wants a word.'

Blake checked himself once more before the mirror and sallied forth. Gloria was dressed in silver and gold. Smooth men in dark suits encircled her at the bar. She was the only worthwhile legacy of Blake's absconding American bankers. A blonde Californian financial consultant, recently widowed, elegant in her sorrow, she braved an evening or two in Blackwood's every week. She spoke to everyone in exactly the same low sympathetic voice, surveying them with her astonishing almond-shaped eyes. Blake himself aspired to her in a gentlemanly way, but although she hung on his words she was not yet ready for commitment.

Gloria introduced bankers and business moguls to the club. She also handled some nifty offshore investments for selected acquaintances, with returns so high you could even afford to pay the tax, if that was your idea of fun. Had even recovered money from one of the vanished partners' accounts, and was investing it on Blake's behalf. Doing remarkably well, somewhere in the blue Caribbean.

She caught his eye, smiled sadly across the distance that divided them.

When, five minutes later, he forced himself to re-enter the den, the Robin and Pat were huddled together, sniggering. Pat rose to his feet and stuck out his hand. 'Lookit, boss, I'm sorry about the thing in the bedroom. I had nowhere else to take the girl. Me ma would do anything for me, but she won't let me take girls home. It's agin her religion.'

Blake gave his fingers a friendly slap. 'Think no more of it, young reprobate.'

'Sure how were you to know,' Pat grinned, 'about the cheap tart being Robin's first cousin?'

Blake's stomach was suddenly empty. 'I'm frightfully, I really had no idea –'

'No harm done,' chuckled Pat. 'What did the bank fella want?'

'Insisted on writing me this cheque for his membership fee. I said it would be two hundred and fifty. Did I do right?'

Pat pocketed the cheque. 'To be filed,' he grinned. Blackwood's had offered trial membership to the chosen few. An annual fee was to be invoiced at some vague

7

point in the future. Blackwood's was unusual in this and in other respects. As the city spawned ever more glitzy facilities for the moneyed, this club remained doggedly conservative. The French chef came in the evenings only, carrying string bags full of market produce, and cooked exactly what he felt like cooking. Tonight, a salad of walnuts and ducks' gizzards.

Still the Robin sat silent.

'I'm planning a recital for the ochre drawing-room,' Blake babbled. 'I'll have the Bechstein tuned.'

Not a word.

'The Cape reception was a roaring success,' Blake continued, as though they cared. 'You really should drop in, Robin, meet the gang. They'd like you. I'm sure they would.'

The Robin leaned his wiry frame back in the rosewood carver, gazed over Blake's head. Pat O'Hara chipped in helpfully: 'They like your tickets, anyway. Paul Blake is a bleedin' magician, so far as they know.' The Robin supplied unobtainable seats for plays, for ballets, for concerts, for matches, which Blake passed on to club members at cost.

The Robin frowned. 'Who owns this place?'

Blake swallowed. 'Technically, it's –'

'I said who *owns* it?' The Robin's voice was rising in his throat.

Pat cut in nervously: 'Lookit, Robin, it was a misunderstanding, okay? Plus, Mr Blake is after solving your delivery problem.'

'*Et voilà!*' Blake crooned. 'Completely slipped me noggin. He's calling around in the morning for a chinwag. Fennessy. Jerome Fennessy, professor of modern languages. Pure serendipity. We were schoolmates. An assignment such as yours would suit him to a tee. Here on a flying visit.'

The Robin, still motionless, asked: 'When could he go?'

'Any time.'

'Why would he do it?'

'I advanced Jerome a little cash once. He doesn't have the wherewithal to repay. He'd be interested in the fee. We go back a long way.'

'Professor? Where does he teach?' The Robin peered unblinking into Blake's eyes.

'Language academy in London. English as a foreign language, for senior business folk, very high-powered.'

'And you met him in Oxford?'

'No, at school, as I told you.'

'Not a Balliol man, then?'

'No, indeed.' Blake laughed indulgently. 'But passes for a gent.'

'What age is he?'

'Forty-two, forty-four, give or take. Been in London two, three years. Got tired of his old job.'

'Which was where?'

'Boarding school in County Cork.'

'Married?'

'Not any more, I'm afraid. Where do you want him to go?'

'Paris. There's papers have to be brung. Tell him be at the Midshipman, eleven in the morning.'

'Our rendezvous is for ten. I'll send him straight on.'

The Robin stood up, pulled on brown leather gloves, settled his heavy blue coat around his shoulders. Standing up made no great difference to his height. The coat hung about him like a vampire's wings. Frankly, an anorak would have suited him better. 'Okey-doke,' he said. 'You gave the man a loan. How much?'

'Jerome? Owes me five hundred. Irish pounds, of course.'

'Call it six-fifty euro. We'll wipe that out.' He counted thirteen fifty-euro notes from his back pocket, handed them to Blake. 'Start even.' He turned to go.

Blake harrumphed. 'Look here, I don't want to be awkward, but are you sure this is safe? Chap was arrested coming in from Amsterdam two weeks ago.'

The Robin nodded, bored: 'He got off. Did you not read it?'

'Indeed. And another chap's on trial at this very moment.'

'He'll get off too. And do you think I'd get into stuff like that? I keep my nose clean, Paul. Plus I said Paris. That's in France, Paul. Amsterdam is in Holland. Tulips. Did they not learn you that at Balliol College?'

There was a cheap little tin box on the corner of the walnut desk, that priceless heirloom that would forever remind Blake of the home from which despicable Désirée had barred him. The tin box had a design proclaiming Junior Fidelissimo Havanaise, by Rossini of Amsterdam. No tulips, just tobacco leaves. The Robin stubbed out his cigarillo in the tin, closed the tin, pocketed it. He always smoked those cigarillos on his visits to Blackwood's Club. He carried no key to the club. He knew the combination for the back entrance.

'I'll see you to your car,' Pat O'Hara said. As the two little trolls departed the premises, Blake patted his cheeks with a scented splash of Eau de Contadour, replacing the bottle in the top drawer of his walnut desk, where he also kept such treasures as his old Oxford University Calendars, his special address book and the nifty six-shooter he'd brought back from South Africa, which was perhaps not strictly legal.

He slipped out to the bar, poured himself a shot of Courvoisier. Meeting the Robin always made him feel ghastly. But he must rally. A man is bigger than his own problems. One has to move to pastures new. In today's world, security comes from imagination. In his case, sound business ideas. For example? An Irish gentleman's club in Mayfair. Crying out for it. He could talk up his Dublin experience.

Gloria was on the landing now, in her good black coat, flanked by admirers. As he moved towards them she started to drift away, trailing pleasant laughter. He caught up with her and escorted her to the door. She pressed his hand regretfully, as if only circumstances prevented her from committing unspecified intimacies upon his person.

The guests were trickling out. Pat came back to close the bar and count the cash. Blake took himself off to the private suite. The other bedrooms were being renovated. Nobody staying tonight but himself.

He put the money away in the safe, got into his nightshirt, brushed his remaining teeth, thought once again about things as they were, as they might have been. How unpalatable those fellows were. Having been educated by *soi-disant* gentlefolk, for a time, he naturally resented the Robin for being common, and patronizing him, and talking in a flat Dublin accent, not to mention wearing brown shoes with blue blazers. But he told himself not to be such a jolly old snob. And being realistic, what were the alternatives? He had been left high and dry. So what if he was living in the Robin's pocket? He enjoyed a handsome salary and a flexible budget. He was still top dog. There were, of course, some blots on the landscape. He suspected Pat O'Hara of purchasing contraband spirits for the bar. And Pat had recently usurped jurisdiction over his personal space. Just one week previously, Blake's own bed had hosted a tryst between a Kokoschka-painted Russian courtesan and a Welsh arms-dealer, while he himself had had to put up at the Shelbourne like some sort of commercial traveller.

Still, let us not exaggerate. Tonight he had done well. Reprimanded Pat, and given the Robin a minor lesson in style – although the little runt was almost beyond redemption.

Poor Jerome Fennessy! Was it fair to take advantage of his indigence?

The Robin would have to be dealt with, firmly, one of these fine days. Remind him what's what. Assert one's authority.

The forthcoming weekend's assignment, far more important than any of these folderols, was a jolly good heart-to-heart with Dee Dee and Felicity. Without overdoing it, of course. Children may be unforgiving little beasts, but they must at least be helped to understand. That is our last duty as parents. They would enjoy their surprise trip to London. He would show them Merchant Tailors' School, entertain them to lunch in the Aldington. They would stroll through St James's Park, take in a show, talk lightly about life and its multiple ironies. Rebuild. Reconstruct. Revalue.

Prepare to disappear, if required. Resurface in sunnier climes.

Paul Blake fell fast asleep, dreamed of ocean breezes south of Monterey.

{{{{{{○}}}}}}

'Frankly, he's a joke,' said Billy O'Rourke.

'So why did Frye appoint him?' Trixie repeated.

'Don't think of Joyce as a human being. Think of him as a bespoke suit.'

'So why should Frye appoint him over you?' she insisted. 'Why aren't you the head of the iDEA? And was it Joyce that chose that poncy name?' She laid her notebook on the coffee table.

'God, no,' said Billy. 'That was the Minister himself. Wanted the Yankee effect. Drugs Enforcement Agency. With a small little "i" for Ireland. Our people on the switch have instructions not to pronounce it "idea", but to spell out all four letters: "I-D-E-A, how-can-we-help?" All part of the image.'

Billy was such a hunk. Big, rough, yet with that touch of gentleness. One of those sources you want to be close to.

'And the head of the agency? Why Joyce?'

He considered her question. 'OK, here's how it went. Paddy Goldborough has his heart attack. Finance, as usual, trying to shut the agency down. Frye wants me, but I'm an animal. Plus I'm too young. Only a boy. Bit of a thug. Couldn't be Director. So he parachutes in Séamus Joyce, committee star and performing seal, fresh from Europe, to be our bishop and sit on his arse in the back office drafting policy documents with fancy titles like "Europe Without Drugs" while I'm out in the rain playing Action Man.'

Trixie discreetly refilled his glass. 'And the sole purpose of the iDEA is to hoist Richard Frye into the European Union Narcotics Directorate?'

Billy nodded. 'We're here to line up photo-ops. Preferably heroin, because who cares about hash, and cocaine is for yuppies, but heroin rots your teeth and makes gougers from council flats come and clean out your dez rez to feed the habit. So we capture a few working-class heroes, one or two big pushers, the odd dago master criminal, and Frye is winning all the way. At last, a Minister who's hitting the drug barons. Meting out Dublin justice to the godfathers. If we screw up, it's all Séamus Joyce's fault. If Joyce personally screws up bad enough, he doesn't get confirmed as head of the iDEA. But if he's a really, really good boy, Frye brings him back to Europe. And Joyce knows his way around Europe. He's well regarded. Half of them think he wrote *Ulysses*. And if he does get back, his iDEA stint will stand him in good stead, because when that European druggernaut finally hits the road, it's going to be run by diplomats negotiating with greasy foreign governments over drug supplies, without sending in the Marines, because Europe won't be doing Marines.'

Billy's delivery was rapid and gruff. There was no variation in his facial muscles to indicate when he was being ironic. And those eyes, weighing her up. The hidden anger.

'Print any of that stuff, Trixie,' he warned, 'and I'll put you across my knee. The *Gazette* is to treat Mr Joyce with the utmost respect. I will not have my boss upset. Not when he shows such fatherly concern for my welfare. Not when his Minister is howling for convictions, and all poor Séamus can offer is acquittals. Not while his wife is sick.' He stood up to go.

'What's wrong with the wife?'

'Apart from being rich and fat and dressing in pink and sleeping with the great and the good?'

'No, really. What's she got?'

'Diverticulitis. It's when your large intestine –'

'Stop it, Billy!'

'You're not a fellow sufferer, are you, Trix?'

'Tell me about yourself,' Trixie begged. 'About what really happened last year.'

'It was in the papers.'

'Yes, but I was on *Woman's Eye*. I wasn't paying attention.'

'Here, I'll show you my chest.' Billy undid another button of his tartan shirt. Her eyes widened. His skin was crisscrossed by long jagged scars, starting from the neck. 'Thoracic Park.' He buttoned up again.

'They pulled you out of hospital,' Trixie said,

'questioned you for days, then gave you a medal. Manky or what?'

'You come to expect that sort of thing. Top brass didn't like the Inner City Racketeering and Drugs Task Force.'

'ICRAD. I know.'

'Course you do, Trix. An old hand like yourself. Top brass reckoned we wuz too political, too media-friendly, too rough on the poor criminals. Also, they thought we were on the take.'

'What actually happened in that house?'

Billy shook his head.

'Please. Off the record.'

He closed his eyes for a moment, sighed. His voice a rapid monotone: 'All right. ICRAD is putting pressure on the Mahers. So the Mahers start feeling insecure. Losing their grip. So they decide to make an example of a newsagent's son, because the newsagent, an Asian gentleman married to a Wexford girl, is making complaints about them to his local councillor.' Billy paused. Trixie sat forward, breathless.

'They lift the young lad, near his home, take him off to this derelict house. Some old one phones the fuzz. Thank God. I'm driving through the neighbourhood, and I hear it on the intercom. I know that house. Leo Jordan hears the same call, but he's coming from Drumcondra. I go in along the lane at the back of the building, through the basement window, nice and quiet. They're up in the front first-floor room.' Another sigh. 'Leo pulls up on the pavement. Hops out of the car and starts trying his master keys in the front door. Fozzy

Maher hears the racket and comes out to investigate. Fozz is carrying a piece. He's the eldest son. Twenty-five. Sees me on the stairs, takes a blast. I return fire, to put him off his aim. Nick his arm. Pure fluke. Fozzy drops the piece, runs into the first-floor room, holds a knife to the child's throat, and when I get to the doorway he says "Throw it away, Billy." But I don't. I can't. Completely unable to, actually.'

Billy's breath is catching. Trixie says nothing. Billy sighs and goes on, as if dragging a rake through gravel. 'Of course I should have dropped the gun, started negotiating, waited for reinforcements. Softly softly. But Fozzy is a mad bastard. Harmed a boy once. I can't trust him. And we're allowed to shoot in order to preserve life. That's what the rules say. I raise the gun nice and slow, shoot him, clean. Old man Maher carves a few noughts and crosses on my chest with a hunting knife. I go down, but I get my left hand to the gun and blast him in the stomach. Then I collapse. Loss of blood. Leo meanwhile kicks in the front door and comes up the stairs like a herd of elephants auditioning for *Riverdance*. Old man Maher is still alive, unfortunately. Reaches for my gun and wastes poor Leo. Fires a second shot into the nice Georgian plaster ceiling. Then dies and goes to hell.'

'But you saved the boy,' Trixie breathed.

Billy nodded. 'At a cost. Three dead, and I'm not feeling too good myself. I was out sick for seven months, and Decko Dowd snaffled Leo's job. Decko was our big rival at the time. He closed down ICRAD. When I came back they put me guarding Richard Frye, while he was still a junior minister in Justice. Then Frye got promoted and set up the iDEA. Decko still hates us. Nice man.'

'Why were they so suspicious?'

'Three bodies. Not the way we do things here. Marked a new high-water mark in the annals of Dublin gangsterism. Bad for trade. And it wasn't just the cops and the tourist board; the whole nation was shedding salt tears for the Maher family.'

'They believed you in the end, though.'

'I was the only witness.'

'What about the boy?'

'Partially sighted. Not the full shilling. Old man Maher believed in soft targets. But yes, of course I should have dropped the gun, taken the chance that Fozzy would act reasonable. I did wrong. That's what the internal enquiry said.'

'Another drink?' Trixie asked.

He shook his head. 'Calls to make. We never sleep. That was off the record, mind. Official Secrets Act. Unspeakable punishments.' Billy tapped her lightly on the wrist and was gone.

Trixie closed the window. He had insisted on fresh air. The cold draught had given her the beginnings of a sore throat, but she didn't mind. Suffering in the line of duty. She lit another Silk Cut.

{{{{{{o}}}}}}

There was a delay. The Dublin flight would leave ninety minutes late. A short reprieve.

Séamus bought a *Figaro* and glanced at the front page. The stories refused to settle in his brain among the sediment of the day gone by: the formulae of bureaucratic politeness, the dull presentation they had come to hear, his own naive questions, the chairman's sardonic interventions. All eclipsed by the fax from the clinic.

He shook his head and found a seat in the departure lounge. A little girl came and sat beside him: cropped black hair, dark skin, big ears, brown eyes, long purple skirt. Aged nine or ten. Arab? Persian? Jingling some coins, counting them, turning them over. She stood at the coin-operated Coke machine and fed a coin into the slot, pushed a button, retrieved her coin from the return tray. Did the same again. Looked at her coins and moved to the confectionery machine. Fed a coin into the slot, pushed a button, retrieved her coin from the return tray. Came and sat again, turning the coins in her lap.

'Can I help?' But who ever heard of a kid needing adult help to work a coin-op machine? The girl paid him no attention. Séamus realized that her euro coins were of different national origins. The Greek owl, the German eagle. The coin you get back is not the one you put in. Hawkish Dante Alighieri eyed Queen Beatrix with distaste.

Séamus groped for his wallet and found a coin bearing the Irish harp. 'Would you like one of these?'

She turned and smiled. An older girl in blue denim, slim and close-cropped, swooped to bear her away. Sister? Mother? Au pair? They had a plane to catch, or else she needed to remove the little one from the toxic attentions of an older man.

{{{{{{o}}}}}}

On a morning such as this, with the warm brickwork of Merrion Square picked out by sidelong sunlight, and a clean blue sky offering a cold picture of spent summer, and along the Georgian vista, far away, tweedy blue hills rising gently, Dublin seemed a good place to be. Not for Jerome Fennessy, of course. Never had been. Never would.

The place did look prettier. That much was true. Prosperity and rampant good taste: Dublin was burgeoning without losing its roots. Venerable squares, carefully preserved and restored, stood like the ghosts of the old brick tenements he remembered, north of the river.

Blackwood's was one of the larger houses on the Square, with iron and woodwork smartly painted black. Jerome tried the bell. The door was opened by a dark teenage ballet dancer, in a tight black tailleur, circa 1965. Jerome explained that Paul Blake had asked him to drop by. Mr Blake had just popped around the corner. She led him upstairs – those coltish legs! – but she was not his type, her face soured by adult make-up. She pranced him into a rose-coloured drawing room, backed him into a chintzy armchair, handed him a *Financial Times*. He opened the Weekend section and gazed uncomprehendingly at a garden on Long Island, where someone had designed a patch of old England in a haze of clematis, salvia, cosmos daisies and Tibouchina. Too many words for his wandering mind, his brain still tender from the breakfast interview. Those hungry businessmen at the Merrion Hotel had pricked his veneer of professional competence. His gimcrack qualifications had been probed, his experience dismissed, his lack of vision exposed. They had winced as he drank jugfuls of orange juice. He was not fit to be Deputy Principal of their new College of Language and Cultural Studies. He had let everyone down. Paul had done him a reference, and he had failed to shine.

Lifting his eyes, he spotted through the open door a dishy redhead, running a tap behind a mahogany bar. Jerome essayed a shy smile, which she returned with freckles. A moment later she was in his midst, wearing a voluminous yellow silk dress with puffed white sleeves and carrying four china jugs full of variegated flowers which she laid out on tables across the room. Jerome forced himself to speak:

'Crowflowers, nettles, daisies and long purples.'

His creaky voice sounded sinister, even to himself. The little moon-faced girl frowned. 'Are you a teacher?'

'Is it written on my face?' he asked in some dismay. He had somehow hoped that this day at least, in his Norfolk jacket and broad-wale corduroy slacks, he might have passed for a minor country gentleman.

'Don't worry,' she said. 'I won't tell.' She stoked the little fire with coal, whistling under her breath, dipped him a curtsey, and disappeared in a flurry of yellow silk.

Where on earth had she got such a dress? From a theatrical costumier? Such a contrast with her slim workmate, now handing him a cup of bitter coffee and trying not to laugh.

He sipped the coffee, went to the lavatory, dried his hands on the softest of towels, tried the bristle clothesbrush. Paul Blake came bounding up the stairs. 'Romy! Large as life and twice as handsome! Sorry to hear the news. They phoned to let me know. You did make an impression. Have the sylphs been pampering you? Come to my boudoir.'

Jerome followed him. From the top drawer of his antique walnut desk, Paul extracted a sheet of cream-coloured paper with the familiar heading: *AAA.AAA – Anglo-American Academy of London – Accademia Anglo-Americana di Londra*, and flourished it like a conjuror's handkerchief.

Jerome's throat went dry. He knew the shape of that ancient letterhead. He had chosen the name so as to head the Yellow Pages listings of language schools. Ceased trading. Money owing. People to be avoided, all over London.

Paul tore the paper twice, lengthwise, dangled the four strips in the air. 'Wiped out, Romy,' he smiled. 'Obliterated.' He dropped the pieces into the paper bin.

'No, really.' Jerome held up his hands. That IOU had been haunting him. The last six months had not been kind. Brit-Lang had cut his hours, and his young ladies were growing expensive. To be released from an unpayable debt was a blessing, and a new obligation.

'No call for it in the first place,' Blake went on in confidential tones, drowning out his friend's feeble protests. 'Your credit was always good with me, Romy. And as it happens, I don't need the cash. Tell me about the interview.'

'Dreadful,' Jerome confessed. 'They chewed me up. But to forgive me this debt. I hardly know –'

'Think nothing of it, Romy. You'd do the same for me, were our circumstances reversed. And as luck would have it, you are poised to do me a signal favour. If you're available, of course, I need someone to pop over to Paris, on behalf of an associate who has a delicate piece of business to transact. All above board, it goes without saying, but super-confidential. I recommended you.'

'When can I do it?'

'This very day. *Hic et nunc*, as they say.'

'Oh. Yes. I have a flexible ticket.' He would return to London on Monday instead of this afternoon. He could do something to repay. A sense of relief began to spread through him like milk.

'Do you know the Midshipman?' Paul asked. 'The public house?'

'Ah. I think I've seen it. Tara Street or thereabouts?'

'Thereabouts. South Brunswick Street. My friend will see you in the snug at eleven o'clock.'

'Whom shall I ask for?'

'He'll know who you are. I've described you. Flatteringly, I assure you.'

Jerome consulted his watch. 'Gosh, just in time.'

'Attaboy! I value your support.'

Paul Blake watched him fondly as he receded along the Square, looking like a superannuated donkey in his cast-off tweeds.

{{{{{{o}}}}}}

23

The crew of the Midshipman was bracing for Saturday lunch. Tables were being set, the shiny carpet vacuum-cleaned, a sweet smell of wax polish blending with the ineradicable pub aroma of stale beer and cigarettes.

'Pro-fessor Fennessy?'

A small fat man wearing a grey suit, grey shoes and a grey hairpiece emerged from the shadows, beckoned Jerome and floated back into the secluded area from which he had come. He subsided onto a velvet bench. 'Cup o' tea?' A high, throaty voice from somewhere west of the Shannon. 'Or maybe somethin' stronger? Sammidge? The sammidges here is grand, so they are.' He himself had set up a double-decker, glistening with salad cream.

'Nothing for now, thanks.'

The little fat man took a large bite and masticated vigorously. 'Mulhone,' he mumbled through the crusts. 'P. J. Mulhone.' He gulped a mouthful of tea and chomped his now amphibious sandwich with redoubled vigour, gulping more liquid to clear his gullet. 'You're sure you won't be having a sammidge, Pro-fessor?'

'I'm all right, thanks.'

'You won't mind me polishin' this off, then?' And P. J. Mulhone tackled the remains of his snack with animosity, as though chewing the nape of an ancient enemy. Jerome settled into a seat and waited until it was all over.

His host washed down the last noisy morsel with a final aspiration of tea, sucked the tips of his fingers, dabbed his lips with a pink serviette. 'Smashin',' he sighed. 'Scrumptious, so 'tis.' He reached under the

24

table, produced a briefcase, fished out a padded envelope and placed it on the table next to Jerome. 'Now, Pro-fessor,' he said. 'This is the thing.'

He peered around to check for eavesdroppers, and proceeded.

'Doc'ments, d'ya see?' He tapped the envelope. 'Vital doc'ments. We have to complete this property deal, pronto. Stric'ly confidential, like. We're after reservin' your air ticket, you're to pick it up at the airport, I'll hand you this envelope again at the departure gate at two-fifteen sharp. D'ya get me?'

'More or less. What sort of documents?'

'Planning permission doc'ments, copies of title deeds, official tenders, plans and drawings. Top secret, d'ya see, though it's all legal like, but I'll tell you anyhow because you're an educated gen'leman and you'll want to know what you're gettin' into. There's a lot ridin' on this, Pro-fessor. Not just money, but jobs. Loads of jobs. For the young people of Dublin. And months of work. Our plan' – here he dropped his voice, as though swallowing an obscenity – 'is to build a shoppin' centre, d'ya see? In a deprived area. We been assemblin' the site for two years, so we have. The centre means work for boys and girls, and it means urban renewal and all the rest, so it does, but the real pain in the arse, pardon me French, is if we don't secure the site by tomorrow night it gets bought in as an investment by some shower of shaggers in an English feckin' bank and sits there idle for the next five or ten years doing no good to man or beast.'

'And these documents have to be signed in Paris?'

'Not Paris, Pro-fessor. Holland. The thing is because

there's one little parcel of land we need to complete the site, like. That little parcel is controlled by a crowd of Hollanders. Our bid for it is late, d'ya see? We're after missin' the shaggin' deadline, Pro-fessor. The Dublin lawyer having carriage of the sale, as they say, is after leavin' town last night, he's over beyond in the Nether-lands. He'll be meetin' the present owners of the land tomorrow night, in a town called Eindhoven, did you ever hear tell of that place? He's taking a train down there from Amsterdam, so he is. He's agreed to put our bid on the table, but only if we get all the paperwork to him fully completed by tonight, so's he can go over the doc'ments, make sure they're in order, because he's supposed to have done all that in Dublin, d'ya see? He's doin' us a favour, d'ya see? The dirty eejit.' P. J. Mulhone opened his round eyes wide, searching Jerome's face for signs of comprehension.

Jerome was puzzled. 'I'm delighted to help, of course. But suppose I made some silly mistake. You'd be safer delivering –'

'No, no, no, can't be done at all, man. The English bidders, d'ya see, thought they had the whole thing sewn up last Tuesday, when the tender deadline was after passin'. Which wasn't our fault, mind you, but stric'ly speaking the lawyer fella shouldn't be acceptin' the documents off of us at all at all. If our competitor could prove that one of us was over beyond in Holland this weekend, they could undermine the whole shaggin' biddin' process and get an injunction to stop the sale going through, so they could. Or if they could prove we used a firm of couriers, same thing. We'd be rightly bunched then, d'ya see? The beauty of you, Pro-fessor, if you don't mind me sayin', is I never saw you before in my life and I hope I'll never meet you again, heh heh. We're total strangers, so we are. And of course we'll pay you for your time. Did I mention that at all?'

'Thanks indeed. May I see the documents?'

'They're sealed. Has to be. Why would you be wantin' to see them anyways?'

'Well –'

'What's your problem, Pro-fessor?'

Jerome bit his tongue.

Mulhone groped for meaning, twigged, waxed indignant. 'Man dear! D'you think we're askin' you to do something shady, like? You think Paul Blake is after leading you astray?'

'No. Of course not.' Jerome saw how silly he was being. 'Forgive me.'

'I'll take no offence, then, so I won't.' But his voice had gone cold. He cleared his throat. 'Your cash, Pro-fessor.' Still scowling, Mulhone handed Jerome a bundle of hundred-euro banknotes, with a small index card clipped to the front. 'Eight hundred in all. Not your fee, but your expenses, d'ya see? You use this stuff to buy your ticket to Amsterdam today, and pay for your room in the Hotel Poorbuis. The names is all written down on this card. You're booked into a room with a bathroom off of it, and its own colour television and even a trouser press, like. The lap of luxury, d'ya see? We're after writin' the reservation codes for the plane and the hotel on that card. The plane takes off at three o'clock. Now, the Hotel Poorbuis is on the Meijerlaan. It's written on the

27

card. You take the number 7 tram from Amsterdam central station, get off at Leidseplein. Sit yourself down in the hotel lobby at eight o'clock tonight, with this bag on your knees, so's the lawyer fella can recognize you when he calls in. He'll give you a receipt for the doc'ments. You'll hand me that receipt, here in this room on Monday mornin' at eleven sharp, and I'll hand you nineteen hundred smackers as your professional fee. Cash. Between you and me and the Revenue Commissioners, d'ya see?'

'Perfectly,' said Jerome. Nineteen hundred euros. Unbelievable. At current rates of exchange, he would be almost twelve hundred richer in sterling. This was a new start, a heaven-sent opportunity. Carlotta Monelli: the pearl-drop earrings! Her shivering smile.

{{{{{{o}}}}}}

Séamus Joyce, Acting Director of the iDEA, was not behind his desk, but at home in the spacious residence, set in an acre of gardens on the suburban slopes of Glenageary, that he shared with his wife. His mind was snared in a mess of trackless emotions, as he padded through empty bedrooms and bathrooms, consulting his list and packing her Samsonite bag with nightdresses, bedjackets, dressing-gowns, lavender perfumes and soaps. Theresa would not be home today. Autumn was sinking towards winter.

Around the house, Wharfedale speakers poured out Ivie Anderson's glorious whine – 'I Got It Bad And That Ain't Good' with the Duke Ellington orchestra –

while the supersweet saxophone of Johnny Hodges trailed airy tendrils all around her, in Hollywood in the summer of 1941, a full decade before his birth. Séamus had discovered it on a French compilation, bought in Bordeaux on a weekend break, during his European days.

He would soon be on his way to Saint Aidan's Private Hospital, with a bunch of her favourite chrysanthemums – flowers of the dead, said the French. He would sit with Theresa, take instructions for paying the roofer who had re-slated the Kilmacanogue house, and the painter who was finishing up in Bluebell. He would gossip about the office, about the Minister, about Eileen McTeague, his personal assistant, who had been enquiring with ladylike delicacy about her condition.

He would make an excuse and leave her lying there, to keep his appointment with Dr Maguire Gibson. After weeks of tests, they were circling the cause of her illness.

Theresa had made him what he was. He was moulded by her, bonded by something stronger than love. He was her creature. This was his identity, the cage of his existence.

What's the point of freedom? Take chickens. They have no use for it. Captivity comes from nature, not circumstance. Released from death row and redesignated as free-range poultry, chickens would still be caught in chickendom.

Theresa's things were everywhere: silver thimbles on the occasional table in the sitting room, ebony figurines on the bookshelf, lacquered vases on the windowsill, a grey Angora cardigan on her chaise-longue, colour swatches in the workroom, and the crochet hook she might never again pick up. All strange, these familiar effects.

The minutes were slow in passing. The house was heavy with the scent of plants. Séamus thought about being alone again. Wished he hadn't been born a chicken. Listened instead to long-dead Ivie Anderson singing 'Jump for Joy', just for him. Glanced in the mirror, caught sight of his mother's smooth face. Averted his eyes, patted his flat thinning hair. Picked up the crochet hooks and wool, plunged them into her bag, zipped it up, made for the open air.

{{{{{{o}}}}}}

Davnet's dusting was finished. It being Saturday, no members had shown up. Mr Blake had nipped out again, so she sat quietly with Jenny, and they worked on their homework together. First history, then biology. Jenny recited the questions and Davnet had all the answers, yet they both knew it was Davnet who needed Jenny. These were the best bits in her entire life.

The doorbell rang. Jenny skipped downstairs. Davnet leaned over the banisters. The scrawny teacher was back again. Pink flamingo skin, ingratiating twinkle. Davnet watched his reaction to Jenny as she twirled around. No surprises there. Beauty and the Beast. But his sad eyes flickering over Davnet were equally yearning.

'If it doesn't inconvenience you,' he was saying, 'I'd like to wait for Mr Blake, just in case –'

Davnet showed him into the reading room. He

refused coffee, settled into an armchair, pretended to read the *National Geographic*.

She perched at the bar, putting Jenny through a mock oral examination while they polished the warm glasses from the dishwasher. Jenny's throaty voice stumbled over the nasals and fluting sounds of French. After six years, she still had trouble differentiating *vous* from *vu*. A strand of dark hair fell across her hazel eyes. Davnet fixed the moment in her image bank.

Jenny changed her clothes, hugged Davnet around the neck, kissed her cheek, clattered off to catch her bus. Davnet, pumped full of happiness, filled the ice-buckets, stored them in the freezer, poured fresh water into ice-cube trays.

'Am I holding you up?' The oldster was teetering on the drawing-room threshold.

'Not really. I don't have to be home until three.'

'It's just that I'm anxious to have a word with Mr Blake. Where did you get that wonderful dress, if I may make so bold as to ask?'

'Secondhand shop. Mr Blake wants us to wear period costume. Even in the mornings. It's part of what he calls the look and feel. He gives us cash to buy the clothes. No jeans and combats. Jenny goes for slinky stuff. I go for the puffy look. Guess why. Am I talking too much?'

'Not at all. Did anyone ever tell you you look like a painting?'

'Rubens? I tend to hit people who say Rubens.'

'Gosh. No, Rembrandt. It's in the National Gallery, on Trafalgar Square. Rembrandt thought your name was

Saskia. I'll send you a card of it when I get back home. I teach in London. You should come and see yourself. Oh, by the way, I'm Jerome Fennessy. What's your real name?'

'Davnet O'Reilly.'

'Where do you live, Davnet?'

'I never give my address to strange gentlemen.'

'You think I'm strange,' he said, 'you should meet my wife.' And wished he hadn't.

{{{{{{o}}}}}}

Paul Blake was returning to base after a sortie. Road-testing a credit card, he had picked up a scarf in Kevin & Howlin, and a box of Strauss in HMV. He had also reserved three tickets to Heathrow for the weekend – business class because the plebs had stuffed up the steerage. Dee Dee and Felicity would enjoy the champagne, even if they refused to talk to their father. The tickets were flexible, which was just as well as the trip had yet be negotiated with barking Désirée. No hurry about that. Sufficient unto the day. His immediate plans involved a Havana cigar and some Viennese waltzes, and possibly a peek into the *Financial Times* colour magazine, entitled 'How To Spend It', which frankly had never been his number one personal problem. Put things behind him. Besides, the timeshare brochures were starting to arrive. He needed to plan his retreat on the Algarve. Nothing lavish: a simple white-walled villa. Four weeks in the year. A small glass of madeira to put him in the mood?

He fished out his key. Young Davnet had made a super job of the brasses.

When suddenly the black door swung open and there floated up before him like a corpse from a harbour the frozen mackerel face of Jerome Fennessy, about to jump ship.

Blake did his best to smile. 'Don't tell me they turned you down!' An unfortunate phrase, considering Jerome's employment record.

Jerome simply crinkled the corners of his eyes, the way he always did. 'Paul, I was afraid I'd missed you. Thanks awfully for fixing this trip for me. I wondered if there's anything you'd like me to bring back for you.'

'That's most awfully kind. Why, come to think of it, they do packages of jolly nice lark's liver pâté at Roissy Charles de Gaulle.'

'It's Amsterdam, actually,' said Jerome.

A horrid vision of doom began to materialize. Damn and blast Fennessy!

Little Davnet pushed past them. She had changed into loose-fitting jeans. 'Nobody in,' she said. 'I'm gone.' And she ambled off, a carefree sunlit child.

A worm turned in Paul Blake's gut.

'Ah, if it's Amsterdam,' he boomed, 'there is one item you could fetch. Tin of cigarillos. Present for a friend. Not duty-free, actually. Available exclusively from Rossini's of Amsterdam. You'll find their address in the phone book. Ask them for a tin of Rossini Junior Fidelissimo Havanaise cigarillos. Got that? Tell them they're for Mr Hughes. They know the sort he likes. A medium tin.'

'Medium tin. Junior Fidelissimo. Dr Castro, I presume. I'll remember that. And thanks again, Paul. About the loan, too. I mean –'

Blake thumped him benevolently on the back, clasped his hand, wished him luck, watched him go. Oh Romy, Romy, wherefore art thou Romy? Such a priceless chump.

{{{{{{o}}}}}}

Séamus Joyce sat on a straight chair in the ante-room. Studiously secular artworks littered the beige walls. Sunflowers, roses, a landscape with burgeoning trees. On a veneered table, a swelling cactus in an earthenware pot. Surveying all these growths, Séamus wondered how long the cancer had been rooting inside Theresa.

Why was Dr Maguire Gibson making him wait?

He was back in the Dean's study in St Justin's, waiting for Lulu, braced for interrogation about the glasshouse window. Elias Gore had smashed it with a football. Lulu, Dean of Residence, was planning a fresh assault on the third-year dormitory. His favoured technique was to fasten on some minor crime and demand that the culprit be delivered up for chastisement. When the boys refused, Lulu would whip out his rod, line them up at the banisters and rhythmically swish his way along their buttocks. Once Kevin Scott, who was tough as well as brave, had stepped forward and taken the blame for another boy's misdeed. Lulu pulled Kevin's hair until he cried, drew blood from his legs with crisp cuts of his cane, made him kneel in the dark upper corridor for two hours before the plaster statue of the Virgin Mary. After that, there was tacit agreement that they should all share Lulu's attentions.

The door opened. Instead of Lulu's excited snarl, the grave old headmaster told Séamus in a dull voice that his father had unexpectedly passed away.

That had been the end of the old life. He had never gone back to boarding school, because his mother did not hold with wasting money. She wanted to set him to work straight away as a hotel porter, but his older brother Daniel, who had left home years earlier and was doing well in Manchester, insisted on sending a remittance to pay for Séamus's schooling. He finished his Leaving Certificate at a technical college in the godforsaken market town of Ballynahane. His English teacher had taught him Latin, made him sit the Civil Service examination. He passed with flying colours. All the requisite words, facts and figures skipped into place; he simply wrote them down.

His mother had packed his father's brown suitcase. Father had been an agricultural inspector. She had always hated Father.

Séamus was assigned to Customs and Excise in the port of Dublin, which allowed him to enrol for an evening degree in Arts at King's College Dublin. The dilapidated campus in the Phoenix Park could not compete with Trinity College or the National University, but it had a certain seedy atmosphere and one or two inspired teachers. When the first-year results came out he was granted a scholarship and became a day student. He joined student societies, discovered jazz, even went to dances until a brassy girl called him a feckin' country hedgehog. Then, to his amazement, he became briefly involved in a romantic liaison with a dramatically beautiful student, all scarves and boots and shocking frankness. She was the most intensely physical and the most intensely spiritual girl he had ever met: too pure, too uncompromising to stoop to simple gratification. He made discreet visits to pharmacies, took to baths and talcum powder. Lovely Fionnuala innocently led him on, to the point where his little stock of condoms was almost called into service. Then, the shattering moment when he discovered that she was spending afternoons in bed with the middle-aged professor who was supervising her final-year thesis. A smug manipulative slob with an invalid wife. Séamus felt violated.

Theresa was different. They met in the hallway outside his bedsitter, queueing to use the payphone. Theresa was soft and lovely and circumspect. She was home in Ireland after years in Nottingham, where her widowed father had emigrated. She had found employment in the Dublin office of an electrical wholesaler, a business she knew well because her father had run a radio and television shop. She was to be married to Thomas Rawlings, a quantity surveyor currently working in tax-free Saudi Arabia. Séamus found her measured English accent restful. She enquired politely about his university course and future plans. She patted his arm in a sisterly fashion. She was wiser in the ways of the world.

He bought good shoes and a Harris tweed jacket, persuaded his barber to give him a Caesar haircut. The effect was more ridiculous than ever, like a pig in a pet shop, as his mother told him when he went home to visit. She never wrote, but cashed his cheques the day they arrived.

He asked Theresa to tea, showed her his collection of jazz records. She got him a tiny portable cassette recorder, to record jazz sessions. This he did in Sheeran's Lounge where Reinhold and Christopher played, and did it again, illegally and surreptitiously, when Gary Burton played at the RDS concert hall. Nobody noticed the microphone inside the sleeve of his overcoat, and the sound quality when he took it home was as good as the worst of the commercial recordings in Disc Finder's jazz section.

Aided by a relentlessly sharp memory, which made up for his lack of original thought, he took a very good degree and was promoted to the grade of Higher Executive Officer. At that time, Theresa decided to marry him, and started to become yielding and flirtatious.

He could barely believe his luck, as a certified guilt-ridden hedgehog, when she shyly let him know how her feelings were changing. She had broken off her engagement; Thomas Rawlings wanted to stay in Saudi. She invited Séamus to dinner, and cooked beef strogon-off in her tiny kitchenette, wearing a silk blouse with a floppy bow. He brought a bottle of Piat d'Or, but she was not a drinker. Theresa's little flat was furnished with much the same cheap junk as his own bed-sitting room, transformed with tasteful lamps and rugs. Her cookery books were ranged in alphabetical order, on a shelf which also held a tidy row of folders labelled Bills

(Domestic), Bills (Personal), Building Society, Correspondence, Electrical, Family, Mementoes, Records. He never saw inside those folders. She remained an inveterate hoarder of documents, while Séamus, though his filing was haphazard, was cursed with endless recall.

Their wedding was subdued, partly because Theresa's father had died, and partly because Séamus's mother, who did not hold with Englishwomen, had strongly opposed the marriage, redoubling her objections after meeting Theresa, whom she classified as a scheming bloodsucking devious moneygrubbing whore. That judgement was delivered in the carpark of the Frenchman's Arms in Ballynahane, after she had refused to eat lunch with Séamus and Theresa. Even Daniel had missed the wedding, claiming pressure of work in the building trade.

When Séamus's mother had her first stroke, Theresa took charge, nursed the speechless old woman, booked her into the best geriatric ward in the country, where she suffered a second stroke and died. Daniel flew home for the funeral, insisted on paying for everything, including a proper gravestone for both his parents. Mrs Joyce had not held with gravestones.

Her will, lodged with Leneghan and Company, the new solicitor in Ballynahane, left everything to her sister-in-law Mary Joyce, specifically excluding Séamus and his wife from any part in her inheritance. Daniel was left a token hundred pounds. Theresa unearthed Séamus's father's will in the offices of the town's longer-established solicitor, Beggs and Stokes. Under the terms of that earlier will, it was clear that Mrs Joyce had enjoyed the use of her late husband's property only during her own lifetime. Auntie Mary threatened to have the law on them, but Theresa promised her a gratuity of two thousand pounds from the sale of the house and contents. That was real money in small-town Ireland at the time.

Why remember all this now? Theresa had stopped treating Séamus with contempt since her illness had struck, and yet he needed to recall the earlier times, when she was strong and sharp and full of fight. The money from that will had got her started: first a run-down cottage by the Dodder, tarted up and sold within six months for double the money. Next came a big house in Rathmines, where they lived in the basement while she renovated the three upper storeys with a squadron of scurrying tradesmen. With the proceeds of that house, she bought two more, one to live in and one to renovate. Séamus was sidelined.

As she traded her way up, there were consequential changes. She invested in good clothes and hairstyles, wore them with a quiet elegance, refined her accent, made good connections. She fundraised for charities, patronized art exhibitions, did the colour schemes for the Haven Homes apartments, contracted with MB Quality Hotels to procure artworks and *objets* for their chain. She took a stake in a furniture boutique, travelled abroad to trade fairs and exhibitions in Frankfurt, Milan, New York. She did the showhouses when Daniel started building housing estates on the edge of Manchester. She became a director of Daniel's company, brought him to Dublin for visits, served as matron of honour when he finally got married, in late middle age, to his long-time receptionist Rose, a loud cheerful Yorkshire woman who left him after six months, following which Daniel sold up and retired to Spain. Daniel must have been a born bachelor, after all.

Séamus marvelled at Theresa's achievements. He had a feel for musical sounds, a long memory for phrases and figures, but no visual sense. To her, shape, texture and colour were second nature. As was price. Her mind was a catalogue of bargains.

What did all this matter? Because it was her life. She had bought their present house ten years back, at what was now a bargain price. She loved that house like a baby, lavished her care on it. She had stayed there during all the time he was in Europe, attending the Permanent Liaison Committee on Security Affairs. She had come to visit him now and again, but not quite often enough.

We cannot turn back the clock.

Now the door was swinging open, and Dr Alphonse Maguire Gibson entered with his characteristic slow-motion stride. The specialist's demeanour was bland and judicious, neither friendly nor cold. He explained in some technical detail the nature of the preliminary findings, indicating the presence of some growths in Theresa's stomach and another little crop on the oeso-phagus, undoubtedly a contributory factor in her recent difficulties with swallowing. Further tests would indeed be required in order to determine whether those growths might be termed benign or malignant, and if the latter, what degree of malignancy might be involved. Such tests would be initiated at once and carried forward with all due speed, having regard to the lady's post-operative condition. Meanwhile, a stable condition would be maintained by means of a carefully calibrated cocktail of medicines. Only on completion of the investigative process could the correct course of treatment be embarked upon. It would be premature at this stage to venture a prognosis, but Dr Maguire Gibson was always hopeful. Always hopeful.

The word 'cancer' was never mentioned.

Ah, yes, and by the by, thanks to the fine surgical work of Mr al-Hussein, that diverticulitis problem had been definitively resolved. At this juncture there was no further call to fret about diverticulitis.

{{{{{{o}}}}}}

Jerome loved Amsterdam. The nostalgic whiff of hashish in the railway station, the canals, the brick houses, the bicycles. A civilized version of England.

His three o'clock flight had made perfect time, and he had taken a little wine for his stomach's sake. With a free city map from the airport, he found the Poorbuis without difficulty. The room was cramped but comfortable. A cool shower sobered him up.

At Rossini's cigar shop, they knew of Mr Hughes and his preference for Junior Fidelissimo Havanaise cigarillos. They handed Jerome a brownish tin with a pleasing tobacco-leaf motif, and put up a spirited resistance to his production of his credit card to pay for the purchase. He won the point, signed with a flourish, and walked away feeling quietly satisfied with the world

41

and his place in it. He sampled a glass of white Dutch beer on the way back to the hotel.

P. J. Mulhone's fat padded envelope was collected at eight o'clock by a thin black-haired young man from the lawyer's office. 'I'm to meet you here again tomorrow. One o'clock, on the dot,' declared the young man.

'No need to meet me,' Jerome said. 'My part is done.'

'No, no, they got to get a receipt,' said the young man. Dublin youth accent, sharp as lemon-juice. 'We're to give you countersigned copies, and you're to hand them over to Mr Mulhone tomorrow evening.'

'Why didn't he tell me that?'

'He didn't know, that's the why. They're to produce the countersigned documents in Dublin on Monday morning. Mr Mulhone'll be waiting for you at Dublin Airport. If you don't give him the receipted documents, they won't pay you for bringing them over here, and they'll be wanting their deposit back, what's more.'

'Just asking,' Jerome said. He did not much like this whippersnapper.

'Just answering,' sneered the black-haired boy, and off he went with the padded envelope.

Determined to enjoy his holiday, Jerome wandered out into the city, found a trattoria where they served a stodgy Italian meal and soft Valpolicella. Then a saunter through the red-light district. The pink girls shrined in the illuminated windows looked stale on closer inspection, though hardly as mouldy as himself. He wandered back towards the hotel, but was ambushed by a pleasant pub with newspapers and curaçao.

Next morning he rose early, overdosed on coffee, left his bag at reception, and made for the Rijksmuseum. He took a circuitous route, fetched up at the wrong entrance, managed to trip and fall in the new car park. Feeling foolish, he dusted himself down and circled the building to the main door.

Dutch interiors, Dutch exteriors contained in a Dutch interior, the understated drama of Dutch lives cocooned in muddied watery Dutch light. A group portrait of tourists assembled devoutly before each famous work.

Pausing to admire a tiny painting of a pub scene by Jan Steen, peopled with blob-faced drinkers like himself, he overheard an academic Englishman assuring an academic Welshman that this, and not Cézanne's homonymous work, was the painting that had inspired Philip Larkin's scatological poem 'The Card-Players'. Jerome liked Larkin, had even used 'The Whitsun Weddings' for advanced learners.

At the end of a broad corridor he glimpsed Rembrandt's *The Night Watch* through the crowd. The gloomy canvas featured a press of posturing vigilantes, and in their midst a red-haired child in a yellow ball gown, staring at the two leaders of the patrol, one of them clad in a matching yellow uniform. He thought of Davnet in her bright silk dress. Davnet, the fresh Irish beauty, so unspoiled. With a girl like that one could be a real teacher, once again.

In the museum shop, among the postcards of Dutch masters, he selected *The Night Watch*, addressed it to Davnet O'Reilly, care of Blackwood's Club, and scribbled a playful message on the back: 'Watch Out For Me! Love, Jerome.' Perhaps that was going a little too far.

The visit had taken longer than he had thought. He hurried back to the hotel. The black-haired young man was waiting, tense and waspish. 'I've a train to catch, you know. We're to be in Eindhoven by four.' He thrust the envelope into Jerome's hands and made himself scarce.

Jerome bought a stamp at reception, posted his card to Davnet, wandered off and lingered over lunch in a café, drank more white beer, daydreamed about the conciliatory letter he should long ago have written to his wife, came back to the hotel, picked up his bag and headed home.

{{{{{{o}}}}}}

Paul Blake blocked Pat O'Hara.

'What's this palaver 'bout Amsterdam?' he demanded.

Pat had dropped in late on Sunday afternoon to deliver a case of Glenmorangie. Period costume was not for Pat. Off duty for the weekend, he was dolled up in a blue suit, white shirt, shiny grey shoes. Gold rings and a gold bracelet completed the picture of the minor pimp about town.

'What's which about where?' Pat smirked.

Blake stood firmly in the doorway. 'Amsterdam, young Patrick. Amsterdam. You said Paris. Robin distinctly said Paris. Jerome has been dispatched to Amsterdam.'

Pat lowered the case of whisky carefully onto the carpet. 'Was he on the phone to you or what's the story?'

'No. He told me before his departure that it was Amsterdam. Not Paris. Amsterdam. Spot the difference.'

Pat shrugged. 'Amsterdam. Benidorm. What odds?'

'You deceived me, there's the rub. And I don't like it. If anything happens to Jerome, I'm holding the pair of you responsible.' He knew he sounded slurred, fought to steady up. 'I won't hesitate to go to the authorities, you know.'

Pat considered carefully for a moment.

'Lookit, boss. I better tell you. The cops are in on this. Mr Fennessy'll be in a bit of hot water, but it'll work out grand.'

'What the blazes are you insinuating?'

'Did you ever hear tell of the Snowman?'

'No.' Although he had, of course.

'Evil bastard. The cops want him put away. It's a sting. First off, your friend will be got for carrying smack.'

'You said nothing about that.'

'Don't worry, no harm will come to him. The cops will let him walk the moment he identifies the guy who sent him.'

'Why me?'

'No, boss, not you. The man he met in the pub. The Snowman. Matt Wellan. They'll let your friend off with a caution.'

Paul was not mollified. 'How can they do that, if he's carrying drugs?'

'Because the value of drugs isn't fixed, you see. It all depends on the purity. They can shrink the dose down to the level where he'll get probation if he plays ball.'

'And just suppose I came into court and gave evidence that Jerome had been tricked into taking part?'

'Ah.' Pat shook his head, sighed: 'Then, you see, we'd have to start talking about Lambourne Blake Motors of Gillingham, and the Brentford Building Society.'

There was a moment before Blake could speak. 'That's outrageous and irrelevant. Those things happened years ago, even before I went to South Africa. How do you know about them?'

'Robin had enquiries made. Tracked you all the way from age ten. Borstal an' all. Thing is, he still trusted you. He still put money in your club, didn't he? He thinks the world of you. Loves the voice, the style, the Oxford ties, all that. So you've nothing to worry about, Paul, just so long as you don't rat on him. Robin's a broad-minded bloke, he doesn't mind guys having a few blots on their copybooks, spinning the odd yarn, but the one thing he won't take is people ratting on him. He gets upset. Do you understand what I'm saying? I'm telling you for your own good, even if you are the boss itself.'

Blake understood, all right. It was not his first time in this kind of position.

He would have to find a way of making it up to Jerome. Discreetly.

Oh what a tangled web we weave.

46

He subsided onto the chaise-longue. Pat O'Hara stashed his bottles behind the bar, then left. Blake was on his own tonight, ready to play the genial host. Sunday nights were generally quiet.

{{{{{{o}}}}}}

The flight from Amsterdam was dead on time. At eight o'clock Billy O'Rourke stood inside the small interview room with its one-way glass while Bosco Woulfe slipped into the baggage-collection area.

Dublin airport was bursting at the seams, as usual. You could easily lose someone in that crowd. But Bosco wouldn't do that.

The mark's reaction when tapped on the shoulder was to let his shoulders go slack and hang his pink face like a grazing tortoise. He came quietly into the interview room, murmured his full name – Jerome Patrick George Albert Fennessy – and lapsed into a chair while Bosco opened the leather bag and slit the padded envelope with a Stanley blade.

Asked to identify the white powder in the cellophane wrapper, he chuckled as if sharing a private joke: 'Absolutely no idea. But if you're asking, it's presumably because you already know.'

Billy cautioned him. Fennessy said, 'Perhaps it will be helpful if I give a full account.' He put his fingertips together and began to describe, in a carefully modulated gentlemanly undertone, how on a brief visit to Dublin he had been recruited in a Dublin pub and promised nineteen hundred euros for carrying documents to

Amsterdam. He agreed that the offer was generous for a legitimate transaction. 'Absurdly so. I thought I was getting a paid holiday. Culpable stupidity.'

He started on the story that had been fed him by Mulhone, who was due to meet him outside just now, in the arrivals area. Billy went through the motions of looking for the elusive Mulhone, with the help of the airport police. Not a trace. They had Mulhone paged. No response. They paged 'the person waiting for Mr Jerome Fennessy, a passenger from Amsterdam'. Again, no response. Billy went back to the little interview room, where the prisoner and Bosco Woulfe were looking at picture postcards from an art gallery. Bosco was a culture vulture.

Decko Dowd of the Garda Drug Squad came hammering on the door, doing his standard impression of a rabid sheepdog, demanding to take custody of the prisoner. He obviously had friends among the airport police. Billy telephoned the senior officer who sorted out turf wars between Drug Squad, the iDEA and the customs authorities. After five minutes' blustering, Decko backed off, sincerely hurt. Decko always looked earnest to the point of tears.

Billy clapped the prisoner on the shoulder. 'Come along, Jerome boy. We're going to take a proper statement, and catch the dastardly fiend who sent you to your doom.' Billy led the prisoner out to their car, with Bosco Woulfe bringing up the rear. Bosco drove, while Billy sat in the back with Fennessy. No need for handcuffs.

As they crossed the Liffey by the East Link bridge,

the prisoner looked wistfully out at the dark water and the lights.

{{{{{{o}}}}}}

Séamus Joyce had suffered through a social Sunday afternoon with Tom P. Stringer, the earnest Texan seconded from the European liaison section of the Narcotics Policy Institute. Grey-skinned, grey-suited, grey-haired, Stringer was going to be with the Department of Justice for three months, and needed to know all about the iDEA.

Stringer's visit to the office during the week, with its relentless inquisition into the minutiae of budgets, policies and personnel, had been bad enough. He had prowled around their antiquated headquarters, pale eyes prying. Had grilled Mary Rice, the office supervisor, on the details of her filing procedures. Had cross-examined the computer section about statistics and sampling techniques. Had cornered Gilbert Covey, the Minister's spin-doctor who maintained an office in the iDEA building, and compared notes on worldwide opinion polls concerning narcotics. Had perched on a straight chair in Séamus's office and reviewed the failed drugs policies of successive Irish governments over the past fifteen years. Eileen McTeague, doyenne of the secretarial dames bequeathed to the iDEA by the Fisheries Commission, had brought in tea and biscuits. The visitor had quizzed her about security in the office computer network. Eileen had smiled and shaken her head as though being addressed in Chinese.

Today was a compressed repeat performance, over drinks with Stringer on the lawn of his rented house beyond Rathnew. They had lunched at Hunter's Hotel, and Séamus had drunk rather too much. Now, Stringer stuffed him with martini and olives and probed him on Theresa's diagnosis before turning to serious business. He wanted Séamus's view of the prospects for European policy co-ordination, and his personal assessment of the effectiveness of anti-drug agencies in other small European countries. Every answer was met with a tight nod.

At last Stringer released him, presenting him with a cellophaned bunch of wilting flowers to bring to Theresa, together with his good wishes for her recovery, and promising to call into the iDEA during the week, after the tour of regional crime-fighting facilities that the Minister had arranged for him.

Séamus set off towards Dublin. The rainless Sunday afternoon had drawn Dubliners out into the Wicklow hills, and the returning traffic was heavy and slow. He rummaged in his tape box, found his bootleg tape of Getz's Dublin concert, the one time he had seen Getz in the flesh. 'Early Autumn', then 'Here's That Rainy Day'. Calm descended.

In the hospital car park, his mobile phone shrilled. Máire Benedict, the Minister's private secretary, tense as ever, enquired if Séamus could call to the Minister's house in Dalkey for an urgent briefing. He promised to be there within the hour. It would mean missing evening Mass, but he had not enjoyed Mass for some years now. Missed it as often as not, unless Theresa went with him.

It wasn't the scandals in the Church he minded, the cruelty, the child abuse, the knee-jerk conspiracies of the chief priests. Séamus's quarrel was with God, who made the world.

Propped up on pillows with a selection of lifestyle magazines fanned across the coverlets, Theresa opened one eye and surveyed Séamus without dislike. Facing into next week's further procedures and the unspoken prospect of early death, she had shed the edgy antagonism with which she had punished him these last few years. She wrinkled her nose at Stringer's bouquet, but had the nurses put it in a vase in case the donor might take a notion to visit her.

Séamus could not bring himself to speak. He sat and gazed at her thinned face, dark-ringed eyes, fine golden hair grazing the pillow. She was sleeping now. Being bony did not suit Theresa. That change had first alerted him to her illness. Which in turn could have been precipitated by his recall from Germany and the threat of disgrace over his disputed expense accounts. Or perhaps it was mere coincidence. Had he deserved any better? He was her creature, but had he been a good creature? Had he given thanks? He had done his work conscientiously, earned his salary, done whatever she asked. But was there more that he should have done? Theresa had taken care of things. He had lived like a prince, with walking-around money in his pocket, credit cards in his wallet, and beautiful suits that combined with his prematurely greying hair to lend him a spurious air of distinction.

As his career progressed, he had often wondered how

far she might have eased his rise. The original transfer to Justice was probably due to his own merits, as was his stint as private secretary to the long-serving Minister, Mucky Smith. But his nomination as the Irish observer in Aachen could well have been due to Theresa's influence. Why else would Theresa, with her aspirations to gentility and her entrée to the best social and financial circles, ever have cultivated a connection with Mr and Mrs Mucky Smith? Mucky was a slewthering, pig-ignorant ward-heeler who had made a deeply incompetent and disreputable Minister for Justice. Mrs Mucky was a bloated battleaxe. When Theresa had gone through her phase of soirées, the Smiths were included in her guest lists. Mucky travelled everywhere with a thuggish enforcer who, like his Minister, was a boozer. Drunk-driving arrests had been papered over more than once during Séamus's tenure as Private Secretary. Later, on weekend visits home from his European posting, he had found his sitting room invaded by the Smiths carousing with business leaders while caterers replenished their glasses with Alsatian wines that Mucky proceeded to piss all over the bathroom carpet. They should never have carpeted that bathroom.

Theresa had not entertained his concerns about these matters. She had lived her own life. Her early middle years had been, at least in his eyes, a time of mysterious beauty, before illness had started to sap her physique, and her temper had turned against him.

She was awake again. He felt her eyes upon him. In a tired monotone she quizzed him on his laundry, his diet. He could barely remember. She instructed him to buy three new cream-coloured shirts in Thomas Pink of Dawson Street, reminded him of his neck size. In an almost friendly voice she enlisted his help with the crossword puzzle in the *Gazette* – the nurses had been stymied by SERAGLIO. She told him to give her regards to the Minister.

He drove like an automaton. He could see no further than Theresa's operation. He went through a red light, for the second time in a week. Nobody saw.

The Minister's house was on a quiet road, set back from the sea, a Victorian neo-Gothic pile. Spotlights lit the foliage of tall specimen trees. The guard on the gate recognized him, waved him through. He parked on the gravelled apron under a tropical pine. Richard Frye was standing in the ecclesiastical gothic doorway.

'Short notice, I'm afraid. How's your wife? Miss Benedict has had to go.' He led the way swiftly into a sombre baronial hall, at the end of which a television screen flickered with silent images from CNN.

'Dry?' A schooner of Tio Pepe was placed on the long dining-table. The last time he had come here, on the night he was appointed Acting Director (Interim), they had drunk Chablis and talked about Sicily. This time, the atmosphere was different. Richard Frye rested his tapering fingers on the back of a tall oak chair, faced his visitor and bared his teeth.

'Europe Without Drugs? State of play?'

'It's early days yet, Minister. Favourable reactions from Scandinavia. The British remain sceptical. The Germans will reply next month. The Mediterranean countries like the idea, but haven't quite accepted the idea of Ireland as the sole sponsor of the programme.'

The Minister made no comment on this, but fired a second question: 'Mr Tom Stringer?'

'A clever man, Minister. Inscrutable. Very well informed. Not greatly impressed by our information systems.'

'He should tell that to Finance. They want us to use quill pens. Mr Dowd of the Civic Guards pours poison in their ears, moaning about duplication and waste and other bad words. Nonetheless we remain upbeat. May I have your personal overview of the iDEA's current performance?'

He struck a listening pose. How much did he want? Séamus made a start, mentioning the education campaign, the website, the archives, the drugs information sharing agreement. There would be a full draft of the iDEA's five-year strategy document by Tuesday morning. Gilbert Covey's pamphlet, *The Drugs Problem: An Irish Solution*, had been sent to ninety-six newspapers in Britain, Europe and the United States, and already there had been several articles praising the Irish government, in papers ranging politically from left to right.

Richard Frye nodded at each point, waited for more. Séamus ploughed on. Heroin on the streets showed a continuing decline. Assaults with syringes were down twenty per cent, as were vigilante attacks on addicts. Neighbourhood Concern's nine local groups were providing reliable information on Dublin's dealers, and helping communities to fight against drugs within the law.

The Minister nodded. 'Continue, please.'

Still more? Séamus detailed the increased number of addicts receiving treatment, the falling rate of drug-related crime. He outlined the work of the Tough Love Treatment Centres, the first two of which had already received funding. Total projected capacity, two hundred and eighty places.

Richard Frye finally cut in. 'That is all very nice. But our core function, in strictly political terms, is repressing narco-distribution. Arresting and convicting the traders. In this, we are falling short. Certain issues have arisen.' The Minister inspected his fingernails. 'Next week I shall have to take some tricky parliamentary questions about the measurable effectiveness of our efforts in this field. My opposite number, Mr Comerford, aims to show that the iDEA is a waste of money. He is clearly being fed the Declan Dowd line, and has absorbed it well. When I delivered my "Dublin Justice" speech last May, I made it clear that our capital city was to be rendered an unattractive place to dump narcotics. We do not need the passing trade. This country is appetizing to foreign investors today because we offer a clean, educated, young workforce.'

'Yes, Minister.'

'I will not have the motivation of this generation of Irish youth – the first with a real chance of taking its place economically among the nations of the world – swamped with cheap stimulants imported from the slums of Latin America and Afghanistan. I promised to deal out Dublin justice to those who –'

'Indeed, Minister.' He had heard this speech verbatim on being appointed Acting Director. He had read it in the newspapers when it had first been delivered. He had been given a photocopied typescript of it by Gilbert Covey, who had written it for Richard Frye while still working for Pandarus Limited, Public Relations Practitioners, before his move to the public sector.

Frye did not like being interrupted. 'You will appreciate, Mr Joyce, that having given these very public commitments I need to show that I am choking off the suppliers, the importers, the middlemen who infect our young people. I need to chalk up major successes in the war on pushers.' He fixed Séamus with his laser gaze. 'Mr Joyce, I have done everything possible to facilitate you. Fought for resources. Authorized informer fees. Obtained warrants for telephone intercepts and confidential investigations. I have deliberately thrown out ten years of smug consensus and woolly research, and gone for the jugular vein of the problem. When we sail close to the wind, when we cast off the comfort of the familiar, that is because we wish to make real advances. What results can you show? What trophies, what scalps, can we lay before Mr Comerford?'

'You can point to a number of significant arrests, cutting into –'

Richard Frye raised a finger. 'A sore point. Our two major arrests have resulted' – pained smile – 'in two unfortunate failures.'

'Just one acquittal so far, Minister. And that was well outside our control.'

'Where did we fall down, Mr Joyce? Where was the weakness in our case?'

'We did not fall down, Minister. Mr McIntyre was a

respectable bank messenger working for a reputable German bank. He arrived in Dublin carrying a parcel which had been given to him by a temporary clerk in the despatch room of his bank in Amsterdam, addressed to a reputable banker in the Financial Services Centre here. The parcel contained heroin. Billy picked him up as he entered the Mangan Building. Everything was done correctly, and the facts were not in dispute. His case failed purely on the question of *mens rea*, meaning that the courier's criminal intent was not proven beyond –'

'Thank you. I know what it means. And the current case?'

'Mr Craig's defence is based on attacking the procedures that were used in recording the seizure – not our procedures, but those followed by Customs and Excise. Also, the value of the haul was disputed. But no decision has been taken by the trial judge. She adjourned on Friday, and –'

'Miss Justice Wade will announce tomorrow morning, Monday, that she is throwing out our case.'

'How can we know that?'

'Because she leaked it to her tipstaff, who mentioned it to another person, who informed Mr Covey, who passed the glad tidings to me. Unofficially, but reliably. To lose one case may be regarded as a misfortune, to lose two looks like carelessness. What does all this suggest to you, Mr Joyce?'

'That we've done a good job, but the judges don't like the legislation.'

Richard Frye nodded. 'They want to shaft me,' he

said. 'They wish to assert their independence. They presume to challenge the government's right to make the laws that rule this state. They intend to reduce my policies to tatters. We are giving them too much space, Mr Joyce. Next time, I want them to be faced with an open and shut case. Black and white. I want their noses rubbed in it.'

'We will certainly keep trying –'

'Succeed, Mr Joyce. Succeed. When do you anticipate your next outing?'

'Billy O'Rourke is picking up another courier tonight. The paperwork will be watertight.'

'But will he get the right sort of confession? Will the street value be over the threshold? Will the culprit be nailed, as the term is?'

'I expect so.'

'Don't expect, Mr Joyce. Ensure. You are the man in charge. Your two recent cases have compromised all that I set out to achieve. Last month, a retired Guard in West Kerry –'

'I am aware of that, Minister.'

'A retired Guard in West Kerry,' Frye reiterated deliberately, 'with the memorable name of Larry "Lugs" O'Laughlin, came across a dinghy that had drifted ashore with two and a quarter million dollars' worth of cocaine, and it made the television news on three continents. A comic Irish tale. If we're such lucky leprechauns, Mr Joyce, why do we need the iDEA?'

'Because luck is not enough, Minister.'

'Indeed not, Mr Joyce. Now we cannot close down the iDEA in its inaugural year. Which raises a subsidiary question: if the agency fails to perform, should we make changes? You are on secondment. You could go back to your desk, make way for a more productive chief.'

'That is entirely up to you, Minister.'

'The stable door must be properly shut, Mr Joyce. Your position as Acting Director would become untenable – *untenable* – should the next case fail.'

A telephone chirped in the Minister's pocket, and he went into his study to take the call, closing the door and leaving Séamus Joyce standing in the great baronial hall.

Again he remembered his first visit to the Minister's house, less than four months ago, to be confirmed as Acting Director (Interim), saved from his cramped office in the maintenance section, tantalized with the prospect of getting back to Europe once again. Because that was the real carrot. Richard Frye was bound for Europe. He had started his career as a rising star of the Brussels bureaucracy before moving to Washington and a consultancy with a conservative think tank. Everywhere, he had made allies. His contacts with British politicians and institutions were legendary. Money from the States funded his election campaigns.

Even so, how on earth had Richard Frye ever got elected to the Irish parliament? How had he become a Minister? In a party of back-slapping demotics, he was a patrician: handsome, cool, slender, favouring button-down collars. The antithesis of poor old Mucky Smith, now confined to an asylum for the terminally drunk. Richard Frye lived alone, although he was reputed to have a Belgian mistress. He spoke perfect French and good German. His Cabinet colleagues disliked him. Everyone was pleased that Frye was the front-runner to head the new European Union Narcotics Directorate. His only rival was the English candidate, Sir Alfred Edwards, and the British themselves were lukewarm about Edwards. The Sicilian candidate was not being taken seriously. The Danish woman, being a Green, was frankly unacceptable. Frye was the man to watch. And if he had to jettison a cypher like Séamus Joyce to further his rise, he would do so without a second thought.

The study door opened. The Minister emerged, smiling like a tray of ice cubes. 'I do apologize, Séamus. I've been neglecting you.' He brandished the sherry bottle.

'No, thanks, Minister, I'm driving.' His glass of Tio Pepe remained on the table, untouched.

'Good of you to call,' said Richard Frye. 'I know you will crack this legal problem. We will show Mr Comerford, and the judges, who is in charge here. In addition, we will strike a blow' – an unexpected shake crept into his voice – 'against the proliferation of stinking plague rats who infest my country and contaminate it with their little doses of poison and drag our good name down with their internecine feuds.'

Such emotion was surprising in this disciplined man. Séamus glanced at him with new interest. 'We'll do it,' he promised. He moved towards the door. The Minister accompanied him, laying a hand on his forearm.

'I'm continuing to take an active personal interest in your case with the auditors. I've had a word with our own financial people. I have no doubt they will see sense, and quickly. The charges were purely technical. It is regrettable that you have this as well as your wife's difficulties. I know what you're going through.'

'You do like fuck,' said Séamus to himself.

{{{{{{o}}}}}}

When the car stopped in Booterstown, Fennessy looked around. 'Wasn't this the old Vocational School?' His eyes were dry now.

Billy made no answer, stood close to the prisoner as Bosco Woulfe opened security locks, tapped in electronic codes. They hurried their captive through dark, deserted offices, up the creaking stairs, into the bare attic room. Billy switched on the lights, flung windows open.

Bosco left the room. Billy leaned over the table: 'Listen here, Jerome. That stuff you carried has a quote unquote street value of over twelve thousand seven hundred euros, meaning you face a mandatory stretch of ten years in jail. Cut and dried. On the other hand, if you help us catch the boys who sent you, then the contents of your bag might turn out to be worth a bit less. Street value is a grand flexible term. Your haul could be valued at twelve thousand. Eleven and a half. Ten.'

Fennessy observed him distantly, as though the situation did not greatly concern him.

Billy plugged in the electric kettle. 'You're an educated man, Jerome. Here's the deal. All we need is a statement, naming the man who set you up. We'll bring you in

61

front of Justice Moore. Man's a bleeding heart. His mother was a schoolteacher. Only last week he gave a suspended sentence to one of your kind. And not a word about your earlier troubles. You'll get probation. You can go back to London.'

Jerome held his peace.

'What's the problem, Jerome? Afraid he'll come and get you?'

'No, that's not it.'

'Because he'll be well out of the way. You won't have to worry about him.'

'It's not that. I'm afraid of implicating an innocent person.'

'We only want one name, Jerome boy. The man you met in the pub. Mr Mulhone, as you call him. He's not innocent.'

'Nobody else?'

'Nobody else. You see, Jerome, there was nobody else involved. Do you ever take a drop too much to drink?'

'It's happened, once or twice,' Jerome admitted.

'Well, that's what you did yesterday. You were feeling a bit low, for some reason –'

'I'd done a disastrous job interview.'

'Good man yourself. So you went to the Midshipman to drown your sorrows, like any decent Irishman would. Next thing there was this dastardly fiend, Matt Wellan, whispering temptation in your ear –'

'Matt Wellan?'

'Mr Mulhone's real name. Otherwise known as the Snowman. What did he say was in the packet?'

Jerome blinked, focused on the question. 'Papers. For a shopping centre.'

'Opium Arcade,' Billy said. 'Morphine Mall. Cast your eye over these beauties.'

He slapped a photograph album on the table. Jerome turned the pages, found Matt Wellan's picture, stared at it for a long moment. Flipped through the rest of the album, turned back to the Wellan page. Billy poured a mug of tea, slapped him on the shoulder. 'Bullseye, Jerome boy.'

The prisoner shook his head miserably. 'Look, I told you I can't implicate an innocent man in my own stupid conduct. The man I met in the pub was got up to look like this. But it's not the same person. Mr Mulhone was wearing a hairpiece, whereas this man has a full head of hair. It's not the same person, and I can't in all conscience say it is.'

Billy snapped the album shut, swept out of the room, leaving the door ajar. Jerome drank some tea, sat quietly on his own. Irrelevant questions buzzed in his tired skull. Was it really only yesterday that he had been in the Merrion Hotel? Would those businessmen read his name in the papers, and dine out for years on how they had interviewed a drug courier for a teaching job? Would everybody have forgotten the case in ten years' time, when he came out? But surely nobody actually served ten years. Sentences get commuted, don't they? There's time off for good behaviour, and Jerome was always well behaved, unfortunately. Was the fake Matt Wellan a policeman? Had Paul known what was going to happen?

The answer to this last question, at least, was instinctive: at school, Blake had been known as a dodger. Mr Carrington had dubbed him a 'moral relativist', an accolade that Paul had worn with pride. But he was not treacherous by nature.

It was cold. He roused himself, went to close the window. Billy came in quickly, followed by Bosco Woulfe.

'Shot while attempting to escape,' Woulfe snorted.

'Any further thoughts on the pictures?' Billy asked. 'That was an old photo, you know; his appearance has changed. And we're only looking for one name. Just the Snowman. Nobody else.'

Jerome faced him. 'You are trying to frame an innocent man, and I will not be party to it.'

Woulfe gave a bark of genuine laughter. 'The Snowman? Innocent? I don't think so.' He choked with amusement. 'Pure as the driven snow!'

'Can I go to the lavatory?' Jerome asked.

'You'll have to wait,' Woulfe sniggered. 'Guest toilets reopen in the morning.' Jerome sat down at the table. Woulfe poured a second mug of tea, no longer hot. He placed the mug clumsily on the table edge. It tipped over. Tea sloshed over Jerome's beautiful corduroys. Woulfe snorted. 'Wet yourself, Mr Hennessy?'

'Fennessy,' said Billy.

Jerome said nothing.

Billy stared into his face. 'Mulhone. Wellan. It's the same man. We'll give you a week to think about it. You'd be surprised how your memory can change over seven days. Especially when you think of getting out at the end of the week, or else spending an extra ten years behind bars.' There was an unfathomable force of anger in Billy's blue eyes. Not directed against Jerome, but at something beyond.

Jerome made no move to wipe the tea from his trouser front. 'You have your own agenda,' he said at last. 'You may have good reasons. But I'll say nothing without my solicitor.'

'You'll be waiting a long time,' Woulfe put in. 'Nice new laws they gave us.'

Jerome nodded. 'So be it.'

Woulfe caught Billy by the elbow, drew him away as if warding off violence. They went out, closed the door. He was alone again, but he knew they were watching.

He would hold out. He had to. Nothing else left. He should have gone to the toilet on the plane, before it had started its approach to Dublin Airport. Time and tide . . .

Banging and creaking from downstairs. And the sound of Billy's voice, no longer tight and loud, but surprised, subservient, dismayed. The door swung open.

In his smooth grey suit and sober-patterned silk tie, the new arrival made a meek impression. He was carrying a walkman and wearing a large headset around his plump neck. 'Aren't you going to introduce me?' he asked in a mild voice.

'Mr Jerome Fennessy, language teacher and occasional smuggler,' Billy announced. 'Mr Séamus Joyce, Director of the Irish Drugs Enforcement Agency. I'm negotiating with Mr Fennessy to see if we might be able to get him off the hook. We want to follow up his contacts with the people who sent him. If he plays ball, we might be in a position to help.' He handed Fennessy a towel to wipe his trousers.

Joyce sat down heavily on a kitchen chair beside the prisoner. 'They call me Director,' he confided, 'but I'm just the Acting Director. A civil servant, by the by, not a policeman. Apart from the enforcement side, we look after legislation, policy, schools, all sorts of stuff. I see you're wearing a wedding ring.'

'Oh.' Jerome clasped his hands, hiding the ring. 'She wants to re-marry.'

'My wife is seriously ill,' Séamus Joyce said, blinking.

'I'm sorry,' Jerome said.

There was a pause. 'What's wrong with her?' Jerome enquired, to keep up his side of the exchange.

Before Joyce could answer, Billy O'Rourke cut in. 'I'm trying to get this man probation, Séamus. He could nail one of Dublin's –'

Séamus Joyce held up a soft hand. 'Sorry, Billy. I'm afraid there's no probation.'

Billy was incredulous. 'Not even if he can snaffle the Snowman for us? Jerome would make a lovely witness. Not your average gangster.' Again the anger in his voice.

Joyce looked embarrassed. 'No deals. The agency is fighting an all-out war on drugs. That's what the Minister wants. We must fight every case. On what evidence did you arrest Mr Fennessy?'

Billy looked blank for a second. Then he stepped out of the room, returning almost at once. Like a magician at a children's party, he shook Jerome's overnight bag upside-down over the table. Out tumbled the padded

66

envelope, Jerome's pyjamas, his toothpaste and tooth-brush, his postcards and catalogue from the Rijks-museum, the tin of cigarillos from Rossini's, and a second padded envelope that Jerome had not seen before. Billy opened the second envelope, drew out its contents: another plastic wallet of white powder, and a glossy magazine showing a naked child, perhaps two years old, holding a toy alligator in front of her crotch. The magazine's title was *Pudeurs Enfantines*.

Billy flicked open the magazine, riffled its pages. Séamus Joyce studied the look of mingled surprise and revulsion on Jerome's face.

'This your usual reading matter?' Billy enquired.

'I never saw it before.'

'And the extra sachet of smack?'

'Planted, of course. As is the magazine. The museum catalogue and cards, on the other hand, I bought. Like-wise the cigarillos.'

'Would you like to smoke one now?' Séamus asked.

'Can't be done,' Woulfe said in the background. 'They count as evidence.'

'Anyway, they're a present,' Jerome said. 'For a friend of a friend. But thanks all the same.'

Billy paused for a moment, as if a thought had struck him. He picked up the tin of cigarillos, read the label, put it down, then dangled the plastic wallet of powder in front of Jerome's face. 'Do you know, Jerome, this extra bag of horse more or less doubles the street value.' Billy shook his head. 'The news is bad. Change of plan. Nothing to be done.' He started to gather up the items he had scattered on the table-top.

'I didn't believe you anyway,' Jerome said. 'And I'm not talking any more. I'm tired. I need to go to the lavatory and you won't let me.'

'Of course we will,' Séamus said. 'No problem about that. I need to go too. I'll accompany you.'

As they washed their hands, Jerome asked, 'Would it be helpful if I prepared a full written statement?' He spoke like a professional man offering his services. 'I don't want to implicate innocent people, but if I wrote out everything –'

'It would be extremely useful,' Séamus assured him. 'We're not going to persecute innocent people. We have plenty of the other kind.' He led the prisoner into his own office, fetched some sheets of paper from the desk, pulled up a chair at the conference table, switched on an Anglepoise lamp. 'Make yourself at home. Take your time. Put in whatever you think is relevant. Another cup of tea?'

Billy O'Rourke came in. 'We thought you'd shinned down the drainpipe. Writing your memoirs, Jerome?'

Jerome took a fountain pen from an inside pocket, scratched at the paper. 'Empty, of course.'

'Not to worry,' Séamus said, rummaging in a drawer. 'I think there's a bottle.' Indeed there was. Pelikan black ink. Poor Paddy Goldborough liked to have the best. 'Here you are, Mr Fennessy. Work away.'

'I have to caution you,' Billy said formally, 'that you are not obliged to say anything, or to write out any statement. Anything that you do write or say can be used against you in a court of law.'

'That's fine,' Jerome assured him.

'I'll be outside,' Billy said, 'in case you need me.'

Jerome Fennessy filled his fountain pen, while Séamus Joyce covered his plump ears with the headset of his CD walkman and settled back into his chair with the benevolence of a hanging judge.

{{{{{{o}}}}}}

Paul Blake plopped the spent champagne bottle into the waste-paper basket. Non-vintage but drinkable. Half past midnight by the grandfather clock. The last group of members had decamped some time ago, seeking the fleshlier pleasures of Dolly's. Blackwood's would not stoop to dancing and vulgar music. Even Pat O'Hara agreed that lap dancing was for losers.

Blake drained his glass, debated whether to venture forth himself. Since Ruth had thrown him out, he had been experiencing a temporary shortage of womenfolk. He was getting to the age when casual pickups were no longer appropriate. He needed something longer-term.

No sign of Gloria tonight.

Ruth had been his best liaison, after Désirée had unreasonably ejected him from the matrimonial home. Ruth was very much younger, which was of course wonderfully refreshing, but it did eventually lead to problems of compatibility. That much had to be admitted.

Gloria, now, might be something entirely different. The age differential would be negligible: no more than a dozen years. Less if he trimmed a bit. All's fair in LBW.

Had he perchance been too diffident with Gloria?

69

He must engineer an occasion. These American dames prefer the forthright approach. It's like the National Lottery. If you're not in you can't win.

He slipped into his second-best dressing gown, uncorked the Grand Marnier and glugged himself a miniature glassful. He wasn't about to break open a second bottle of champers at this hour. Not all by himself. That would smack of excess. He reached for the remote control. On the sound system, Cecilia Bartoli was locking her tonsils around young Wolfgang Amadeus. What a gal!

Perhaps he could persuade Gloria to accompany him to the opera. In Salzburg, say, or Prague. Why not? Buy a couple of tickets to a gala evening, pretend he'd received them as a gift, casually ask Gloria to accompany him. The worst she could say was 'no'. And if that happened, he would be as urbane and gentlemanlike as ever. He would never make her feel uncomfortable. She would surely be pleased to have been asked.

Which did not, however, solve the immediate *impasse*.

He poured himself another snifter. Ah, this yearning for female company! He had always been a man who liked ladies. Genuinely. Singular and plural. Older and younger. Not the sort of foible one can explain to daughters. They have to find out by experience. He really would have to confront Désirée, first thing in the morning, and negotiate that trip to London with Felicity and Dee Dee.

In the meantime, should he risk telephoning ruthless Ruth? Last time she had been furious to be called after midnight, and had said some rather wounding things, but then, one never does know with women. She might be ready to forgive, perhaps even ready to give him another whirl. Why not? If he didn't try, he'd never know for sure. Which would be a crying shame. Ruth, in the right mood, was a prize worth having. Lesser men might quail. He knocked back a throatful of warming liqueur, poured himself another splash, and feeling like a First World War trooper about to go over the top, reached boldly for the receiver.

A footfall on the landing surprised him.

Surely Pat had beetled off hours ago? Long tall Jenny had left at midnight, with taxi fare plus a little *pourboire* to signify one's appreciation.

The door opened, slowly.

'Robin! *Quel honneur!*'

The Robin was quivering. Paul had never seen him nervous before. He smiled to reassure him. 'Step right in.' He felt curiously like a headmaster receiving a miscreant in his study.

'I just want to know,' the little man stammered, 'was it you sent him to that shop?'

Paul knocked back his Grand Marnier in one gulp, replenished the glass, and steadied his focus on the matter in hand. 'Whom? Pardon me! To whom are you referring?'

'Keep your voice down, for Jeez sake. The man they nicked. He was carrying drugs. Was it you got him to buy the cigars? Or is he on his own game?'

Paul sighed. This thing would have to be faced, after all. 'So it's true, what Pat said. Poor little Romy. Unconscionable. Treated like a common criminal.'

'That's what he is,' squeaked the Robin. 'He's a dope dealer. They nicked him. And he's singing. And not the tune he was supposed to sing. And why did you have to do that fuckin' stupid thing with the cigars, Paul? I trusted you.' His supplicant demeanour might almost have been amusing in better circumstances.

Blake stood tall, glared down at him with the contempt he deserved. 'Trust? Trust, you say? You guaranteed,' he pronounced, 'or rather Pat guaranteed, that nothing deleterious would occur to Jerome. If you'd kept your word, you'd have had nothing to fear from my little *démarche*.'

'You thought you could set a trap for me?' The Robin was still shaking. 'You sent him to the shop to mix me up in it. But that can't be done, you see, 'cause I keep a clean sheet. My dad did time, my brother did time. My uncle was hung in his cell. Not me. They'll drag me down if they can. But I stay clean. Paul, I trusted you, and you went behind my back.' His voice had risen to a nagging petulant girlish whine. Just like blasted Désirée at her worst.

Paul Blake rose up. A red mist, tinged with fumes of Grand Marnier, swam around his eyes. But he knew he must meet this challenge. Long overdue, in truth. Controlling himself with an effort, he drew a deep breath and took firm command of the situation, laying a friendly hand on the Robin's shoulder.

'Now look here,' he began. 'Romy and I were at school together. I simply can't abandon an old chum to the tender mercies of your associates, can I? I mean to say. Notwithstanding which, I hasten to add, I have no quarrel with your good self.' Quite a fine speech.

'You planned it,' wailed the little man. 'You lousy prick.' He shrank back out of reach.

Paul cleared his throat. 'It's what we call a fail-safe mechanism. Without telling him what it was for, I instructed Jerome Fennessy to buy those cheroot thingies that you favour. Even requested him to mention your name in the Rossini cigar emporium. I'd glommed the name from one of your tins, little dreaming how useful it might be, one day. My actions were neither reckless nor gratuitous. And this is the way it's going to have to be, henceforward. Jolly old worm has turned. Here I stand. Literally, and figuratively. All I ask – a modest requirement enough – is that you rescue Mr Fennessy from his present difficulty, and leave me, henceforward, to manage Blackwood's in my own style.'

'And if I don't?'

'If you throw down the gauntlet, Robin, I shall regretfully have to testify that in my opinion you not only arranged the recruitment of Romy as a traveller in illegal substances but did so with the deliberate intent of entrapping him. Frightfully sorry, you know, but a chap can only take so much.'

'I know how much a chap can take, and there's some takes more than what's good for them.' There was a noticeable change in the Robin's tone. He had stopped shaking. 'One last chance, Paul. You'll have to swear you never met the man.'

'Testify I never met my old china?' Blake bellowed with honest mirth.

'Or,' whispered the Robin.

'Or what, pray? Are you threatening me, perchance?' Blake poured another shot of liqueur. His throat was dry. 'You don't dictate to me, Robin.'

The little man nodded, as if he had finally reached a decision. 'All right.' Stepping forward, he flicked the glass out of Paul's hand. Grand Marnier spattered the brocaded upholstery. No matter. Grand Marnier leaves no stain, and the smell is rather pleasant. Like superior wax polish.

Paul Blake moved back unobtrusively towards the desk. His gun was in the drawer. 'You really mustn't attempt to intimidate me,' he told the Robin as he glided towards his objective. 'I've got contacts, you know.'

The small man emitted a jagged bark. 'You think they love you, because they drink my free booze. Let me tell you, Paul, the only way to find out how popular you are is watch who comes to your funeral.'

Unpleasant thought, this, but he had finally reached the desk drawer. He pulled out the gun, a great big ugly thing, and slipped the safety catch.

'What's that for?' The Robin was pulling on a pair of gloves.

'Protection, Robin. That's what.'

'You're goin' to plug me or what?'

'Not unless it's strictly necessary,' Paul assured him. 'I have no wish to harm you, Robin, but I must ask you to leave the premises forthwith.'

'Too fuckin' late, Mr Blake.' The little man reached into his trouser pocket.

Paul squeezed off one shot, into the bookcase. A warning. He had forgotten how deafeningly loud the gun was. The books showed no sign of damage. Those fine leather bindings must have absorbed the impact.

The little man was holding a pistol of his own. Small, appropriately enough.

Past the point of no return.

Having no alternative (he would explain this later to the jury, with his customary mellifluence), Paul aimed quickly at the little man's chest, fired once, twice.

The roar of the gun filled the room.

He would never have believed himself capable of that. One learns one's own strength in moments of crisis.

The Robin was still standing, which was more than odd. Now he was screwing a silencer onto his pistol.

Paul took careful aim, wincing, at the head. Fired again.

'Cigars,' said the Robin, 'can damage your health. Did you ever hear tell of that?' He let off a silenced shot, shattering the ornate French gilt mirror that leaned against the wall. 'Does your gun not work?' he asked. 'Mine does.'

Paul fired his last two shots in rapid succession. Then the trigger clicked, and clicked again. There was silence in the room for half a second. Fear rose like an iceberg in his brain.

'Pat loaded it up with blanks,' the Robin explained. 'He thought you might do harm.' He squeezed his trigger again, and the grandfather clock gave a horrified thud of splintering wood and echoing brass. 'Right, Paul. I don't have much time. Open the safe.'

'Why?' He formed the word, could not hear himself pronounce it.

'To see the dosh you got from the Snowman.'

'Not a tosser, I do assure you.' This was too shaming. Too absurd to be terrifying. Paul fiddled with the wall safe, miraculously recalled the combination, swung the door open. If only he had been clever enough to hide another weapon in there, he could be dropping to his knees at this instant and spraying the room with real bullets, like Bruce Forsythe. Forsythe? Chap in a singlet. Of whom Dee Dee had a poster in her bedroom. 'Come on down! Make my day!' Sadly, real life was not as well choreographed as the movies. He stepped back from the empty safe. 'See for yourself, Robin. Not a sausage. Scout's honour.'

'Clear out your pockets. Quick.' The little man pointed his silenced pistol while butter-fingered Paul littered banknotes and coins across the desktop.

'Now the credit cards. Go on.'

Five of the little monsters. Three too many, to be perfectly honest. Paul spread them out with a croupier's flourish, though his hands were shaking with a life of their own. Combined credit limit: a tiddly bit over forty thousand. Unsustainable. He would have to reform, regroup, refinance. But he was going to die, here, now. Or perhaps not.

The little man surveyed the lot, cocked his head on one side like a real robin.

'So long, Paul.' And shot him in the upper thigh.

Paul Blake was catapulted into a new world of un-believable pain. There was a suddenly remembered younger Paul, needing only to leap through the bonds of reality into the realm of opportunity. An alternative self to be reached by different paths. A life to be lived by the laws of pure potential. Losing his balance, the real Paul pitched forward across the desktop. Money rolled onto the carpet. He was going to be sick. How embarrassing. Far too far away, coins were rolling and sinking out of sight.

'A robbery,' mocked the Robin, 'gone wrong.'

And put a full stop to Paul Blake's complex, con-flictual and largely illusory life with a single executioner's bullet through the skull.

He then adjusted his safety catch, pocketed the gun, stepped carefully around the wreckage of the body, quickly scooped up money from everywhere.

Cecilia Bartoli sang sweetly on. The Count was not to have his way with her tonight.

The killing of Blake was afterwards judged to have been an overreaction. In fact, a definite mistake.

{{{{{{o}}}}}}

Séamus Joyce settled back in his reclining desk chair, eyes closed, head turned away from the light. Paddy Goldborough had ordered the chair from the Back Shop. It did not quite fit Séamus's back.

The Stan Getz tape came to an end. He let the silence grow.

Anything was better than being at home. The house was unbreathable without Theresa. Last night had been dreadful; he had lain on his bed as in a burning coffin, unable to rest. Tonight the sound of a scratching pen might keep him awake. Better than silence.

Even the memory of Heidi could not relax him now. Usually, he was comforted by the warmth of that sinful afternoon in Taormina, when she stood on honey-coloured tiles, slipping out of her white clothes and tossing them softly aside. But these nights Theresa, not Heidi but Theresa, was lying in the false comfort of her hospital room, on a white prison-barred metal bed that meant neither sleep nor marriage nor love but death and only death.

And yet that first afternoon in Taormina returned to his memory with the mythic intensity of pure fiction. It could not possibly have happened, but it had. After the florid welcomes and the dull meeting and the lavish lunch, the group had trudged up the hill to the amphitheatre, and white-haired Heidi, from the German secretariat, in her white dress, had slipped and twisted her ankle. Séamus had caught her elbow as she fell. They had walked back to the hotel together because she suddenly decided against the trip around Mount Etna by tour bus, and on the way she had leaned on his arm (so lightly) and asked him about Ireland. She told him that she had always wanted to talk to him, ever since he had first come to the Permanent Liaison Committee headquarters in Aachen. She asked him to help her upstairs. She unbuttoned his shirt.

He looked across at the prisoner, writing steadily like a well-prepared examination candidate. The man faced prison and disgrace for the thing that he had done. And yet he seemed perfectly content. When you are guilty, capture comes as a relief.

Séamus had never been with a woman other than Theresa. His student fumblings had come to nothing. Heidi was a feral cat. He had assumed that after Taormina she would never speak to him again, he had been so inadequate. Instead of which, she had pursued him when they got back to Aachen. She wanted him to come and stay in her cottage outside town. He was afraid. What on earth could she see in him? Was she a spy? She never asked him to make a break with Theresa, although he had revealed that he and Theresa had had no sexual life together for more than five years. That was unforgivable. Theresa was entitled to his discretion.

He had gone to Heidi's place for a weekend, once, and was avalanched by happiness. Might even have gone again.

Then everything had changed. Mucky Smith, his nominating Minister, had collapsed with alcohol poisoning at a dinner in Dublin and gracelessly retired from the political scene. The Department's internal auditors had pounced.

It was a stupid story. The details went around in his head like convicts tramping a prison yard. The Permanent Liaison Committee had allocated an entertainment budget to those of the national delegates who did not receive such a budget from their nominating governments. This scheme had been designed to assist the Eastern European observers, who found Germany impossibly expensive, but it also topped up the household incomes of the observers from Ireland and two other small nations, who did not enjoy full diplomatic rank. One was not expected to spend one's entertainment budget on entertainment. It was a slice of tax-free salary. Mucky Smith had told him so, in so many words. The auditors knew nothing of that, or so they claimed. The exact sequence of their inquisition was printed in his brain. After an exhaustive enquiry, they had reported the case to the Comptroller and Auditor General, and also convinced Hewdie Doherty, the retiring Secretary of the Department, that Séamus Joyce was a fraudster and tax evader. He had been ignominiously recalled, and not replaced, because in the view of certain opposition parties the Permanent Liaison Committee on Security Affairs was of no conceivable use to the Irish taxpayer, being merely a means of sucking neutral members of the EU and the Council of Europe into NATO's sphere of influence in the wake of September 11.

He had relived the whole episode hundreds of times, arguing it to himself indignantly many different ways in the darkest hours of the night. He remembered the auditors' names, their telephone numbers, the numbers of the files they had sequestered. A civil service training is not conducive to sound sleep.

Séamus had at first suspected that somebody in Dublin had got wind of his affair with Heidi, and that he was being punished for that. It could even have been Theresa. He had longed to challenge her, but was stifled by guilt.

His superiors had shunted him from job to job: procurement, personnel, immigration, maintenance, pensions. Nowhere was he given any responsibility, because he was not trusted; in fact each new superior officer had clearly been briefed to keep an eye on him. Home was lonely, too, because Theresa had started spending more time in her holiday cottage in Kerry, which she was restoring and decorating. Séamus had gone back to a diet of packaged dinners. His weight was creeping up.

Then Paddy Goldborough had his heart attack, and Richard Frye, the new Minister, plucked Séamus from obscurity and disgrace and offered to place him at the helm of the iDEA. Séamus had felt bound to raise with the Minister the advisability of appointing him while still awaiting the outcome of the auditors' report. Frye had congratulated him on his scrupulousness, and airily assured him that nothing would come of the case. At most, a technical reprimand might be issued. Mr Smith's penchant for unorthodox arrangements was well understood. No blame would attach to Séamus for following the former Minister's instructions.

That was a lucky break, if you like. Although the auditors' case was still unfinished, the atmosphere changed overnight. Séamus was seen again as a rising star. Colleagues started speaking to him. People who had brushed past him in corridors were now pursuing him across car parks to seek his valuable opinion. He hated them for that.

Other parts of his life were in rapid downturn. Theresa had come home from Kerry, looking thin and disorientated, but unwilling to accept that she might be seriously ill.

How long ago had it been? It felt like years, yet it was

only months. This was her first time in hospital since her distant miscarriage.

No use trying to rest. The scratching pen was still at work. He sighed and sat up. The prisoner took no notice of him. Séamus started up his desktop computer, logged on and started to search the Internet. The screens changed with agonizing slowness, because the iDEA was still connected over a dumb telephone line. Better things were promised. Still, it worked. After some false starts he surfed onto the shores of oncologychannel .com, an American site. This corroborated what Dr Maguire Gibson had told him about oesophageal cancer, and some of the likely treatments. Theresa had already had a barium x-ray and biopsy. After her test results were known, she would face surgery, possibly combined with chemotherapy, depending on what stage the cancer had reached, if indeed it was cancer.

The prisoner asked him for more paper. Séamus gave him a thick sheaf. He was writing fast and fluently. Séamus scrolled back and forth on the computer screen, his mind fully awake although his body was numb. Further searches brought him to a French site where the technical language was far beyond his grasp. He returned to the American site and printed out some pages. He pictured the auditors tracking his Internet hits and accusing him of converting state-owned resources to private use. He would go and see someone in the Irish Cancer Society. Or he could ask for a second opinion. Suppose Dr Maguire Gibson had got it wrong? But no, the news was bad, therefore true.

He switched off the computer. Jerome Fennessy was

staring into space. As Séamus watched, he bent his head and started writing again. Papers were scattered around the table. Some drafts, with heavy crossings-out, had slipped to the floor.

Séamus sank back into his chair, closed his eyes again, tried to think about things outside of himself and Theresa. But his mind wandered back. Drugs were a cancer in society. His job was to clean them out, through surgery and radiation and chemotherapy. Chemotherapy: good drugs fighting bad drugs. All treatments destroy what they try to preserve. The trick is to target, to cut, to blast life only where life itself is threatened. To allow the body's natural resistance to fight against the alien cells. No: cancer is not an alien contamination. It comes from within. Unborn babies can carry it in their little bodies. That must give God something to laugh about.

Still the scratching pen, the sounds of night-time traffic. He followed the sound of a retreating engine until it was lost in silence.

Daylight was seeping through the blinds. Billy's voice: 'Am I too early?'

'I've been asleep. What's the time?'

'Seven o'clock.' Billy's voice was light and relaxed, as if he had rested. The prisoner was motionless, his head resting on his folded forearms, a sheaf of handwritten papers trapped underneath. He might have been dead, but for the muffled whisper of his breathing.

'I'm writing out my report,' Billy said. 'Once we have the paperwork done, I'll get him into the queue for the district court.'

Séamus opened the blinds, gazed out at the gathering

Monday-morning traffic. There was just time to visit Theresa before the office opened.

He drove to the clinic, muzzy with exhaustion, forcing himself to focus on the tasks of the day. Three urgent letters to dictate, and a request for regrading by the new librarian to be processed. Then to collate the last editorial changes to the five-year strategy document. Mary Rice would tackle the corrections. This was supposed to be Eileen's job, but poor Eileen was reduced to smiling helplessness by the very sight of a computer screen.

The shooting of a nameless Englishman made a brief item on *Morning Ireland*. The body had been found in a gentlemen's club on Merrion Square.

The nurses gave him a cup of tea. Theresa was pale and sleepy, seemed barely aware of his presence. He stayed for fifteen minutes, said nothing of where he had passed the night.

Back at the iDEA building, the prisoner was reading through his sheaves of paper and numbering the pages sequentially. Billy and Bosco were hovering at the office door. Bosco was white-faced, his eyes ringed with black like a koala bear. Billy was impatient. 'Ready yet?' he wanted to know.

'I'll ask.'

'Kid gloves, though,' Billy said. 'We don't want to frighten him.'

Joyce went into the room. 'Slept well?' he asked.

'Enough, thanks.' Fennessy's crinkled face still looked carefree. Séamus almost envied him. What did he have to lose, now?

'Finished?'

'I'll just add a codicil, if I may.' Jerome shook his fountain pen gently to get the ink flowing, then as Séamus watched over his shoulder he wrote carefully but without hesitation, as if he had already determined the wording: 'I may be guilty of nothing more than foolishness, but extreme foolishness is itself culpable. I am thus willing to accept the consequences in so far as they relate to me. I believe myself to have been gulled by the person who introduced himself as Mr P. J. Mulhone. My valued friend Mr Paul Blake, who unwittingly involved me in this sorry affair, is entirely innocent of criminal intent. Of that I am certain.'

He signed 'Jerome P. Fennessy' in a clear, smooth hand and handed the papers to Séamus, who riffled through them. There were fourteen numbered pages, on top of a sheaf of draft pages traversed by bold diagonal lines.

Billy O'Rourke came in behind them, carrying a tray with a pot of coffee, a Greenpeace mug and a plate of fig rolls. These he placed in front of Jerome, and looked at the sheaf of papers. 'Did you write in the time?' he asked. 'They'll want that.'

Séamus found the last sheet without crossings-out. Jerome consulted his gold watch, and inscribed below his signature: 'Monday morning, 8:26 a.m.'

Billy poured a mugful of coffee for Jerome. 'Maxwell House,' he said. 'Mild and satisfying. I'll be back up with a safety razor, then we'll go see the judge. Your coffee is upstairs, Séamus.'

'Do you think the judge might give me bail?' Jerome was asking as they left.

Climbing the stairs, Billy showed Séamus a copy of *The Irish Times*. 'Bail? I don't think so.' He pointed. 'Seen that? Club owner shot dead. Mr Paul Blake. The guy Fennessy now claims recruited him for the trip to Amsterdam.'

Séamus glanced at the story. 'Is that the Englishman whose body was found?'

'Bingo.'

Séamus stopped. 'And Fennessy knows he's dead?'

Billy nodded. 'Sure. Heard myself and Bosco talking about it while you were out. There was something on *Morning Ireland*, and Bosco was on the phone to one of his mates in Garda HQ. The *Times* puts Blake's murder down to robbery, but it sounds more like a Mafia hit. Jerome is cashing in on the coincidence. He's not quite the innocent gom he's been letting on. He'll get the ten years all right.'

Séamus thought of Theresa condemned to death, and of his own life stretching ahead in the distance. 'Ten years?' he said. 'Is that all?'

Part Two

Things got better. The strategy document passed its final vetting. Eileen McTeague stayed back late to finish spiral-binding the copies for Cabinet. For all her fear of computers, Eileen was a demon with a binding machine.

And Theresa recovered her morale. When Séamus finally got back to the clinic in the evening, Sister Mary was leaving the ward. 'We've been praying,' the nun confided. 'Saint Thérèse of Lisieux will intercede.' Theresa was lying back against the pillows, fanning herself with a handful of holy pictures. 'My passport to heaven,' she said. It was a long time since he had seen that glint in her eye. She talked about the interior decoration of the house in Bluebell that she was preparing to sell. Séamus joined in as best he could, left her asleep, floated home ten tons lighter, went to bed in a daze of happiness and slept like a baby.

Tuesday's morning papers noted the iDEA's success in arresting a drug courier – all the sweeter since yesterday's *Gazette* had contained a distinctly snotty piece by one Trixie Gill, suggesting that despite the presence of dynamic officers such as Billy O'Rourke (winner of the Walsh Medal for bravery), the Agency was poorly led and amounted to little more than a public relations exercise for the Minister. This morning, the same Trixie Gill was leaking snippets of the five-year strategy, which she hailed as one of the most imaginative plans ever to come out of a government agency. Covering the Fennessy arrest, she put the street value of the haul at twenty-nine thousand euros, and billed the case as a major step in breaking the drugs distribution empire of one of Dublin's leading criminals, popularly known as the Snowman.

Séamus's office was invaded by Mary Rice, his capable administrator, and her troupe of electricians. They were installing cables for the new computer network. Each office was to have Ethernet wall sockets. The library suite, Gilbert Covey's offices and the statistical section would have DSL lines. Not that this made much sense, as the iDEA would shortly be moving to new premises. Still, there was talk of selling the present building on to the Dún Laoghaire–Rathdown local authority, which might find some use for the cabling.

Eileen loaded the strategy document printouts into cardboard boxes, which the Garda driver carried down-stairs. Half an hour later Séamus placed a sample copy on the Minister's desk. Richard Frye flipped through the pages, pleased. 'Worth all the trouble, I think,' he purred. 'More to the point, we've converted Miz O'Sullivan.'

Sal O'Sullivan was the first female Secretary General in the Department of Justice, a job long viewed as impossible for a woman. Sal was tough enough to do it. Séamus had attended a meeting on organized crime at which she had crisply shredded two senior officials. She had been appointed just before the new Minister, and it was known that their relationship was uneasy.

Sal had not shunned Séamus during his period of

virtual disgrace. Neither had she been supportive. She had simply remained herself, politely distant, like a Siamese cat. He respected that.

He left the Minister's office in high spirits, called in again to the clinic on his way back to work. Theresa was returning from her morning tests. Still faintly smiling, but her skin was ivory-coloured, like polished bone.

He bought two bunches of flowers in the hospital boutique and walked back to the iDEA building. It was a glorious early winter morning, with sunshine brightening cold air and just the hint of damp that brought out the delicious smell of fallen leaves. He felt almost redeemed.

Séamus was not naturally clubbable. He had never been entirely at ease, with himself or anyone else. His apparent academic abilities had hoisted him into the civil service; once there, he had found little in common with his coarser colleagues, and was afraid of the abler ones, so he had remained a fish out of water. His aloofness had done his career no harm, as it was assumed to stem from self-possession. His lengthy German posting had broken many of the social contacts he might have built up. And Theresa had never been one for mingling with civil service wives. But the iDEA was different. These were his people. He entered the building with a tentative spring in his step, holding the flowers discreetly. Everybody pretended not to notice them.

Gilbert Covey was fuming over a radio programme by somebody called Peter Simons, on a Dublin independent station, which had insinuated that Richard Frye was directly funded by the Responsibility Foundation Institute, a right-wing US lobby group with links to Indonesia. Vicious lies, said Gilbert. Billy O'Rourke had arrived and was slinking around the place, a triumphant glint in his eye. He watched from a corner of the main office while Séamus made his little speech thanking Mary Rice and Eileen McTeague for their great efforts in preparing the strategy document, and presented the two bunches of hospital flowers.

'A word?' Billy was bursting with suppressed excitement. In Séamus's room, he flourished his newspaper clippings. 'What do you think of these?'

'Very gratifying,' Séamus said.

'You ain't seen nothing yet. Because we' – Billy dropped his voice – 'are about to snaffle one of the biggest bags of horse in the history of the state. Valued in the millions. Forget Neighbourhood Concern and the other chickenfeed. The horse will arrive into Dublin Airport on a cargo plane from Cyprus, and we'll grab it – if you give the go-ahead, of course.'

'What do you need?'

'More muscle than we've got, unfortunately. We're going to have to involve Decko.'

'Are we on speaking terms these days?'

'Not quite. But if we throw Decko some credit for this, he might stop trying to bugger us. Especially as he's been out to get this particular importer for years.'

'Who's the importer?'

'You might have read about him in Decko's so-called intelligence reports, since Sal got us put on the circulation list. The man's name is John F. Hughes, but his friends call him the Robin.'

{{{{{{o}}}}}}

Davnet was tired. The investigation of Mr Blake's death had fallen to a chimpanzee in a blue suit. He kept Jenny and Davnet waiting for aeons in the bar of Blackwood's Club, then took Jenny into the drawing room and shut the door. When Jenny came out he summoned Davnet, put her sitting in the brocaded wing-backed armchair, puffed clouds of pipe-smoke at her (in the yellow drawing-room!) along with a barrage of silly questions in a sing-song Donegal accent – had anyone threatened Mr Blake, how did people get along with him, had there been break-ins in the past, had suspicious characters been snooping around, for example anyone claiming to represent the gas company or the electricity board? Any health inspectors? He wrote in his black notebook. What he didn't seem to realize was that Mr Blake's daughters would never see their father again, and Jenny and Davnet were going to lose their job working together.

Jenny left first, on her way to meet a guy in Trinity College, and Davnet did not want to witness that. She collected her yellow dress from the staff cupboard. Ridiculous. It reminded her of dressing up when she was a small child. Taken in, it might fit her sister Maureen, who could do with some cheering up and had once done ballroom dancing. She stuffed the folds of yellow silk into a Blarney Woollen Mills bag, then went slowly downstairs for the last time. The club was strangely silent. She heard floorboards creaking. She would never come back.

Afternoon post lay on the mat. Bills, circulars, more timeshare brochures, a handwritten mauve envelope for Paul Blake Esq., this week's *New Yorker*. Davnet gathered everything up, to be laid out on the mahogany credence, and then noticed the postcard addressed to herself. 'Watch Out For Me! Love, Jerome.' Jerome who? The card was titled *The Night Watch*. She turned it over. A fat girl in a yellow dress, surrounded by armed men. Jerome. Of course. The skinny perve who had called in on Saturday morning. Who did he think he was? That child on the postcard was no more than ten years old. Still, she liked the jumble of life in the painting. Jerome was a friend of Mr Blake. Maybe he would come to the funeral. She pocketed the card, opened the big door and walked out into the sunshine, slamming it behind her. Jenny had faded from sight. Davnet trudged through Merrion Square gardens, then lingered over a cappuccino in the Leinster Coffee House before going to catch her bus. She walked slowly through Trinity College, but there was no sign of Jenny and her date.

At home, there was the usual menagerie: Maureen glooming around the kitchen with a cup of hot chocolate, Pa slumped in front of the horse races on television while conscientiously administering a can of Beamish to his long-stemmed glass, Ma in the scullery wearing her purple overcoat and slapping a steam-iron at a succession of shirts. 'There was a man,' Ma drawled, taking a drag on her filter-tipped fag. 'Phoned. Desires to speak with you about Mr Blake.'

'I've just seen him. A chimp with a Donegal accent. Are you going to wear that coat?'

'This one didn't have a Donegal accent. Kerry, I'd say, or Limerick. O'Rourke, he calls himself. Blackwood's, Thursday morning. You have my permission to go.' Ma was perfumed with Cork Dry Gin, as usual at this stage in the afternoon. Her voice was loud and deep and cracked, like the wrinkles on her jowls. Her lanky grey hair was wet from the shower.

'Not going,' Davnet said. 'Got school. Anyway, I already talked to the chimp.'

'O'Rourke says a man name of Fennessy, busted for heroin smuggling, claims to have met the said Blake Saturday morning last in Blackwood's, in full view of the skivvies. O'Rourke wants to verify with you and Missy Long-Legs.'

'He told you all that?'

'I wasn't letting you off school without a damn good reason.'

'Responsible parent.'

'Gee thanks. Give this to Pa.' She handed Davnet a half-ironed shirt, formerly white. 'Ask your useless sister to rustle up some food.'

Fat chance. Cooking reminded Maureen of marriage, which brought on fits of weeping. Davnet would do it herself.

Ma lumbered off towards the bus stop. Even through a haze of alcohol, her brain was razor-sharp, which was perhaps why Mr Gutman got her to do the books for his continental sausage emporium.

Pa looked at the shirt with disdain.

'What's it for?' Davnet asked.

'Medical exam, for the disability,' he croaked. 'Five-thirty.'

'Don't show up pissed.'

'No indeed.' He drained his glass, stood up, removed his pyjama top, got into the shirt. 'Where did they hide me good tie?' he demanded, tucking the shirt into the waistband of his old dark civil service trousers.

Davnet produced the tie from the sideboard drawer, and the dark jacket from the back of the kitchen door. Pa straightened himself up like a soldier. 'Best be moving,' he said. 'No sense in being late.' Which meant that he planned to drop in at the Cardinal Richelieu.

Alone in the house except for Maureen, Davnet glanced again at Jerome Fennessy's card. Heroin smuggling? Fennessy? Prissy old fruit. Hardly his style.

She looked up *The Night Watch* in *World Masterpieces of Western European Painting*, the mouldy tome which had come down to her from sensitive Uncle Stephen who died accidentally by sticking his head in a gas oven after forgetting to light it. A brownish reproduction was accompanied by several paragraphs of sludge. The painting was dated 1642. Commissioned by some scabby old burghers who protested that it contained too much action. A yard of canvas had been sheared off one edge when it was transferred to the Amsterdam Town Hall during the eighteenth century. In the estimation of Professor Serebryakov, Rembrandt's masterpiece represented, more powerfully than any other civic painting, man's pride and fragility, his hopes for security and his justified apprehension of self-inflicted damage. Notice how the weapons slice diagonally through the canvas, menacing the group they claim to defend. Notice the expression of domineering incompetence on the face of the group's official commander, Frans Banning Cocq. In modern civic culture we know how empty are our leaders' pretensions to heroism – yet we continue to require leaders and to impose those same pretensions upon them. This is the paradox of authority in the democratic age. Notice too the strained expression on the face of the little round-faced girl, whose over-lit yellow dress echoes the yellow uniform of the commander's henchman. A semi-divine figure of youth, she is a mascot bearing the contradictory ideals of her civilization. In the prescience of that anxious visage, the viewer may almost intuit how the protection of civilian values will be used in subsequent epochs to justify every atrocity.

After a speechless dinner of Dougherty's Irish Curry with Maureen (Pa had not returned), Davnet sat at the kitchen table and revised her European history, reducing her notes onto index cards. Maureen was reading *Men Are from Mars, Women Are from Venus*, which her counsellor had lent her. She turned one page every ten minutes.

{{{{{o}}}}}

Mr Manley came to visit. He stood in the far corner of the interview room. 'Your Mamah is bearing up,' he breathed. 'Indeed she was looking remarkably well when I saw her. Very nice home, I must say. I believe she proposes to bunk out and attend the trial.'

'Give her my love,' Jerome said. 'Tell her I'm not guilty.'

'Ah. Mmm. Technically, of course, you are. Perhaps unwisely, you've admitted as much, in your very full and comprehensive written statement. Morally, on the other hand, you may well be innocent.'

'Will the court believe us?'

'Ah,' Mr Manley regretted. 'It's not really my bag, you see. Indeed I haven't taken a criminal case in quite a few years. But I've found you a fellow who, I am given to understand, does little else. Young solicitor, terribly keen, called Ó Neachtain. Fiachra Ó Neachtain. That's Naughton in English, I presume. Ó Neachtain's entire practice, I am reliably informed, is built upon criminal defence.'

'Why can't you take the case?'

'Wouldn't do it justice,' Mr Manley murmured. 'Too rusty in the criminal law. Horses for courses, as they say. Not the best man at all. By starting your statement, you see, with an extended account of your education and teaching career, I fear you have laid yourself open, and if the prosecution decide to exploit that material, it may prove difficult to enlist the sympathy of a judge and jury. Now, if it were a civil matter, torts, conveyancing, property rights, I flatter myself that I would be adequate. But in this case it's best I bow out. I'll pass the papers to Mr Ó Neachtain without delay. There's no time to be lost. You're on the "fast track", don't you know, part of this new "speedy trials" nonsense. They plan to come to court within ten days.'

'I won't have time to prepare my defence.'

'Ah. But they won't have had time to prepare their attack. They'll be going off at half-cock. You'll be right as rain. I shouldn't give it too much thought, if I were you.'

He bowed out.

{{{{{{o}}}}}}

Mr Blake's funeral took place on Wednesday morning. Most of Davnet O'Reilly's class trooped along, in sympathy with Felicity and Dee Dee Blake. They were escorted by five teachers. In the grey church the acoustics had been designed to preserve the mysteries of the Faith by reducing the priest to a bellowing echo. Mother Polycarp, the old religion teacher, sat beside Davnet, wearing civilian clothes so awful that only a nun could have bought them.

The widow and daughters occupied the front right-hand row, as is customary, Pat the bar manager and his friend Mr Hughes knelt at the back, and Davnet could identify three of Mr Blake's recent girlfriends on the left-hand side. Ruth Harris was the only one who looked sad. The other two were horsy hags, and were treating the occasion as a fashion event.

Mr Comerford, the politician, sat in the front left-hand row. He had been a member of Blackwood's, but rarely came. Gloria Mennon left early. She spoke to Davnet for a moment. She had a sore throat, and her eyes were hollow in their puffy lids. Davnet wondered whether Mrs Mennon might have been secretly attached to Mr Blake after all, and dismissed the idea.

After the ceremony, outside the church, as the coffin was wheeled to the cavernous black hearse, the whole class hugged Felicity and Dee Dee. Mrs Blake had sympathizers of her own age. The hearse was a Rolls-Royce, which Mr Blake would have loved. Among the wreaths being placed carefully on top of the coffin was one with a card from Jerome Fennessy. Davnet recognized the handwriting. The chimpanzee policeman was hovering at the edge of the crowd. Catching her eye, he looked through her as though she were a ghost.

{{{{{{o}}}}}}

Fiachra Ó Neachtain was a thin child with a wispy beard. He went through Jerome's case like a scavenging terrier, brandishing papers and holding them up at the end of his nose. 'Duress,' he barked at the written confession. 'Abuse of procedure. Did they harass you? Cause you discomfort? Subject you to verbal abuse?'

Jerome's tales of the spilled tea, and the promise of a lighter sentence should he incriminate Matt Wellan, and the delay in letting him go to the bathroom, all filled his new solicitor with savage indignation. 'We'll nail them on this,' he snarled. 'This won't wash, zero tolerance or no zero tolerance. You know what they say: treat us like shit and we'll hit the fan.'

Jerome did not much like that idea.

Next day his new solicitor was back with a whiskery tramp, enormously bloated and unsteady on his feet. 'Mr

Senan Roche, Senior Counsel,' Ó Neachtain announced proudly. 'The captain of our ship. One of the most experienced men at the Irish Bar. You heard of the Harrington case.'

'Ten years ago come November,' Roche said. He had a deep actorish voice, rurally accented, and rolled his 'r's like an Italian. For some reason, Jerome imagined him living on a diet of raw parsnips. 'I proved that his cousin had maliciously incriminated him,' Roche declared. Jerome was too polite to ask for details.

'Tell him about the St Alexis case,' Fiachra Ó Neachtain urged.

Roche harrumphed. 'Ah, yes. Fourteen years ago, Hubert St Alexis came home from Australia to claim his inheritance. Victorian castle and twenty-five acres of land, zoned for light industry. Except that it wasn't Hubert, but his sister Penelope, ha-ha, in man's attire. Hubert had left the family home, was living in a boarding-house in Brisbane, Penelope had abstracted his passport. We produced the true claimant on the fourth day of the case. Now your situation, Mr Fennessy, is what I would call a piece of cake. Chicanery, entrapment, conspiracy, plantation of evidence. I shall drive a coach and four through their machinations. For a start, I'll have your written statement ruled inadmissible. You may rely upon Senan Roche.'

{{{{{{o}}}}}}

Skipping school on Thursday was a small compensation. Davnet and Jenny stopped for fruit juices in Nude on

Suffolk Street. Jenny was planning to get a Christmas job in Brown Thomas. She wanted Davnet to apply too, and Felicity and Dee Dee. The last bit sounded good to Davnet. Christmas would be tough for the Blake sisters. They had hated their father, mocked him to their friends, refused to work in his business or take his money. Now they could never come to terms with him.

The club's front door was locked, but Davnet still had her key. She relocked the door behind them and Jenny led the way upstairs.

Raucous laughter wafted from the drawing room: 'No sweat. The Jesuit's on his best behaviour. Total pussycat. He's in love with me, actually. No. Not mutual, not quite. And no need to let the three-legged Rottweiler out of her kennel just yet. We'll turn on the tap, drippy drippy drippy –'

The two girls reached the creaking stair. A tough man appeared at the drawing-room doorway. 'Kiddies have arrived. See you in Madigan's.' He lounged against the door-frame, pocketed his mobile phone. 'Which one of you is O'Reilly?'

'Which one of you is O'Rourke?' Davnet returned.

'Talk to you first,' he said to Jenny. 'In you come.'

Jenny didn't budge. Davnet said, 'We'll see you together.'

'Whatever.' He sat at the bar, pocketed his mobile phone, produced a notebook and a gold ballpoint pen and started firing questions at them: names, ages, addresses, how long they had worked in the club, how they had come to work there, what their duties had been, their weekly pay, their RSI numbers, the amount of income tax deducted, their average weekly take on tips. He laughed when they explained that tipping was not allowed, this being a private club. 'That's your story,' he said. 'Don't be scared, I don't report to the Revenue.'

'There's nothing to report,' Jenny said.

'Who owns this club, anyhow?'

'Mr Blake,' Davnet said.

'Where did he get the money?'

'He was a businessman in England.'

'Was he, now? Tell me about the members.'

'Middle-aged guys. Bankers and stuff.'

'Generous?'

Jenny sighed: 'We told you.'

'Any females? Hostesses? Go-go dancers?'

'It's not that sort of club. A few women came in with the men. Wives. There was only one actual female member.'

'How did she get in?'

'She was a personal friend of Mr Blake.'

'How personal is personal?' O'Rourke was jocose.

'She handled his investments, I think,' Jenny replied.

'She flirted with him,' Davnet put in, angry at the recollection. 'He was fond of her, but she couldn't care less.'

'How do you know? Think she had him killed?'

'Of course not. Aren't you going to ask us about Mr Fennessy?'

'Do you know what he's done?'

'He's accused of drug-running. He's not the type.'

'There's more than one type. Fennessy claims he was a bosom buddy of Mr Blake.'

'That's true. Mr Blake called him Romy. He was pleased to see him at first.'

'How do you know? Did you hear their conversation?'

'Not the first time. But he dropped in again later. We got talking –'

'I bet you did –'

'About art. He's a teacher.'

'Was a teacher. Shagged out of his job for paedophilia. Did you know that?'

'He didn't mention it. Mr Blake came back just before Mr Fennessy had to leave for the airport. He asked Mr Fennessy to bring him something from Paris airport, and Mr Fennessy said he was going to Amsterdam. Mr Blake looked sick.'

'What did he say, exactly? His precise words?'

'Didn't hear. I was on my way home. I heard them talking as I came down the stairs.'

O'Rourke turned to Jenny: 'And did you hear this conversation too?'

'No, I'd gone home earlier.'

Billy O'Rourke finished writing. 'OK. Uncorroborated. Unreliable. Back to school, girls.'

'That's not how you spell my name,' Davnet said.

'Sharp-eyed, aren't you? Clever-puss.'

'They taught me reading.'

'Sure of yourself, too. Passed your Junior Cert?'

'She got nine A's,' Jenny put in. 'We averaged four and a half between us. I'm thick.' She fluttered her eyelashes.

O'Rourke stared at Jenny, earnest and unsmiling. 'I prefer thick people myself,' he said, as though stating some high moral principle. 'You've both got the full use of your faculties. But boneheads and retards have to live too.' He turned back to Davnet. 'What's wrong with your name?'

'There's an "e", not an "i",' Davnet said.

'You write it in, then, since you're so particular. I might do it wrong, being a dumb cluck and all.'

He handed her the notebook and his gold ballpoint pen. She wrote her name. Her writing was horrible, round and back-slanting, looking silly and childish under Billy O'Rourke's adult italic script. For such a brute, he had delicate handwriting. The pen was a Cross, finished in rolled gold, with a black top, and the name *Mowbray's* incised on the clip. Six months previously Davnet had used her personal savings to buy a silver-plated Cross ballpoint in the Pen Corner on Dame Street, for Pa's birthday, and Pa had promptly lost it at the pub, although his name was engraved on the barrel. Pa always lost things that Davnet gave him, because he didn't love her like he loved her sister.

{{{{{{○}}}}}}

As Billy O'Rourke pocketed his pen, yapping noises rose from below. Davnet went to investigate. Désirée Blake surged upstairs in a black trouser-suit, eyes narrowed, jet-black hair combed into a lacquered helmet. Behind her tripped a pink baldy in a grey pinstripe. 'I'm sorry,' he was huffing, 'it's out of the question.'

'You're trying to tell me there's nothing to be had, the mortgage is unpaid, my husband's investments have vanished. I am Paul's heiress, and you're trying to tell me I'm ruined.'

'Sadly, the contents did not belong to him personally,' the baldy insisted. 'They belong to the company, except for those items you had loaned to him. If you will kindly point those out to me, I am prepared to make an approach on –'

He fell silent, noticing Davnet on the landing. Désirée continued, more loudly:

'Are you trying to tell me, Mr Finnegan, that the furniture is mortgaged as well as the building?'

'Unfortunately, Madam, this is not a mortgage situation. If your late husband had purchased the furniture personally, even with borrowed money, title would have passed regardless of whether he had repaid the loan. In the present state of things, Kleistrad Limited has title to the furniture. Any attempt to dispose of company property as though it were personal would be tantamount –'

He fell silent again.

'This is Davnet O'Reilly,' Désirée said, going over to her and clutching at her shoulder. 'Davnet O'Reilly is my daughters' best friend from school. Davnet, this is Mr Timothy Finnegan from my late husband's firm of solicitors. Mr Finnegan is trying to make out that I'm a thief.'

'Nothing could be further from my intentions,' fibbed the baldy. 'I have every sympathy for your predicament.'

She burst into tears. Davnet put her arms around her. 'I'm sorry, Mrs Blake. Come into the drawing room. Jenny's here too. Can we get you a cup of tea?'

'Who's this?' Désirée noticed Billy O'Rourke.

'He's a policeman. He was going over some stuff with us.'

'I'm sorry for your trouble,' said Billy O'Rourke. 'I was just asking these young ladies about a man who claimed to be a friend of your late husband. A Mr Fennessy. Jerome Fennessy. Do you know him?'

'My husband never introduced me to his friends.'

'I won't intrude any more, then,' O'Rourke said. 'I'll be off about my business.'

'How did you get in, anyway?' Davnet asked him. 'You were waiting for us when we arrived.'

'Seán Óg Dempsey gave me a lend of his key. I'll return it to him.'

'Is that man investigating my husband's death?' Désirée asked as he left.

'No, another case. A man arrested for smuggling was here last Saturday morning.'

'And are they trying to make out that my husband was involved with smuggling?'

Mr Finnegan pricked up his ears.

'Not at all,' Davnet said. 'Mr O'Rourke didn't even think they knew each other.'

Jenny reappeared with a tray bearing a teapot and four cups. 'We're in luck,' she prattled. 'The kettle was nice and hot. Afraid there's no milk, so I went for the Earl Grey. Okay for everyone?'

Jenny never looked lovelier than when she was acting stupid. Davnet fell for it every time.

Even Mr Finnegan took a cup of tea. Davnet found the shortbread tin and passed that around as well.

Désirée dried her dark eyes, carried on in a quieter tone:

'Thing is, I'm skint. Paul hasn't been keeping up. As per bloody usual. Two months late. He kept saying he had investments, but Mr Finnegan denies all knowledge.'

'If you could just point out the items,' the solicitor began again, 'of which you wish to dispose.'

'There was his desk for a start.' Désirée emptied her teacup, led the way across the landing and into the den. She stopped on the threshold, dramatically. 'Gone!'

'I think that might be evidence,' Davnet said awkwardly. 'There was a mark on it.'

She had seen the desk carried downstairs, its sides gouged, its leather top soaked in gore. It would not be a saleable item, unless to a museum of horrors.

'And was there anything else?' Mr Finnegan wanted to know.

'My Victorian caricatures.' She gestured around her.

'Ah, yes, now those are extremely nice,' the solicitor said, looking around the green walls of the den. 'Potentially valuable. I'll certainly take those up with Kleistrad. And?'

She did a slow-motion pirouette, scanning the furniture and fittings. 'I don't know. I'll look around, I'll tell you what I find.'

'Just so long –'

'As I don't steal anything.' She looked dangerous again. Mr Finnegan retreated: 'Now, Mrs Blake. That was not my contention. Now, I've got a luncheon appointment. I'll leave you in capable hands, Mrs Blake. I'll be in touch.' He slid away while the going was good.

'Another cup of tea?' Jenny rallied around. They

steered Désirée back into the drawing room, settled her in an armchair. She lit a cigarette and glared at the overdone opulence of the room. 'How am I to provide for my girls?' she demanded. 'We're banjaxed. He led us up the garden path.'

'Actually, he may have had some investments,' Davnet said nervously.

'Where?'

'I think one of the members was advising him.'

'Which one?'

'An American lady. Mrs Mennon. She works in a bank.'

'What bank?'

'European Pacific Trust.'

'I'll go and ask her. Now.' Désirée stood up. 'Where's her office?'

'I'll come with you,' Davnet said quickly. 'I can introduce you.' She couldn't bear to think of poor Désirée, alone and unchaperoned, making a fool of herself again.

{{{{{o}}}}}

They found the address in the telephone book, and Davnet called the number. An American receptionist announced that Ms Mennon was momentarily out of the office. What did it concern?

Désirée took the receiver. 'I'm Paul Blake's wife,' she said. 'We're coming round.'

The place was in the Financial Services Centre. Désirée drove her old Rover. It needed a silencer repair. They dropped Jenny at one of the Trinity College gates, and parked illegally across the river. Désirée sprang from the car and pranced away, moving like a cavalry horse on a flanking action. Davnet skipped along beside her.

By the time they found the building, Gloria Mennon was ready for them. Every blonde hair in place, a compassionate handshake. She led them into a wood-panelled conference room, offered refreshments which Désirée declined, produced a buff cardboard file, extracted some papers which she placed on the glass-topped table. She smiled at Désirée, a complicit smile, woman to woman. Davnet braced herself.

'Mrs Blake, your late husband entrusted me with the management of certain financial resources.' Gloria was somewhat hoarse. 'I positioned his funds in a range of portfolios managed by an offshore bank. The ultimate investments are in the Far East – Korea, Singapore, and Taiwan. These have performed better than average for the region, so there will be –'

'How much?' Désirée interrupted. Her eyes were slits.

Gloria blinked. 'I know how you must feel, Mrs Blake, so I'll cut to the chase. At maturity, your husband's investments were due to yield one hundred eighty-four thousand dollars. As we are not yet at that point, our strategy is to negotiate the best possible surrender value. Usually the bank is hard-nosed about early withdrawals, but I have explained the tragic circumstances of your late husband's passing, and because I place considerable business with them, they are prepared to allow us one-fifty-seven immediately, if you will sign a release form.'

'How do I know they're not worth more than that?' Désirée asked.

'Right now the investments could be worth a lot less,' Gloria replied in the gentlest of tones. 'The bankers are not being unreasonable. They could insist that you wait another fourteen months, or accept a forfeit value of eighty-six thousand dollars. That's the narrow contractual position. They could also insist on waiting for probate and delay paying you for up to six months. Instead, they will accept my personal assurance that you are as of now the beneficial owner of the account.'

'If I sign, when do I get the money?'

'By close of trade tomorrow. Paid into a bank designated by you.'

'I'll do it.' Désirée scrabbled in her shoulder bag. 'Bloody biro,' she exclaimed. Gloria placed a form in front of her, and a gold-coloured ballpoint pen. Désirée scrawled her signature without reading the text.

'Thank you, Mrs Blake. And again here, if you would. Will you witness the signatures, Davnet?'

'I'm under age.'

'So sorry, Davnet,' Gloria smiled. 'You're so grown-up. I'll ask Patty.' She pressed a bell.

Davnet wondered if she might have misjudged Mrs Mennon. The woman was certainly sad about Mr Blake. She must have had some feelings for him after all. As well as sympathizing with his wife. Adults were like that. They walked themselves into stuff that they couldn't handle. Or else kept out of stuff they should have got into.

Désirée held up the form that she had signed, peered at the small print, then passed it to Davnet, as if Davnet knew anything about documents like this. Davnet glanced at it politely, under Gloria's amused gaze. Désirée had accepted the sum of US$157,000 in settlement of investment account number IRL77549812/QEA, warranting that the recipient was the legal heir of the original account-holder, and promising to indemnify the bank should this prove not to be the case. The bank in question was Mowbray's Banking Trust, Grand Cayman. Mrs Mennon's gold-coloured Cross pen, which still lay on the table, also bore the name *Mowbray's* incised on its clip.

Patty the receptionist came in, smelling of cigarettes. She signed where Gloria showed her, in witness of Désirée's signature, and filled in her own name and address, using Gloria's gold-plated pen.

'Where would you like the money paid?' Gloria asked.

'My savings account in Jersey,' Désirée said, and recited the number and sort code from memory. Gloria wrote it on a separate sheet of paper.

'Thank you, Mrs Mennon,' Davnet said, filling Désirée's silence. 'You're very kind to arrange all this.'

'Yes,' Désirée concurred. 'I'll tell my girls we can keep the house.'

'Such a loss.' Gloria's eyes were moist. 'Such a charming man.'

'Did you think so?' Désirée's mood was turning dangerous again.

Davnet interrupted. 'Could you possibly run me home, Mrs Blake? I promised to help my mother this afternoon. She's not well, and I promised to be back early.'

Gloria flashed Davnet a look of pure gratitude.

{{{{{{o}}}}}}

Jerome liked prison. Despite his initial jitters about being housed with criminals, he had found everyone in the remand wing very sympathetic. His cellmate too was innocent. He had been falsely accused of embezzlement, just because he'd bought a tiny little apartment in Spain out of some winnings on the horses. Nobody knew of Jerome's disastrous job interview, his dismissal from the convent school, his failed marriage. Being known as a drug courier gave him a certain standing. His denials were taken as evidences of charming modesty.

Fiachra Ó Neachtain, the solicitor, summoned him to the interview room and showed him some documents from the case against him. Jerome shook his head over Billy O'Rourke's first report. 'He says I mentioned Paul only when writing out my statement in the morning. I'd told him about Paul the night before. He broke the news of the murder in the car going to the District Court, at nine in the morning. He must remember that.'

'Look at this later report,' the solicitor said. 'O'Rourke admits that a witness saw you in Blake's club on the Saturday, talking to him about Amsterdam.'

'Anyway,' said Jerome, 'there's written proof. I started writing at midnight, beginning with how Paul sent me to meet Mr Mulhone. Later in the night, I crossed out the rough version, and decided to start the statement with who I am and what I've done with my life, following up with a shorter account of the trip to Amsterdam. Mr Joyce, the Director, saw me working on the rough version. We were sitting in his office all night. Mr O'Rourke took away the rough pages as well as the fair copy. They'll all be in the file.'

'No rough version,' Ó Neachtain barked. 'They only showed me the fair copy. I'll go after the drafts. We'll nail them on that.'

{{{{{{o}}}}}}

Dark in the car, and deathly cold. Engine and lights off, naturally, and Billy's window rolled down because fresh air was needed to stop it misting up. And to listen for the slightest sound. The air carrying the sweet smell of grass and earth. Like childhood, like the grave.

Underneath Billy's unearthly stillness was an iceberg of endurance. That was the thought that drifted into Joyce's mind. He rejected it as romantic.

Where did it come from, then? The sense of purpose you always got with Billy, the feeling of the die being cast, the bridges burnt? What was it that enabled Billy to act without hesitating? Séamus was born to dither.

Tonight they were keeping watch. Billy, to everyone's surprise except Séamus's, had been meek and mild during their conference with Decko Dowd, accepting Decko's invasive demands without a quibble. He nodded sagely at Decko's assertion that the job of picking up the heroin consignment, estimated at more than eight million euros, was too big for the iDEA's resources. He agreed with Dowd's demand that he should handle the main core of the operation with men from his own group, and leave Billy with nothing more than a watching brief. Decko swelled with importance and humble pride.

They had parked here, hours ago, after gaining the rising ground by a long twisting rutted laneway flanked by scrawny bushes. Billy had pulled in under this little clump of trees which left the car half-hidden. It was a brown Opel Vectra, which would not stand out in the gloom, and was sprayed with an additional layer of mud to make it even less reflective. Billy claimed that this effect was achieved by the simple expedient of never washing the car.

They were silent now. Earlier, Séamus had talked uncontrollably about Theresa, how resourceful she was, how well she was coping. Billy had listened for a long time, making no comment, then mentioned that his own mother had kept going all through her last illness, had refused to go to hospital, had baked soda bread on the morning she had died. Slow colon cancer, cut short by a quick heart attack. Good soda bread, Billy said.

Down in the distance, beyond the entrance to the laneway, on a gentle curve, they could dimly make out the smudged silhouette of the small derelict church. Empty for years, it had been named this morning as the drop.

All around, the darkened farmland of north County Dublin waited and breathed.

Somewhere out there, Dowd's men were gathered in

silence, their radios switched off. Tom Stringer was tagging along with them, to see how the Irish handle these things.

Somewhere out there, the Robin's associates were also converging on the church. Or at least that was the hope.

Without movement, the cold seeped into Séamus's bones. His muscles ached. The dull pain in his stomach might have come from bolting his food, or from sympathy with Theresa, or from reading about oesophageal cancer and replicating the symptoms, or from plain old-fashioned stress. Middle-aged men are a fragile breed, as his German doctor used to say.

What was he doing here? He was a desk man, not an operations man. But Richard Frye had opted to blur those categories. The Minister was in expansive mood following his little spat with T. J. Comerford, the opposition spokesman, at question-time in the Dáil on Wednesday afternoon. The two recent acquittals of drug couriers, he had assured Mr Comerford, merely showed the independence of the Irish judiciary, whereas the arrest of Jerome Fennessy was proof positive that the iDEA was continuing to do a first-class job. Did Mr Comerford not comprehend the constitutional separation of powers? Would he prefer a police state, in which convictions follow automatically from indictments? It was not the job of the iDEA to convict criminals. Its dual mandate, in case Mr Comerford had overlooked such niceties, was to make wrongdoers amenable to the courts, and to plan effective policies that would hamper the future operations of the drug barons. The agency was performing on both fronts. Had Mr Comerford not noticed the accolades in the media, hailing the iDEA's five-year plan as one of the most imaginative texts ever to come out of a government agency? Had he perhaps not registered the significant decline in drugs on the street, especially in Dublin? Had he chanced to read the coverage in the *Sunday Times*, the *Observer*, the *Frankfurter Allgemeine*, the *Scotsman*? What of the Swedish editorial welcoming the Europe Without Drugs proposal as evidence that a small country can wield real influence in the new Europe? Why exactly should he wish to undermine the agency's work just now, with his weasel words? Why weaken the winning team?

This lordly put-down might almost have amounted to a famous victory, had it not been eclipsed by scandalous allegations on the lunchtime news, concerning a senior clergyman and a junior rent boy. Gilbert Covey was disappointed, but the career civil servants in the Department of Justice were, if anything, relieved. In their cautious minds, an obscure parliamentary success, under-reported in the media, was always preferable to a famous victory. Sal O'Sullivan, who had sat across the gangway from Richard Frye during his parliamentary performance, had even dared to suggest, during the Wednesday evening meeting of the Department's top brass, that in future encounters her Minister might strive for a less memorable turn of phrase. The Justice portfolio worked best, she contended, when a degree of cross-party consensus was created around it, so that the opposition were left looking disloyal should they tackle the Minister head-on.

Richard Frye had greeted her suggestions with a silent glare.

Séamus Joyce, also present at that meeting, had said not a word, but silence had not been enough to save him. Even after wiping the floor with Mr Comerford, Richard Frye was still pained by his opposite number's stinging depiction of the iDEA as a watchdog designed by a committee, an administrative Pushmi-Pullyu, an operational quango led by desk-bound bureaucrats and largely staffed by semi-policemen under a compromised chain of command. He did not want to lay himself open to such groundless accusations in the future. Therefore, if Mr Joyce could possibly see his way to involving himself in a couple of sorties over the next few weeks, in some sort of supervisory capacity? Show himself to be reasonably familiar with the operational side of the agency's work? Good? Yes? Thank you so much. Now, next business?

Which was why Séamus found himself sitting in a freezing car in the depths of the darkened countryside.

If he had taken the offer of a transfer to the Department of Education, fifteen years ago, he might at this moment be relaxing at home, or reading an improving book, or preparing some harmless position paper that would place no one in danger of death or indeed anything much else.

Billy scanned the horizon, shifting his nightglasses with glacial slowness. Séamus took a turn with the glasses, saw a fox springing across the tussocky field below them, in its own graceful element.

He wanted to talk about Theresa's illness. They were

still doing tests. There would be another small exploratory stomach operation, early Monday morning. The doctors were optimistic. But he bit his tongue. There is no point in discussing things like that with a young man who will never die, however hard he tries.

Instead, he put on his headphones, fished a cassette from his trouser pocket and listened to a Bartók concerto, one of the great recordings that John McClure made for CBS, back in the Sixties. Leonard Bernstein with the New York Philharmonic. Gold and Fizdale, the pianists, blended like a shower of hail. The mikes were a bit too close in on the xylophone, but otherwise the mix was perfect. This was one of the first classical discs Séamus had ever bought. Theresa called it his migraine album.

He was lost in the music. Billy was tapping him on the arm. 'Taking a turn. You wait, okay?'

'Fine.'

Billy eased himself out of the car, stayed motionless for a minute, then crouched his way forward along the hedge, became invisible. Séamus slumped in his seat, closed his eyes, sank again into the jangling ocean of sound. The concerto built to its ironic anti-climax, faded to silence. Séamus took off his headphones and listened afresh to the ambient sounds: creaking boughs, rustling leaves, water running somewhere, the distant hum of traffic from the Belfast road. Yet he heard nothing of Billy's approach until he saw him standing again beside the car.

'Seen anything?' Séamus whispered.

'I saw the wind in the trees, that's all. Decko is keeping

his boys well back. I hope the Robin doesn't leave Decko standing at the altar. A clever little bird is the Robin.'

Séamus suddenly asked the question that had formed in his mind. 'Did you ever think of marrying?'

Billy looked surprised, as well he might. 'Not for Joxer.'

'Why not?'

Billy sighed, leaned down to the window. 'My father wasn't fit to be a parent. Why should I think I'm different?' The subject was closed. Billy reached into the car for the nightglasses, stood against the hedge, scanning the horizon, a darker silhouette against the inky sky.

Séamus's parents had been old before he was born. In retrospect, he was probably a menopausal mistake. His brother Daniel was fifteen years older. He had never visited him in Málaga. They exchanged Christmas cards, but had otherwise lost touch. Theresa was his only family now. And yet he loved Daniel in a way that he would never love anyone else. As a child, he had longed simply to become his older brother. When Theresa died, he would take up with Daniel again.

Billy got back into the car.

'A family would settle you,' Séamus remarked, as if they had been discussing the matter.

'Settle me is right.' Billy looked away.

'Help your career, too,' Séamus insisted. 'They won't let you rise if you're footloose.'

'Who wants to rise?' Billy said. 'I'll stick to this job till I get bored.'

'And then?'

'Drug running,' Billy grinned. 'God knows I'd have the expertise. I'm not the managerial type.'

'You might think that in your twenties. Later, you'll want to consolidate.'

'I'm thirty next week. Ten years a lawman.'

Séamus waited for a moment, then asked, 'How long are we likely to be here?'

'Eight hours max. We've got to maintain radio silence, so there's no way of assessing the situation. If nobody shows up by six in the morning, we'll bugger off home.' He smiled at Séamus's dismay. 'That's stakeouts for you, boyo. Just think of all the overtime we ain't getting paid. I should have stayed in uniform.'

He scanned the landscape again through his night-glasses. Séamus switched to another tape. This was his favourite bootleg recording of Stan Getz, picked up by a nameless German jazz enthusiast in a Danish concert hall on a small directional mike, in mono, surrounded by consumptive Scandinavians, but the sound of the saxophone still spoke straight to what was left of Séamus's heart.

Cocooned again in music, he began to remember disconnected things. Theresa's hair straggling over the pillow under the light of the bedside lamp. The sun setting through the leaves of the laurel tree in Heidi's garden, at the back of her tiny cottage at the edge of the forest, its wooden sign saying *Majestät*. His gaunt withdrawn father, whose house held no place for him. His own half-finished adolescence. In his childish part-nership with Theresa, he had turned his back on adult-hood. Heidi had explained that to him, and she was right. Had Theresa had children, the balance would have been different.

Billy wanted nothing of all that. Billy was like the fox in the field: an outsider, like the criminals he hunted. A confidential report assessed Billy as intelligent and fearless, but also mentioned his unorthodox methods, and the fist-fight in which he had broken a gang enforcer's jaw. His victim had been trying to collect protection money from a special school for disabled children, so nobody felt like hassling Billy. Then there was the claim in the Circuit Criminal Court that Billy had planted stolen goods on Johnny 'The Animal' Fucci, an allegation which the judge had dismissed outright. Billy's fatal shootout with the Maher family had given greater cause for concern. Leo Jordan's widow Val had made some hysterical accusations. But poor Val's mental problems were well known, and questions had emerged about the standing orders paid into Leo's bank account from an unidentified source in Liechtenstein. Had Leo been on the take? Had Val known about it? No smoke without a fire, said some, although Séamus could not subscribe to that view.

Billy's two years in the US Marines, straight from school, were not reckoned as a positive contribution to his career. Why could he not have joined the Irish army, if he wanted adventure? Séamus found this unfair.

A fire would be welcome now. The cold was creeping into his brain. Those youngsters you see sleeping on the streets of Dublin – how do they cope with cold like this, at four in the morning when the blood runs slow?

It was true, though, that Billy would be held back in his career for lack of a family. Personnel worried about men who were not safely pigeonholed. Not that they were censorious. You could be a confirmed celibate, or a married man with a mistress, or even homosexual. But they did look for stability. According to Security, Billy was currently involved with an older woman, the happily married wife of a teacher. A long-standing affair with a doctor's wife had ended some years ago. There were also reports of casual pickups of much younger women, including two flings with female members of the police force, but these were of short duration. The charms of Miss Letitia Bentley of Rotherhithe, who had cut a swathe through ICRAD on behalf of a major drug syndicate, while simultaneously reporting her conquests to the security section, had been singularly lost on Billy, although Letitia had made a special effort in his case and had been heard to remark that he was the one bloke she would have snogged for free. There were rumours about Billy having been involved once with an unidentified nurse from the back end of County Kildare; it was surmised that an unhappy experience with this nurse, presuming she existed, might have put him off marriage for the immediate future. Yet the question mark remained.

On reflection, Billy was more to be envied than pitied. Séamus himself couldn't even keep one woman happy.

Why had he told Billy he should get married? Was it like Aesop's fable of the fox who lost his tail and wanted to persuade all other foxes to share his misfortune?

Why this obsession with foxes?

The music had stopped. He switched off the tape. Time passed without movement to measure it.

Then Billy whispered: 'Toyota Land Cruiser.'

A square vehicle was creeping along the country road below, main lights doused. There seemed to be two men in the front. It glided past the church, stopped, reversed into a gateway, turned and crawled past the church for a second time. It stopped, reversed into the mouth of the lane, turned again and moved towards the church for the third time.

Séamus could hear his heart beating. Billy passed him the nightglasses.

'Half the catch,' Billy whispered. 'When the other jeep rolls up, Decko nets the lot.'

'Which one is the Robin?'

'The midget. The bigger fellow is his left-hand man, Ray Kinnear. Burned a house last year, mother and child died, nothing proved against Ray.'

The Land Cruiser pulled in at the gateway of the churchyard. The occupants lit cigarettes. Minutes passed.

He had left Theresa sleeping. The black circles around her eyes were getting worse, as if she were putting in long strenuous days at work instead of lying in her warm hospital bed.

If he died tonight, how would she survive? Yet she had instructed him to come to this place. Do whatever Mr Frye says, she had replied to his unspoken question.

The sweep of headlights announced the arrival of a second vehicle. 'That's the delivery van,' whispered

Billy. 'Mitsubishi Pajero.' The new arrival rounded the corner down by the church, slowed down, stopped. The lights were doused, then switched off.

Billy got out of the car, leaving the door open. Séamus followed. They watched as two hundred yards away, down beside the churchyard, the drivers climbed from their vehicles and huddled together. The engines were still running. Séamus could not make out the sound of voices. Then a searchlight flickered in the church tower. A crackle of shots.

Billy whistled noiselessly. 'Decko's fucked up.'

The drivers were back in their vehicles, slamming doors. Engines roaring, they took off in opposite directions. There was a distant sound of sirens, another burst of gunfire, and the sound of tyres squealing on the road surface. The Land Cruiser reappeared. Another crackle of shots. The Land Cruiser plunged into the laneway, began to climb towards the high ground.

Billy gave a dry chuckle. 'In behind the hedge, Mr Joyce, if you please, and kindly keep your head well down.'

With big decisive gestures he pushed their car across the laneway, blocking it, then shouldered through the ragged hedge to crouch on the rough grass beside Séamus. 'Ever handle a gun?'

'No.'

Billy produced two pistols from inside his jacket, and another from an ankle-holster inside the bottom of his trouser leg. 'Lesson One. Hold it in two hands, aim with your arms fully stretched, pull the trigger three times.'

He clicked a lever on one of the pistols, and gave it to Séamus.

The engine noise grew to a roar. The Land Cruiser rounded a bend in the laneway and ran smack into Billy's Vectra. A second impact and a scream of acceleration as it tried to push the car aside. After three separate impacts came the screech of changing gears as the Land Cruiser began to back off.

Séamus breathed out, but Billy jumped through the hedge and began to pump shots in quick succession at the retreating Land Cruiser. There were scraping sounds, and the engine died.

Séamus threw himself flat on the grass. Doors slamming. The sound of feet.

Billy dropped on one knee, fired again twice, changed guns, and again twice, and again once, and then not at all. 'Jammed,' he called through the hedge. 'Give me the lend of that pistol.'

Séamus crawled towards him. There was a burst of machine-gun fire. Billy staggered back slantwise through the hedge, fell headlong about ten yards from where Séamus was lying.

The shape of a man came crashing through further up, holding a machine pistol which he swung around in a deliberate arc to point at Billy's recumbent body.

Séamus had pulled his trigger before he could think. Then he remembered to aim.

Without a word the man clasped his neck, sank to his knees, keeled over, lay still.

Séamus was on his feet. Peering through the hedge

he saw another smaller man crouching beside the car. Not armed, so far as he could see.

He stepped forward, completely out of character, and took control.

'Stand up. I'm arresting you under the Offences Against the State Act.'

'Is that a gun?' The small man raised his hands obediently. He was wearing a dark blazer and a blue shirt, for all the world like a bank manager off to play a round of golf. 'Do you not know me, Mr Joyce?' he complained. 'Paddy Mills, Drugs Squad. I was poor Leo Jordan's best friend. Do you remember Leo? I got detached from my group. The other chap ran off down the lane. I couldn't arrest him. I'm not toting a gun tonight. But they'll get him soon enough. Listen, I've got ID in my pocket. Would you like me to show it to you?'

'There's no Paddy Mills in the Drugs Squad.' Séamus kept the pistol steady.

'Except for myself,' the small man laughed.

'Turn around and face the car. Don't move your hands or I'll shoot.' He was amazed at his own aggression. He moved closer, almost touching the small man with the barrel of his pistol.

'Decko Dowd wouldn't thank you for that. If you would just check my ID, we could use my mobile phone to summon an ambulance. Billy needs help as soon as possible. The card is in my outside pocket.'

'Don't try any funny tricks,' Séamus warned.

'Don't worry,' said the small man. 'No comedians in our outfit.' But when Séamus came right up beside him and reached into his pocket, the small man twisted like a fish, grasped the pistol and butted the back of his head against Séamus's chin. Séamus stumbled, went down on one knee.

The small man was holding the pistol jammed against his temple. 'I need a chauffeur, Shaymo.' His voice was high and girlish now. 'Billy shot my tyres out. We'll take your wagon. You drive.'

'I can't. Billy has the keys.'

'Get 'em off him!' ordered the small man. He prodded Séamus in the back, pushed him through the hedge.

Billy was no longer lying where he had been. He had somehow crawled over and retrieved the dead man's submachine gun, which was now trained steadily on the two of them.

'Drop it, Billy,' the little man squeaked, 'or I'll blow your boss to fuck.'

Billy laughed. 'Be my guest, Robin. I'll get a proper shot at you then. Your trouble is, as a target you're a bit on the mingy side.'

'I'll do it! You want me to do it?'

'With that little toy? This here is the late great Ray Kinnear's Uzi. Cut you to pieces in a quarter of a second. Chili con carne. Mexican stand-off, and I'm Montezuma. Throw it down, Robin.'

'Give us the Jesus keys, Billy!' The little man was shaking. 'I've got to get off, Billy. I keep a clean sheet. They'd kill me in jail.'

'Don't be thick, Robin. You'll be a hit in the 'Joy. Mandy will look after you.' The distant sound of sirens was mingled with the noise of motor engines.

The little man wailed: 'You double-crossed me, Billy.

Like old man Maher. After all we did for the boy. We'll fuckin' get you for that. If I go, I'm takin' the two of youse with me.' He jammed the gun-barrel into Séamus's back.

'We're not going nowhere, Robin redbreast. Calm down. You're all right. We're surrounded.'

'Then this is where we all fuckin' die.'

Images blossomed in Séamus's mind, of his life and how it might have been lived, as a whole human being instead of a set of disjuncted fragments.

{{{{{{o}}}}}}

And this is how it feels, then, leaving the world unfinished.

Séamus the Baba was running on the beach at Rossnowlagh behind his big tall father, and smiling at red-haired Sarah Clancy from Hartley's Garage ten years later, the day he saw her in the bar of the Royal County Hotel before she ran away to England with P. J. Monaghan, the motor mechanic, married with two children. Would he see her again in Heaven? What had become of the Monaghan children?

He had never been worthy of life. How would Theresa fare?

He was in the orchard with Daniel. Daniel was holding him up to take a stripey apple. What age? He had never recalled this before now. He longed for Daniel and the strength of his arms.

And when Billy had said he'd seen the wind in the trees, he'd really seen the trees in the wind.

And is there a life after death?

A single shot, and Séamus was thrown on the grass. A fluttering weight bearing down.

Then the weight was gone. The Robin was lying close beside him, staring at the moon.

'Nice one, Tom.' Billy's voice, galaxies away.

Séamus was speechless.

'Steady wrist,' Billy said.

'Practice,' said a slow American voice, 'makes perfect.' Tom Stringer stepped through the hedge, dressed in black, his face smeared with black grease, and wearing a black ski-cap and gloves.

'How bad is it?'

'A bit oozy. Nothing fatal.'

Séamus found his voice. 'You killed the Robin?'

Tom Stringer nodded. 'Regrettable, but I had to take him out. First assessment was Billy could have stopped him without using lethal force. But the man was perturbed at his friend getting totalled, therefore might have acted irrationally.' The calm, flat voice was that of a neutral interpreter conveying an objective message. Tom passed a long-barrelled pistol to Billy: 'You better take this. My Institute doesn't shoot Irish citizens. In fact, we don't shoot nobody. We're disinterested researchers. It's untraceable. Be good.'

Stringer stepped back through the hedge and vanished.

Billy threw a set of car-keys over beside the Robin's dead body. 'Okay, Séamus,' he said. 'Tom saved our bacon. We've got to keep him out of this.' He crawled painfully towards the hedge with the pistol in his hand, and said, 'Here's what happened. I couldn't fire the Uzi because I'd have killed you too, which is against

Department rules, so I dropped it like the Robin said. I threw him the car-keys, then shot him from here with this spare gun, in the side of the head, when he bent down to pick them up. Got that? Now let's not get riddled by Decko's crew. My walking isn't the best, so would you mind awfully switching on the hazard flashers on the car, and sounding the horn? Two short, one long. Two short, one long.'

Séamus did what he was told. Men with blackened faces surged out of the darkness, recognized him, summoned help for Billy, prodded the other two men. 'Dead as doornails, the both of them. The legendary Robin, Lord have mercy on him, and his best boy, Raymondo.'

A helicopter circled, switched on its searchlight, lowered itself deafeningly onto the uneven grass of the field.

'Billy the Kid,' said a voice.

'Is it yourself,' said Billy. 'Did you bring the bandages?'

'Never leave home without them.' The man from the helicopter produced a first-aid kit, cut Billy's trousers with a scissors, rolled white gauze expertly around his leg. 'No probs,' he reported. 'Flesh wound.'

'Just as well I wasn't wearing me good pants,' Billy said.

They wiped Séamus's face with white cloths that turned red. 'Want a ride in a helicopter?' they asked him.

Séamus no longer cared whether he lived or died.

They loaded Billy onto a stretcher. 'No singing, now,' Billy said as the helicopter started to tilt.

Séamus had no children, unless you counted Theresa's stillborn son. And Séamus did count that. Dónal Joyce.

The boy, if God had not taken him on the day of his birth, would have been twenty-three by now. Seven years younger than Billy. And never had a chance.

{{{{{{o}}}}}}}

The accident and emergency consultant, a willowy fellow with pewter-grey hair, inclined his head like a praying mantis, scrutinized Billy's leg through his half-glasses and drawled: 'Nothing to worry us here, I think. Nice and clean. Another inch and we'd have nicked an artery. Two inches, thigh-bone shattered. Six inches . . . Mrs O'Rourke is a lucky lady. We'll have you out and about in a few days.'

'Will I be able to play the harmonium, doc?'

For a moment he was puzzled. 'Can't see why not,' he allowed. 'You'll need to take it easy for a week, though. There is some trauma and laceration.'

'Because,' Billy said, 'I never could play it before.'

The consultant snickered with good-natured amusement at this venerable witticism. 'Mr O'Rourke, you are a card!'

Séamus stood by as they swabbed and bandaged the wound. If he had passed the gun in time, Billy might not have been injured. Séamus's stupid slowness could have killed him.

Billy lay perfectly still, not wincing, just relaxing. A nurse took Séamus aside and cleaned his own bleeding knuckles, which he had barely noticed. He remembered nothing of having scraped them. The nurse's ash-blonde hair smelled of autumn and strawberries. He thought of

Theresa, and the nurses lifting her, so gently. They were in the same hospital tonight, though in different parts. He thought of Heidi's tousled hair.

The Minister, Richard Frye, swept into the ward with his PR man Mick Tanner and his personal private secretary Máire Benedict. The Minister laid his hands on the recumbent Billy like a healer.

'Excellent,' he said. 'Superb.'

'Are you fit to face the media?' Mick asked. 'I gave them a news release, but you're the man they want.'

'Not tonight,' Billy said. 'Maybe Mr Joyce would talk to them.' He saved my life. When Ray Kinnear came through the hedge I was a goner, but Séamus shot him before he could pull the trigger.'

They all turned to Séamus. He felt like the late substitute who has scored the winning goal for his school.

'But I was taken prisoner myself,' he confessed. 'My own fault.'

Billy interrupted seamlessly: 'That was when I had to kill the Robin. I got a clear shot at him. He was trying to take Mr Joyce hostage, and acting a bit hysterical. Couldn't be trusted. Otherwise, we could have picked him up later.'

'You acted correctly,' the Minister pronounced. 'Fine job, Mr Joyce.' Not a word of apology, not a flicker of regret at having placed his life in danger.

Mick Tanner came over to Séamus. 'Do you think you could deal with the reptiles? You don't have to say much. I'll show you our news release.'

The Matron loomed, hissing: 'You'll have to go outside. I have patients trying to sleep.'

And so it was on the cold windswept lawn in front of the hospital that Séamus Joyce took his screen test. He had been on television before, but always in the background. This was different. A small group of reporters, clustered around a camera and some arc lights with cables that ran back to a van. One of their number, a loud young man of heavy build, whom Séamus vaguely recognized, was the interviewer while others thrust their microphones in front of him. 'Saturday, October ninth,' the young man shouted, 'two forty-five a.m. I am speaking to Mr Séamus Joyce, acting director of the Irish Drugs Enforcement Agency. There are rumours of dissent in official circles over the handling of tonight's drug seizure, which was co-ordinated by a regular drug squad instead of by your own agency. Is that correct?'

Séamus stood his ground. Mr Dowd had excellent organizing abilities. His planning had been impeccable within the resources allocated to him. The vehicle carrying the drugs had been intercepted and its occupants arrested without incident. The other vehicle had attempted to break clear, but that was certainly not Mr Dowd's fault. Had it not crashed into Billy O'Rourke's car, he had no doubt that it would have been located further on.

'So you are claiming tonight's incident as a triumph for law and order?' the interviewer demanded.

Séamus held up his hands. 'No triumph. Two men are dead.'

'Is it true that you shot one of them yourself?'

'No comment.'

'And the second man? Is there a shoot-to-kill policy?'

Séamus paused before replying: 'He had disarmed me. We were under attack.'

'You allowed yourself to be disarmed?'

'I am a civil servant, not a policeman.'

'Are you trained in the use of firearms?'

'No.'

'Do you think suspicions will be raised by the killing of two suspects?'

'There will be a full investigation. I have no more to say. Good night.'

They let him go. As he walked across the grass, the arc lights went out. One of the reporters, a female, came trotting after him in the darkness and called out: 'Oh, Mr Joyce, will you tell Billy I was asking for him? Trixie Gill?'

'All right.'

'Will Billy be okay?'

'Absolutely.'

So this was Trixie Gill in the flesh. Nice-looking girl. Much too fragile for Billy. Girls like that never went for Séamus. Why had Heidi?

Back inside the hospital, he conveyed Trixie's greetings to Billy, said goodnight to everyone and walked over to the private wing where Theresa lay in sleep. The nurses brought him a cup of sugary tea, and he sat by Theresa's bedside and listened to her breathing as she dozed, as quiet as a child. They woke her up, gave her the prescribed cocktail of medicines, and she went back to sleep again. When he looked at her, the black circles around her eyes limned the shape of a skull waiting to be set free of the flesh.

We cling to life, in spite of its pain. Yet we waste what we are given.

The taste of blood filled his mouth. Something was changing in him. When he closed his eyes he saw the dark silhouette of Billy falling through the hedge, and heard the high wailing voice of the Robin, not like a robin, more the crying of a seagull. On what grey seas had that man spread his wings tonight?

Is there a life before death?

{{{{{{o}}}}}}

Davnet and her father huddled over the Sunday news-papers. He had bought four of them, each with several sections which he passed to her after skimming them. This was a serious moment. Pa held trenchant opinions on many issues – taxation, urban transport, the Pacific Rim, women priests (whom he called priestesses), funda-mentalists (whom he called blackened sepulchres), European Monetary Union, genetic engineering, South American history – and kept effortlessly abreast of them all.

The trial of Jerome Fennessy was scheduled for the coming week. There were going to be two charges: importation of heroin valued at €24,500, and importa-tion of child pornography which was understood to come from Belgium and to include depictions of babies under the age of three.

'That's the man who came to the club.' She showed the newspaper report to Pa. 'The one who sent me the card.'

'Gallant little Belgium,' he said. 'Worst colonial administration in world history. Reduced the Congo to starvation. You only have to read Conrad's *Heart of Darkness*. Or Roger Casement. They dragged us in to the First World War. They squat in the heart of Europe, raking in the shekels from all sides. Their establishment is riddled with paedophiles and murderers. They export poisoned food. Feed their livestock on excrement.'

'You think the magazine will look worse because it comes from Belgium?'

'Without the shadow of a doubt,' Pa said. 'Here's more about your friend.' He passed her the *Sunday Dispatch*. A news team from the *Dispatch* had doorstepped Jerome Fennessy's wife, photographed in full colour as she pushed the reporter out of her garden. Mrs Fennessy was a youthful, fair-haired woman in a white dress. 'She doesn't call herself Anne Fennessy,' the report began. 'She prefers to be known as Annie Greene, though her maiden name was Scanlon. We tracked her down to her home in an exclusive Dublin suburb. Mrs Fennessy refused to discuss her husband's arrest on drugs and porn charges. Disgraced teacher Jerome Fennessy lost his job at a top-class Cork boarding school four years ago, following a sex-pest scandal involving a 15-year-old girl. Yesterday he was charged with carrying 80 grammes of heroin, worth more than €35,000, into Dublin Airport from Amsterdam.'

Davnet looked at the photograph. The background was vaguely familiar.

'Pretty 29-year-old Mrs Anne Fennessy is the live-in

companion of techno whizz John J. Greene, who sells state-of-the-art computers and office equipment in Clontarf. They share a luxury apartment next door to John Greene's exclusive IT emporium. Anne works part-time in downtown Dublin hairstylists, Gold With Grief.'

At the bottom of the page was a small picture of a shopfront. COMPUQUIP, said the plastic sign.

Davnet knew the shop. Her bus into town passed close by.

'Odd thing,' Pa observed, 'the baby-porn charge doesn't gel with the story about the fifteen-year-old. Perverts who are fixated on babies are never fixated on fifteen-year-olds. Two entirely separate markets. As any fool knows. And note the differing values placed on the drugs. You can't trust any facts presented in the media. Remember that.'

The *Sunday Gazette* had a later story on its front page. iDEA Deputy Director Billy O'Rourke, recently decorated for bravery in the battle against organized crime, had been wounded again last night in a shootout with criminal elements. Heroin with an estimated street value of over nine million euros had been seized.

Billy O'Rourke, who was so anxious to put Mr Fennessy away. Who didn't want to believe that Mr Fennessy and Mr Blake were friends. Whose pen came from Gloria Mennon's bank.

Nine million. If drug barons could shift that kind of value in a single consignment, why would they bother sending Jerome Fennessy all the way to Amsterdam to pick up eighty grammes of heroin?

Davnet wanted to know what Pa thought about this question, but Maureen emerged blinking from her bedroom, and he lost all interest in Davnet. He enquired tenderly after Maureen's health, advised her to go back to bed if she wasn't feeling too well, and mentioned that he'd seen her ex-husband's sister in the pub on the previous evening, which instantly reduced her to whimpering. Pa comforted her, then extracted some five-euro notes from Ma's handbag and took himself off to the Cardinal Richelieu for a jorum, wearing the ridiculous blue beret that made him look like a baboon.

Pa had pinned his hopes on Maureen. She had dropped out of Business Studies to pursue a modelling career (she had been anorexic then), and had fallen for an alcoholic photographer who beat her up on Fridays. Pa had hosted a lavish wedding, attended by wannabees of stage, screen and catwalk. Maureen had escaped after six months, when her new husband broke two of her ribs and locked her in the bathroom. Even now, Pa expected great things of his firstborn. He was actively pursuing a Church annulment on her behalf.

Davnet helped her mother to chop vegetables for soup. Ma loved Davnet, all right, but that didn't count. Ma loved all sorts of things. Even Mr Gutman, though Davnet was not quite certain about that. She thought about Jerome Fennessy. He had looked her over with a kind of paralysed longing that set her teeth on edge. But child pornography?

The exploitation of children was a worldwide evil. At school, earnest Kathryn McKenna was organizing a human rights group. She was constantly bringing in photographs of disadvantaged Africans and Asians. All the girls, including Jenny and Davnet, had signed petitions for victims of oppression in far-flung corners of the world. Men, women and children. If Jerome Fennessy really was a child molester, he could go to hell.

After lunch she told Ma she was going out for a walk. She caught a bus, got off at the Compuquip shop. The window displayed computers, printers, palmtops, telephones, Internet offers, software packages, all spotlit and clean.

Nearby was a front door of the same colour as the photograph in the *Sunday Dispatch*. She closed her eyes and knocked.

Mrs Fennessy flung the door open, almost as if she had been lying in wait. Her freckled face, framed in straw-coloured hair, looked even younger than her picture in the newspaper.

Davnet forced herself to speak: 'My name is Davnet O'Reilly. I used to work in Blackwood's Club, and I met your husband, Jerome Fennessy, just before –'

'What are you doin' here?' A soft voice, but tight in the throat. A Dublin city voice, not at all like Jerome's plummy tones.

'I think he may be innocent,' Davnet began. 'But I don't want to make trouble between you and him.'

'There's no me and him. What's your problem?'

'Was it true he lost his teaching job for molesting a girl?'

Mrs Fennessy stared at her with incredulity. 'What right have you to ask?'

Davnet spoke deliberately: 'It's just that I want to

help him, if I can. The police want to make out he never knew Mr Blake. That isn't true.'

'Mr Blake?'

'Paul Blake. He was murdered this week. I used to work for him.'

'And Romeo is mixed up in that, too?'

'No. Mr Blake was just a school friend of your husband's. Did he ever mention him?'

'He was always goin' on about posh gits he'd known at school,' the fair-haired woman said. 'I never used to believe him, so I did.'

'But Mr Fennessy really did know Mr Blake. Mr Blake arranged for him to go to Paris. Not Amsterdam.'

'What difference does that make?'

'He may have been tricked into carrying the drugs.'

'Lookit, Romeo would do anythin' for money. He borrowed a thousand quid from my mother. He sold a fake feckin' oil paintin' to my uncle. He's a complete and total slimeball. You a friend of his?'

'No. I just wanted to help, if he's innocent. I'm not trying to get involved with him or anything.'

'Are you not?' Mrs Fennessy was openly mocking. 'Well you needn't worry about old Romeo. You can get involved as much as you like with old Romeo, and you'll be safe as feckin' houses. You're welcome to him.' She regarded Davnet with contempt. 'Picked me up when I was about your age, used to buy me cups of coffee and talk to me about feckin' poetry. Then we got married because I was pregnant. Not by him, mind. Old Romeo didn't do things like that. He treated me like a feckin' princess, until I grew up and started lookin' more like an actual woman.' Her hands designed curves around the straight lines of her body. 'Then Romeo started moonin' over young ones again. Never did anythin' about it, of course. The young one that got him sacked was a feckin' liar. And her parents mad for compo. Poor old Romeo was accused in the wrong. Which served him feckin' right.'

A red setter came bounding from the house, and licked Davnet's face. Mrs Fennessy caught it by the collar. 'You can clear off now,' she said. 'I don't know why I'm standin' here talkin' to you.'

'Because we have something in common,' Davnet replied in a sudden flash of insight. 'That's why you're telling me. You and me, we're Jerome's type.'

'Jesus help us if we are.' Mrs Fennessy yanked the dog's collar, dragged it away, retreated inside the house and slammed the door.

Davnet thought about Jerome, trapped in his compulsions, forced to repeat his mistakes – like Mother Polycarp's descriptions of the souls in Dante's Hell.

Jerome was incapable of wanting what he needed. His wistfulness was like a deadly sin, but not one of the standard seven deadlies: pride, covetousness, lust, anger, gluttony, envy and sloth. Frank O'Connor wrote that it is our venial sins, not our mortal sins, that finally damn us. Or so Mother Polycarp said.

{{{{{{o}}}}}}

The Commercial Disasters was the name of the Blakes' rock band, and they were living up to their name. In an almost empty stadium, under flashing lights, Mr Blake, in a pink shroud, was playing the guitar solo from 'Hotel California'. Dee Dee was shaking a tambourine, Felicity hitting drums and cymbals. Mr Dargan, the substitute music teacher, hobbled onto the stage and announced a change of programme. 'Hotel California' was not coming up on the Leaving Cert; instead they must write a ten-page essay: 'The influence of Michael William Balfe on Frederick Bulsara.' Mr Dargan began to ring his little bell. Davnet reached out an arm to switch off her alarm clock. She had the ingredients of a splitting headache. The house was quiet. She tumbled downstairs and drank cold tea with two aspirins and a slice of leftover Guinness cake.

By the time she got to school her head was back to normal. The first class was French, featuring regular verbs. Mr Grennell worked through half a dozen of them in the present, the future and the conditional. Mr Grennell was deeply attached to regular verbs. He lobbed questions around his classroom. Davnet answered only when asked, never volunteering to correct a wrong guess, but she knew all the verb forms and felt them slot one by one into their proper places. She began to feel almost well.

Biology was cancelled, which left her free for forty minutes. She still had an English essay to do for Miss Bellingham. She went into the library and made a start on it.

'The victims in *Macbeth* amount to little more than pale reflections of the protagonist's inner conflicts.' Typical Bella title. *Protagonist* was one of her favourite words.

'This idea only works so long as Macbeth himself is not the victim,' she scribbled. 'But in the penultimate scene' – Bella was partial to *penultimate* – 'when the protagonist accepts his fate, the murderer becomes a victim of the general fate of mankind, and guilty or innocent makes no difference. Aristotle said tragedy purges pity and terror. This play burns out our power to judge. We are forced to identify with Macbeth, the hero, villain and victim. Christ on the cross said "Father, forgive them, for they know not what they do". We can only forgive Macbeth once he really does know. That is Shakespeare's spiritual lesson.'

Literature was Bella's religion, so Davnet was sure of her ground so far. She scribbled on in her horrid childish handwriting: 'There are plenty of victims in the play: the Norweyans, the first Thane of Cawdor, the eagle killed by the mousing owl, King Duncan, Nature, the grooms, Banquo, the Thane of Fife's family, Lady Macbeth, Macbeth himself – and let's not forget the trees destroyed in Birnan Wood.' Bella was ecologically minded. 'All the trouble stems from the three witches sending Macbeth astray, yet they are the only ones spared, which is funny because witches would have been burnt in Shakespeare's England. In putting the blame on them and Lady Macbeth, is this play just another veiled attack on women?' Bella liked feminist questions, though not the answers.

'Some of the victims, when you look, are really hidden perpetrators. The King changes Macbeth's name and promotes him from Glamis to Cawdor. He literally creates his own murderer. When Macbeth kills the king, he is the king's creature and it is by killing his creator that –'

She was stuck. But Jenny strolled in, pure sex in her pervy blue uniform, and riffled through the newspapers on the library table. 'Gadzooks, if it isn't one's boyfriend Mister Fennessy,' she said to Davnet, pointing at a photograph in the *Gazette* of Jerome smiling for the cameras outside a courthouse. 'Drugs case lawyer alleges brutality, by Trixie Gill,' she read aloud in her version of Miss Bellingham's snotty elocution accent. 'Gardaí were last night accused of oppressive tactics in a heroin smuggling case. Jerome Fennessy, a former school-teacher, is to face narcotics and child pornography charges in the Central Criminal Court this week, under the new speedy trials procedure. Last night Mr Fiachra Ó Neachtain, defence solicitor, called a press conference to allege brutal and oppressive tactics on the part of the investigating officers in the Drugs Enforcement Agency. He alleged that his client had been held incommunicado, refused permission to go to the toilet, scalded with hot tea, and accused of involvement in the murder of a nightclub owner in order to make him sign a false confession. A spokesperson for the Incorporated Law Society said last night that it is not standard practice for solicitors to reveal details of their defence plans to the media in advance of a trial. "That may be the way they do things in America," said the spokesperson, "but in Ireland, not."'

Steel-haired, granite-jawed Miss Power had beetled silently into the library. It was too late to warn Jenny.

'Is this what you spend your free class doing, Jennifer

McGlinchey?' Miss Power began in her Black and Decker voice.

'It was lying there,' Jenny said.

'Newspapers are for the remedials, Jennifer, not the Leaving Cert students. Have you no homework to complete?'

'No, Miss Power. And it's Genevieve. Not Jennifer.'

'Don't be impertinent, child. If you have nothing to do, you can clean out the changing rooms. The boys have left them in a filthy state.'

'Let the boys clean them, then,' Davnet said before she could stop herself.

'Miss O'Reilly!' The teacher rounded on her. 'You can help your classmate.'

'No, she can't,' Jenny cut in. 'She has to finish her English essay for Miss Bellingham.'

'Really, I can help,' Davnet said. 'And I'm sorry for being rude, Miss Power.'

'I don't want Davnet's help,' beautiful Jenny said. 'It's not fair.'

Miss Power then launched into her standard pianissimo opening, about how she had never in all her years as a teacher encountered such feckless, impertinent little chits of girls. She raised her voice steadily during the speech, gradually working herself up towards one of her false furies. Jenny's lovely face froze into snow.

This was unreal. Davnet closed her books, clipped her pen to the front of her uniform and stood up to go.

'Stand still, child,' Miss Power shrieked, 'when I am talking to you.'

'Sorry,' Davnet heard herself saying. 'Couldn't be

arsed.' And as Miss Power fell silent in momentary amazement, Davnet walked out of the library, out of the building. Crossing the schoolyard, she could hear Miss Power screaming at Jenny. She wanted to go back and stop her, push her away, hit her. Instead she ran. Cowardy custard. At the school gate she collided with Mother Polycarp, who made a halfhearted attempt to detain her. 'Can't talk,' she gulped, and stumbled to the bus stop.

The *Gazette* offices were in a dingy building near the river. Davnet asked at the security desk for Trixie Gill. They asked if she had an appointment, and offered to see whether Ms Gill was around this morning. After a telephone call, a blonde waif appeared, in a fluffy pink angora top and tight baby-blue jeans. 'I've come to see Trixie Gill,' Davnet explained.

'That's me,' the waif grinned. Her head was too big for her neck, but she was all the prettier for that. Her voice was husky and high-pitched at the same time, reminding Davnet of a talking doll that Maureen had lost.

Trixie seemed really interested in what Davnet had to tell her about Billy O'Rourke wanting her to say that Jerome wasn't friends with Mr Blake. She asked Davnet how she could be sure that O'Rourke wasn't simply testing her story by pretending not to believe her. So Davnet told her about the Mowbray's pen, which seemed to link him with Mr Blake's club in a round-about way. Trixie's eyes widened; she was really intrigued by that detail, and promised to look into it. She assured Davnet that she had no problems about exposing police malpractice. Only recently she had reported a fake overtime scam that had led to the dismissal of a sergeant. 'I'm tougher than I look,' she grinned. She took Davnet's telephone number, promised to be in touch real soon.

Davnet went and drank coffee in Bewley's and thought deep, dark thoughts about life and Jenny's eyelashes.

{{{{{{o}}}}}}

Billy was greatly amused by Davnet's fantasy about the pen. Even funnier than Declan Dowd's talk of sabotage on the night that the Robin was killed. Decko was a bad loser.

The following day's *Gazette* carried Trixie's obituary for John F. Hughes, the compassionate tale of a talented misfit lured into crime. The Robin had been born John Fenimore Hughes in 1959. His middle name was due to his father's having read *The Last of the Mohicans* in a Classics Illustrated comic while on remand in Mountjoy. Young John was regarded by the Christian Brothers as a promising scholar, but left school after his father disappeared in England. His elder brother Tom, described as a slightly organized criminal, brought him out on burglaries while he was still a child. At the age of fifteen, he had hidden behind a pile of packing-cases while a rival gang beat his brother into a coma and stole their takings. When the brother died, little John burned the houses of the rival gang, killed their leader, recruited their camp-followers, and launched a meticulously

planned series of cash robberies. Hence his nickname –
'the Robin' came from robbing, not from his appearance, but so many people thought it was his nickname
that he got called 'Robin' and 'the Robin' indiscriminately. He formed an alliance with a paramilitary gang
that controlled meat-smuggling rackets, and made his
first million by the age of twenty-three. In the mid-1980s
he used legitimate businesses in the entertainment and
horse-racing industries as a cover for criminal activities
which now included the importation of contraband
tobacco. A move into drug wholesaling led to a gang war,
and the Robin decamped for several years, exporting
cocaine from Holland to London. His devoted mother
came out to keep house for him in Amsterdam. Returning to Dublin in 1996, he moved back into local drug
supply, as well as developing a strong line in agricultural
grant frauds and property development. In recent times
he had begun to build up a respectable front in the
licensed bar trade, but his death in a shootout with
police showed that he had never strayed far from his
roots in violent crime.

The article was headed 'Swan Song of a Robin', and
made no acknowledgement of Billy O'Rourke as its
primary source.

{{{{{o}}}}}

Séamus was late arriving for work, after an anxious
wait at the clinic, followed by another inconclusive
consultation. Dr Alphonse Maguire Gibson was not
quite in a position to issue an All Clear. The growths

could conceivably be malignant, although this was not necessarily the case, and the precise grade of malignancy, if any, would take time to determine. Further test results might be available within thirty-six hours, depending on staff shortages in the pathology division, following which they should be in a position to decide on treatment, which could possibly consist of a combination of drugs and further surgery. Equally, however, the news might be better than expected. One must not be premature.

He was still dizzy as he entered the office, helped himself to a beaker of cool water from the new dispenser, flipped through the post in his in-tray. All urgent, which was calming in its own way.

Billy arrived by taxi and strode into the building, limping slightly. No sign of a crutch or stick. He had discharged himself from hospital and was carrying a plastic bag with his overnight things. The secretaries were overjoyed to see him. Three of them had already been in to visit him in St Olaf's ward, bringing him flowers and biscuits and fruit. Séamus had brought a surreptitious hip-flask of whiskey, man to man.

After his lap of honour, Billy came into the director's office and shut the door carefully behind him. Séamus was sitting at his desk, going through the motions of reading a memorandum from the Attorney-General's office.

'Fennessy trial starts tomorrow,' Billy said, 'so there's something you ought to know. They're trying to blacken me.'

'Who?'

'Girl who worked in Blake's club claims I'm framing Fennessy.'

'Who is she?'

'Nobody in particular. She's talking to journalists. Most of them will steer clear of her, but if she goes to Simons the muckraker, he might run it. Radio Free Dublin lives on scandal.'

'Why does she say you framed Fennessy?'

'Because I had a connection with her boss, Mr Blake.'

'A connection?'

'Claims I'm a queer,' laughed Billy, 'and I know something about Blake's murder, and I'm framing Fennessy for the drugs so as to hide my love affair with Blake.'

'Who is this person?'

Billy shook his head. 'She's only a kid.'

'So what do you want me to do?'

'Nothing. Just don't be surprised if someone picks up the story.'

'We'll take them to the cleaners,' said Séamus.

'And you're probably wondering what the Robin meant when he said I double-crossed him.'

'I hadn't given it any thought.'

'I'll tell you anyway. I talked to the Robin three months back, told him the iDEA was going after the Snowman and we'd take the heat off him if he helped us out. He believed me, the fool. Thought I'd let him waltz a wagonload of horse under our noses, in return for him fingering Craig and McIntyre.'

'And was it the Robin who told you about Fennessy?'

Billy grinned. 'No. That was a bar girl in the Midshipman, who recognized Matt Wellan, overheard a bit of the conversation, phoned me on my mobile. I followed Fennessy after he left the pub, tracked him out to the airport, found out when he was due back. Don't tell anyone, though. The bar girl has a baby to look after, and she shouldn't be blabbing about bad boys like the Snowman.'

{{{{{o}}}}}

There was hell to pay, as expected. Miss Power had made a formal complaint to the school principal. Jenny had been given detention. The vice-principal interviewed Davnet, and warned her that such gross impertinence to Miss Power would not be tolerated in future. Leaving the school premises without permission was a serious offence. You could see the poor stiff was going through the motions. Working with Miss Power would be no picnic.

Davnet sulked through German, Biology, Irish, Maths and a double period of English. Miss Bellingham accepted her *Macbeth* essay, late though it was, and proceeded to read it aloud to the class, which was deadly embarrassing.

Mother Polycarp stopped her in the corridor.

'You got bitten by the Power maniac,' she said.

'Sure did,' said Davnet.

'A disgrace to her profession,' the little nun said. 'Turn her to your spiritual advantage.'

'How?'

'Forgive her.'

'Forgive her? What good will that do?'

'It won't do her any good. At least I hope not. But it might stop you getting ulcers.'

Davnet walked all the way home. It took ninety minutes. Mother Polycarp's advice was infuriating. She could disregard Miss Power's bullying of herself, but was she entitled to forgive a wrong done to another person? No, she did not have to forgive the old cow for punishing Jenny.

Transferable forgiveness is a fraud. She could not forgive injustice. This being the case, when she got home she searched angrily through the Golden Pages until she found the number of Fiachra Ó Neachtain, Jerome Fennessy's defence solicitor, practising as Ó Neachtain and De Róiste, and made an appointment to meet him in the Four Courts on the afternoon of the following day, Wednesday, which was to be the first day of the Fennessy trial.

{{{{{{o}}}}}}

'This is a simple matter,' said the prosecuting Senior Counsel, smiling nervously at the jury. 'The defendant is charged under the Criminal Justice Amendment Act with the offence of carrying prohibited substances into the State. We will present evidence to show that Mr Jerome Fennessy, for whatever reason –'

Here he broke into uncontrolled coughing. He was an elderly man, and had an elderly frog in his throat. Mr Senan Roche, Senior Counsel for the defence, charitably passed him a glass of water.

'That Mr Jerome Fennessy,' he resumed after a

minute, 'did indeed so carry prohibited substances. The defendant is also charged with the importation of depraved literature contrary to the Censorship of Publications Act. Ladies and gentlemen, I could remind you of the menace posed by hard drugs and child pornography. I could paint the defendant's character in a dark and sinister light. I will not attempt to do so. It is not our place to be judgemental, ladies and gentlemen. We simply need to ascertain the truth. I would not wish to create any bias in your minds towards the man in the dock. Whatever he may have done, he is innocent until proven guilty. You or I or anyone in this courtroom might find ourselves in a similar unfortunate position one day, and we would not like to face a prejudiced jury, would we? I simply ask you to approach the case dispassionately. What I propose to do is simply to outline the facts, as I know them, and then ask you to reach the verdict according to your own conscience, on the exclusive basis of the straightforward evidence which I shall endeavour, to the best of my ability, to place before you.' He drained the rest of Senan Roche's water.

The courtroom regulars nodded wisely. This was the standard oration (known in the trade as the Simply Speech) with which Mr Gerald McAnnespie SC always launched his prosecutions. The odd thing was, it often did the trick.

Swearing in the jury had already taken up half the morning; the defence had further delayed matters by attempting to have Jerome's written statement excluded from evidence on the grounds that it had been penned without legal advice. Mr Justice McQueen had ruled against them on that: the anti-drugs legislation deliberately restricted access to a solicitor's advice, and for good reason. Mr Roche had then argued that only those portions of Mr Fennessy's statement which related to the present alleged offence should be placed before the jury, rather than subjecting them to irrelevancies about his previous education and career. The judge scotched that suggestion as well; the jury were entitled to know what sort of man the defendant claimed to be, in his self-justificatory statement. Mr Roche further contended that vital parts of Mr Fennessy's writings, meaning the copious notes and drafts which he had made, were not included with the statement, rendering it selective and unreliable. Mr Justice McQueen acidly pointed out that as Mr Roche himself had just now been seeking to conceal part of the finished statement from the jury, he could hardly seek to invalidate it on the grounds that certain extra material had allegedly not been blended into the mix.

Mr McAnnespie's outline of the prosecution case then took almost until lunchtime. He lingered scrupulously over the arrest at Dublin Airport, over Jerome Fennessy's verbal and written confessions, over the laboratory analysis of the substance that he had imported (the two sachets of heroin being identical in their degree of purity and chemical composition, they must have come from the same batch), and over the distasteful character of the Belgian magazine that had been discovered in the defendant's overnight bag.

Mr Senan Roche's opening rebuttal was considerably

shorter and more robust. Here we had, he roared, one of the most savage and unprincipled frame-ups in the history of the State. His client, an honourable man, a teacher who had fallen on hard times, had been cynically picked out as a sacrificial victim, had been tricked into going to a foreign land as a favour to an old school chum, had had heinous drugs and the most filthy pornography planted in his luggage, had been improperly detained and mercilessly interrogated, had been forced to confess to a crime he had never committed, and had seen his words twisted in a way that made him appear like the blackest of criminals. And for why? To bolster the reputation of a wasteful and possibly unconstitutional quango, the so-called Irish Drugs Enforcement Agency, which was designed for no other purpose than to flatter the vanity of an ambitious politician, the Minister for Justice, Mr Richard Alistair Frye. The defendant had been thrown to the iDEA by the drug barons like a piece of fish-bait, in furtherance of their own sinister aims, and the iDEA had gratefully accepted this early Christmas present from the criminal confraternity. If colluding with drug barons to frame innocent citizens was the best they could do, the iDEA should shut up shop.

Mr Gerald McAnnespie sighed, cast his eyes to heaven and was moving to call his first witness when Mr Justice McQueen intervened, adjourning the court until two o'clock.

In the early afternoon, Bosco Woulfe sheepishly outlined his career in the Guards, his secondment to the iDEA, and his attendance at Dublin Airport for the purpose of apprehending a person suspected of ferrying a consignment of drugs on the evening of Sunday the third of October. He had no idea where the information had come from. It was not his job to know things like that. The defendant had been, well, not intoxicated exactly, but a mite tipsy, and had put up no resistance. He seemed a nice gentleman, really. Bosco Woulfe had asked him what the powder in the envelope was, and the defendant had replied 'You know and I know what it is.'

Jerome Fennessy whispered to his solicitor, who passed a note to the junior counsel, Ms Frieda Gallaher, who passed it to Senan Roche, who read it with much nodding and clipped it to his file.

The prosecution counsel halted courteously while this was going on, which spoiled the theatrical effect.

'Carry on, please, Mr McAnnespie,' the judge droned.

'I beg your pardon, my Lord. From the flurry on Mr Roche's side, I had been anticipating an objection. Mr Woulfe, did you have any further discussion with the defendant as to what he knew was in the packet?'

'No. I minded him for a wee while while they went out hunting for the man he said was going to meet him, but we didn't talk about the case.'

'What did you talk about, in particular?'

'Funny enough, we talked about art. There were some artistic postcards in his bag. I do a bit of watercolours in my spare time. Mr Fennessy knows all about Dutch painting. He was after visiting the Rijksmuseum in Amsterdam during his outing. I've never been there myself, though I'd love to go, indeed I would.'

Bosco had guarded the front door of the iDEA building in Booterstown, sitting downstairs in the porter's room, and he had heard nothing of the interrogation.

Senan Roche failed to shake him in his account. He put it to him in cross-examination that the defendant had not said 'You know and I know what it is', but only 'You know what it is'. Bosco Woulfe modestly stuck to his guns. He remembered the phrase exactly, he insisted, because in fact he had been in some doubt as to whether it was heroin or cocaine. He admitted to being a mite short-sighted, and blinked at the jury by way of corroboration. He denied having spilt tea over the defendant. He had brought up a mug of tea all right. Maybe the defendant had splashed it over himself, being tipsy and all. He had seen the defendant writing out his confession in Mr Joyce's office early on the morning of Monday the fourth of October. The defendant had certainly known that Mr Blake was dead before he wrote out the confession, because Billy O'Rourke had bought a copy of that morning's *Irish Times* and he had told Billy, in the prisoner's presence, what he had heard on the radio about the killing, and what his contacts in Garda headquarters had told him about the victim's identity.

Jerome rose to his feet and was silenced by Mr Justice McQueen, who threatened to have him taken down to the cells should he attempt to disrupt the proceedings. Jerome subsided.

'This is a court of law,' the justice reminded him.

A very old woman in the public seating struggled noisily to her feet and tottered towards the door. As she was helped by a chivalrous Guard, she was heard to remark: 'It's a travesty, whatever he may call it.'

'What was that?' The judge affected hardness of hearing.

'I think she asked for the lavatory, or female toilet,' Senan Roche interposed.

'End of the corridor, last on the left,' decreed Mr Justice McQueen.

Jerome smiled. Mummy, at eighty-five, still knew which end was up.

{{{{{{o}}}}}}

There were no trains, but otherwise the Four Courts reminded Davnet of a dingy railway station. Asking the porters for directions, she pushed along crowded corridors until she came to the Fennessy trial, which was going on in a badly lit room with brown churchy panelling. She entered amid hubbub and commotion. The court was rising. The judge swept out and Jerome was led away, head bowed. Davnet stood at the barrier and tried to attract the attention of the lawyers. Eventually, a thin bearded man, mumbling to an old wreck in a wig, turned and noticed her.

'Mr Ó Neachtain?'

'Yes?'

'I'm Davnet. I have an appointment. Could we talk confidentially?'

'In this madhouse? What do you think, Mr Roche?'

'Whisper in my ear, darling,' said the old wreck, stepping to the barrier.

It was a remarkably large ear, none too clean, with a large flappy lobe. She recited the story of how Billy O'Rourke had refused to believe her, and how his Mowbray's pen matched Gloria's bank in the Cayman Islands.

The two men reacted differently. Fiachra Ó Neachtain was jubilant; Mr Roche was dubious: 'It's a matter of tactics,' he murmured. 'If we can get Mr Fennessy off without having to suggest that policemen are twisters, that will be nicer. Juries don't like having their value systems upset, d'you see. They don't mind discounting for a spot of perjury, but the notion of an orchestrated conspiracy by the men in blue tends to put a strain on their faith. Supposing we did want to float this item, could you give evidence for us?'

'If you think it's important.'

'It might be. And you're sure of what you're saying?'

'Of course. Do you believe Mr Fennessy is innocent?'

'As the babe unborn,' Mr Roche said emphatically with no conviction whatever. 'Leave your address and phone. We'll call you when we need you. We must go and talk to the poor man now.'

She found the way out and set off on foot for the city centre and the bus ride home. Her visit to the Four Courts had obviously been useless, and anyway Mr Fennessy was probably guilty as hell, but at least the walk would do her good. She had not gone back to school today. She could not face Miss Power. Besides, she had to read *States of Ireland* for her history essay. Ma had phoned home at lunchtime, enquiring whether Davnet might be in town that afternoon, and asking her to buy three pairs of winter socks for Pa in Hyperbulk. He had been complaining of rising damp in the feet, and his summer hosiery was no longer warm enough. Hyperbulk, near the Jervis Centre, was Ma's preferred supplier of clothing. She alleged that it offered even better value than Dunnes Stores, which was of course absurd, since everyone knows that Dunnes Stores Better Value Beats Them All. Shopping for food at Hyperbulk was impractical, as it was too far to carry heavy items home. Ma ordered her groceries by telephone from a local shop that did deliveries. Pa had sold the car after Maureen's wedding.

She found the socks and paid for them. Hyperbulk employed tired middle-aged female sales staff, with young male trainee managers in sharp suits to bully them. The cashier looked half asleep.

Davnet decided to treat herself to a sticky bun in Henry Street. Diet be damned. But before she reached Bewley's there came a heavy hand on her shoulder and she turned to see a red-faced blob leering into her face.

'Not so fast, young lady!' he chortled. His forehead was covered in pimples. Her first thought, instantly repressed, was that he was a truancy officer who had been infected by spotty adolescents like herself.

'That's the one.' A starving boy in green uniform, with pink skin and scrubby blond hair, was pointing at her Hyperbulk carrier bag. 'In there, Guard.'

'Hand it over!' roared the red-faced man, and snatched the bag, passing it to the uniformed boy, who rummaged in it and produced a bunch of blue socks.

'Where did you get those?' the red-faced man demanded. His strangled voice came from deep in his fat throat.

'In the men's shop at Hyperbulk,' Davnet said.

'This receipt says three pairs.'

'That's right.'

'There are four pairs here,' cooed the red-faced man. And there were.

'I took three off the rack,' Davnet said.

'Did you maybe take four by mistake, like?' the red-faced man insinuated.

Davnet suddenly knew what was happening. She had been right, after all. Mr Fennessy was innocent! Which was what made her suddenly smile as she answered: 'No. Three. Not four. Three. I took three. Paid for three. The lady put three in the bag.'

'Unless she maybe put in four by mistake?' the red-faced man chortled.

'No mistake. She put in three pairs. Not four. Three. Let's go and ask her.'

'We'll take her evidence in due course. I have to ask you to come with me to Kidd Lane Garda Station.' He flashed an identity card under her nose.

'I'm not going anywhere with you.'

'You have to do what I say.'

There was nothing to be gained by backing down. 'Only if you're arresting me, Guard. Otherwise, you know I'm free to go.'

'You've had practice at this.'

'No. We did civics. As in citizen.'

'Okay, frig it, I'm arresting you!' He gripped her wrist

with a huge hammy paw, incongruously adorned by two ruby rings with stones the size of giant pimples. The mangy boy trailed along on her other side. People on the street sensed the situation and blanked their eyes as they went past, except for one velvet-collared prick who hallooed in a greased upper-middle-class voice: 'Well done. Well done.'

Kidd Lane was a small police station close by, ideally placed for the processing of shoplifters. The under-nourished boy was gone. A black-haired uniformed Guard at the desk took her name and address. She stated that she had been wrongfully arrested. He made no reply, wrote nothing down. The red-faced man led her into a brightly lit interview room. Davnet regarded him with contempt, counting the pimples on his forehead.

'First time getting caught?' he chortled.

'May I have your name and number, please?'

He stopped smiling. 'Watch yourself, young lady. Don't get smart with me. You're here to answer questions.'

'No. You've arrested me, so I don't have to answer anything. They must have taught you that in Temple-more. Also, you forgot to caution me. And I want to see a solicitor.'

'There's no call to take that tone, young lady. A lot depends on my report. You could end up in court.'

'You're a poet,' said Davnet, 'and you don't know it.'

'Very funny. You think you'll get probation. But we know the lies you've been telling. When my report goes to the DPP, you'll have a criminal record. I'll be sending it in next week.'

'Don't forget to sign it.'

'We could decide to let you off with a caution.'

'You could.'

'We'll have to send a community liaison officer around to visit your family, tell them what you've been up to. We'll have to look into your family circumstances. What does your father do for a living?'

'Retired civil servant.'

'What will he think of this?'

'He will listen to what I have to say. He will sue you personally. What did you say your name was?'

'Patrick Boyle. You think I'm friggin' scared of you?'

He left her alone in the room. She found a biro and an old shopping list in her pocket. On the back of it she wrote out the exact sequence of events, with a detailed description of her two captors, including the pimples and the ruby rings. Much sooner than she had expected, her father turned up, accompanied by Patrick Boyle and the black-haired Guard from the front desk. 'What have they done to you, Davnet?'

'Planted stolen goods on me. Wrongfully arrested me.'

'But why, pet?'

'To stop me giving evidence in Mr Fennessy's case. It's a criminal conspiracy.'

The black-haired Guard was outraged. 'Now there's no call to be saying things like that. After us sending a car to collect your father. Could you not talk some sense into her, Sir?'

Davnet looked at him. 'Obviously you're not part of this,' she said. 'Maybe Mr Boyle could tell you why he didn't bring his accomplice into the station with me.'

'I saw nobody else but you,' protested the black-haired man.

'That's what I said. I think we're going to be suing Mr Boyle. You should take your own notes of what's happening here.'

Boyle rounded on Davnet's father. 'I don't think you're going to be suing anyone, Mr O'Reilly. Your daughter says you're a retired civil servant. You look a bit young and healthy to be retired, if you don't mind me saying so. You sue me and I'll turn up your medical history. I'll go through your tax records, and those of your wife. Has she a job? Does she contribute to the family income? You'll be right sorry if you come after me.'

The black-haired Guard looked sick. Pa said nothing, but looked shifty and small.

'Tell your friggin' daughter to keep her friggin' nose clean,' Boyle whispered.

'All right,' said Pa, not meeting his eye. 'Come on home, Davnet.'

And he put on his baboon beret. She followed him downstairs. For the first time in her life, she was completely ashamed of him.

{{{{{{o}}}}}}

It started late on Wednesday evening, with Miss Bellingham asking Mother Polycarp to have a chat with Davnet O'Reilly. Mother Polycarp had a pastoral role in the school, as well as teaching religion. The girl's behaviour and school attendance were giving rise to concern, after five blameless years of docility and magnificent results in the Junior Certificate. That such a star pupil should blow a fuse in her final examination year was regrettable, and could damage the morale of her whole class. Of course Davnet was upset at the death of a school parent, but even Dee Dee and Felicity Blake were beginning to adjust.

Mother Polycarp promised to help. On Thursday morning she looked for Davnet, but Davnet was absent again. Then she tried to make contact by telephone. The O'Reilly home was unobtainable. After finishing her mid-morning circuit of eucharistic visits to nursing homes, she drove around to the address that she had been given. She was still in full religious drag, because some elderly patients in the nursing homes were nervous enough about accepting Communion from a female, and the black veil helped to reassure them.

The father, a shifty creature whom she had met at a school concert five years previously, opened the door and stared at her in horror. She explained, untruthfully, that she needed to talk to young Davnet about a voluntary project that the school was undertaking. He had known nothing of the telephone being cut off. He waved her vaguely upstairs and retreated to the television set in the front lounge.

Davnet was lying in the half-dark, her bedroom curtains drawn. She was surprised to see the old nun, and clearly taken aback by her opening gambit:

'Is it a sin to tell a lie?'

'I suppose.' Davnet's voice was weakened as if by long silence.

'That's what they keep telling us,' said Mother Polycarp. 'Naturally, they're lying. They only have to read the Eighth Commandment. What does it say?'

'Thou shalt not bear false witness against thy neighbour.'

'Good girl. So if I were to tell your father that I had called on you to talk about a charitable project for the school, whereas in fact I am calling to find out why you are missing your lessons, would I be breaking the Eighth Commandment, or would I not?'

'No, you would be lying for a good purpose, in order to help your neighbour.'

'Which we are commanded to do. You are, metaphorically speaking, a donkey that has tipped over into the ditch on the Sabbath. So what's going on, young Davnet?'

The girl thought for a moment. 'Come to think of it,' she said in her normal voice, 'I have been trying to prevent somebody from bearing false witness against his neighbour, and that person has borne false witness against me.'

'Tell me more,' growled the old nun. Davnet told her.

Mother Polycarp went ballistic. It hardly showed on the outside, apart from the clenching of her fists. She promised to call again later in the day, and hurried downstairs, waved to Mr O'Reilly lolling on the couch with his glass of stout, stumped out to her rusty Toyota Starlet, and stepped on the gas like a racing driver.

Passing through Fairview, she stopped at an office shop to make two photocopies of the paper on which Davnet had recorded her experiences at Hyperbulk. She also got the address of the iDEA from directory enquiries. A thought struck her, and she telephoned the Hyperbulk store, where they put her through to the Head of Security without offering any resistance. The man confirmed that they still held yesterday's video cassettes from the security cameras.

'Don't record over them,' she said. 'They'll be needed for a court case. Not against Hyperbulk. Against a criminal who tried to take advantage of a schoolgirl. I'll visit you after lunch.'

The doorman at the iDEA let her in at once when she said that she needed to see the Director on a personal matter. Frankly, she had expected him to put up a fight. On the way up the stairs, she noticed the glances of sympathy that several women cast in her direction. A watery blonde ushered her into an office with 'Director' on the door, and wavered off to fetch Mr Joyce. The sense of fishiness increased when a flabby man in a suit teetered in, tears brimming, and held her hand softly in his.

'It's over, then?'

'What?' Mother Polycarp withdrew her hand.

'Theresa? My wife?'

'I'm sorry, Mr Joyce. I don't know your wife.'

'You're not from the hospital?' A tidal wave of relief spread across his face. 'You see, my wife is desperately ill. She's being looked after by the nuns. I thought –'

'I've come to call on quite a different matter.'

'Certainly. Of course. Anything I can do. Please. Do sit down.' He himself subsided into a high-backed rocking-chair.

Mother Polycarp stood. 'One of your staff is conspiring to pervert the course of justice and persecuting a vulnerable young woman. This will stop.'

The Director stopped rocking. 'What young woman?'

'Her name is Davnet O'Reilly. A gifted girl, from a difficult home background, facing into her Leaving Certificate next summer. She is the star pupil of her school. One of the cleverest, also one of the finest girls I have come across in fifty years of teaching. She happened to have a part-time job working for Paul Blake, the nightclub proprietor who was murdered on the same night that you arrested Mr Fennessy. She told the police that Mr Blake knew Jerome Fennessy, and as a result of this truthful statement, one of your men, a Mr O'Rourke, is trying to discredit her. Yesterday he had her arrested on a false charge of shoplifting, engineered by a guard called Patrick Boyle.' She caught the glint of recognition in his eye. 'You know this Boyle?'

'Not personally.' But Boyle's reputation in Justice was less than fragrant. Séamus had heard the whispers.

'Boyle is a criminal.'

'How can you say that?'

'He stole a pair of socks and put them in Davnet's bag. He falsely arrested her. He blackmailed her father. That's just one afternoon's work for Mr Boyle. Lord knows what he does in the mornings.'

Joyce's patience began to fray. 'Look, Sister –'

'Mother Polycarp. Here's my card.'

'You burst in with these wild charges –'

'I do not do so lightly. A young girl's peace of mind and reputation are at stake. You should think of your own children.'

This was a blow to the stomach. He gulped a deep breath: 'Sister, we have no children. My wife is dying, and I have to cope with a malicious campaign –' He bit himself back into silence.

'A campaign, you say? Consisting of what?'

'I am not going to dignify any of these allegations –' Again he had said too much.

Mother Polycarp needled him: '*These* allegations. Why am I not surprised? What steps have you taken to investigate these allegations? What are they?'

He shrank. 'I refuse to say.'

'Involving a gold-plated ballpoint pen?'

'Which?' Shocked to the core. What on earth was he imagining?

'And a bank account in the Caribbean?'

'Nothing of the sort.' His relief was obvious.

'Davnet says that Mr O'Rourke's pen comes from the same bank where Mr Blake held his offshore investments. Isn't that interesting? Do you want to hear more?'

'No, I don't.'

'In that case, you are in dereliction of your duty. You must resign your job or face your responsibilities. Do not be afraid to act, Mr Joyce. Painful though it may be, if we do what is right we may hope that the good Lord will grant us the strength to bear the consequences. And if we fail, what odds? Justice can never be defeated, so long as it is held in the hearts of the righteous, that hope be not destroyed.'

He stared speechless at this raving. She went on, businesslike:

'Here's a copy of Davnet's notes from her false arrest. That is evidence of criminal wrongdoing, so you will naturally want to study it closely.'

He made no move to take the paper. She slapped it on his desk.

'I'll be off now,' she concluded, 'before you throw me out. Never be rude to a nun. It brings seven years' bad luck. I'll pray for your wife. And you.' She pressed his hand quickly and stumped out of the office.

{{{{{{○}}}}}}

Five reporters were assigned to the trial, taking notes for newspapers and agencies. Other crime correspondents, including Trixie Gill, dropped in from time to time. Billy O'Rourke was barred from the courtroom until he had given his own evidence, and he was still resting under doctor's orders at an undisclosed location.

Anticipating an early conviction, Pandarus Limited, the public relations firm that Gilbert Covey had retained on behalf of the iDEA, had arranged full briefings for the chosen few. A Pandarus executive, Cressie Troy, took all the journalists (except Peter Simons of Radio Free Dublin) to lunch in Soupers, and set up an off-the-record interview with Fennessy's estranged wife. On the understanding that she would be left strictly alone in future, Mrs Fennessy talked freely about Jerome's pro-clivities. The parents of Miss T, the schoolgirl from County Cork whom he was alleged to have molested, also came to Dublin on a well-paid day trip and spoke off the record, but they were generally regarded as too grasping to be entirely credible. Juicy snapshots of Jerome presiding over the Junior Girls' Long Jump event at the school sports changed hands for a consider-ation. Miss T herself, now a university student, declined to take any part in this round of briefings.

The case was expected to end in a few days, and profiles of the defendant were already half-written. Catchy headlines were being rehearsed. Given the way the evidence was panning out, the verdict was a foregone conclusion.

Trixie was intrigued to receive a message on her answering machine from some kind of nun, promis-ing important information about the Fennessy case. Probably a crank, but you never can tell.

{{{{{{o}}}}}}

Séamus took two hours on Thursday morning to attend an auction. Theresa was selling a small house in Bluebell that she had bought while Séamus was in Germany. The prospect had revived her. Even at death's door she wanted to know everything: what it would fetch, who would be there, how many bidders would last the course. Her solicitor, Bridie Morgan, had met Séamus at the hospital and cajoled him into going along. 'Sure 'twill take your mind off of your troubles,' Bridie promised.

The saleroom was crowded as the smooth auctioneer launched the bidding at a hundred and eighty thousand euros. By Dublin standards this was cheap, but he still had to drop down in steps to a hundred and forty, laughing gaily at the joke. A young man ventured in, followed by two young couples, and quickly pushed the property back up to one seventy-five. There was a short hiatus and the auctioneer, choking with annoyance, threatened to withdraw the house forthwith if people were not prepared to be serious.

Bridie Morgan whispered, 'Now don't worry, Séamus, the house is worth two ninety. This is only skirmishing.'

A new contender, a tall bearded man, called out 'one eighty'. 'J. M. Rigg, the property developer,' Bridie whispered in Séamus's ear. 'Drops into auctions in the hope of a bargain. He's not short of a few bob.' A flurry of bids around the room raised the stakes to two hundred and seventy-five thousand euros, at which point Rigg dropped out. The auctioneer began to accept additional bids of one thousand. The price crept up to two eighty-three.

'Hold your water,' Bridie whispered, 'it'll make the two ninety.'

There was silence, until a bald man in the corner sang out: 'Two ninety!'

'Didn't I tell you?' Bridie said, out loud.

'I am bid two ninety,' the auctioneer said. 'Any advance on two ninety for this conveniently sized house, with excellent potential, in a prime area, adjacent to –'

'Three hundred,' said a deep voice from the back.

Bridie turned around. 'Be the hokey,' she whispered. 'John Florio. You wouldn't often see him at a house auction.'

'Three ten,' sang the bald man in the corner.

'Three twenty.'

'Three thirty.'

'Three forty.'

'Three forty-five.' But the bald man was beginning to falter.

'Three fifty,' said the deep voice, 'and that's my last word.'

The bald man said nothing.

'Going at three hundred and fifty thousand euros,' the auctioneer announced. 'This lot going at three hundred and fifty. Do I hear any advance on three fifty? Going once. Going twice.' The auctioneer tapped his gavel. 'Done.'

Bridie patted Joyce's arm. 'You're on the pig's back. Sixty K over the odds. And I after telling poor Theresa she was mad to try and auction a pokey tigeen like that. I advised her to sell by private treaty. I hereby eat my proverbial hat.'

{{{{{{o}}}}}}

Mr Gerald McAnnespie SC spent Thursday painstakingly establishing certain key facts. The street value of the heroin haul was set at €25,000 by the expert valuer. Senan Roche, for the defence, attemped to unsettle the witness by asking him how many ounces of heroin he himself had personally auctioned, or seen auctioned, upon the streets of Dublin during the previous month, three months, or six months. Mr Justice McQueen intervened to squash this line of attack, pointing out that if such criteria for determining street value were applied, only criminals could give expert evidence on the value of drugs. 'My exact point!' Mr Roche riposted, earning the unrelenting hostility of the bench.

The Acting Manager of the Fairview branch of the Perpetual Building Society scurried to the stand and gave evidence of six separate giro deposits of identical amounts to Mr Fennessy's account, all made by cash in six city-centre banks in the space of ninety minutes on the Monday morning following his arrest. These totalled three thousand seven hundred and eighty euros. Mr McAnnespie scrupulously refrained from drawing any conclusion at this stage from the fact that the defendant's Irish savings account should have received its largest ever infusion of cash one day after his trip to Amsterdam. Cross-examined by Ms Frieda Gallaher, junior counsel for the defence, the man from the Perpetual agreed that there was no way of knowing who had paid in the six amounts of six hundred and thirty euros each. Sums as small as that would not attract attention individually. It was only when the six instalments were added together that the provisions of the Money Laundering Act would prompt concern among the staff. Ms Gallaher attempted to ask whether it was likely that a criminal gang would have paid money to a courier just after he had been arrested and his drugs impounded. The judge disallowed this line of questioning as based on speculation, and advised Ms Gallaher to stick to the evidence. Ms Gallaher enquired what efforts had been made to retrieve video footage of the persons making the said deposits in the city-centre banks, and was warned by the judge that this was a most unreasonable question to put to the witness, who was merely recounting what he personally had come to know as manager of the branch receiving the money, and was in no way answerable for the actions of the banks which had forwarded the payment.

'No further questions.' Ms Gallaher sat down huffily.

Ms Pádraigín Nic Fhinneadha of Suffer the Children took the stand in both paws and gave a moving account of the damage to Irish society that could be caused by just the kind of pornography contained in Mr Fennessy's briefcase, should it find its way into the hands of compulsive child abusers or paedophile rings. She was led through her evidence by Mr Morrison Cox, the junior prosecution counsel. In her cross-examination, Ms Gallaher pressed Ms Nic Fhinneadha at length on how likely it was that a person fixated on fifteen-year-old girls would also be interested in pornography involving babies. Mr Justice McQueen interrupted to ask how the question could possibly be relevant. Ms Gallaher explained that a whispering campaign of vilification against her client was painting him as a molester of young women. These innuendoes were extrapolated from certain portions of Mr Fennessy's written statement not relevant to the present alleged offence which the court in its wisdom had decided to place before the jury. In Ms Gallaher's respectful submission, the planting of infant pornography in his briefcase was part of a deliberate though self-contradictory programme of general vilification. The judge coldly discounted the imputation that his rulings could constitute part of any so-called conspiracy of vilification, and suggested that perhaps the defendant might have imported infant pornography in order to trade it with other paedophiles whose interests, or collections, lay closer to his own proclivities. Senan Roche rose to splutter at this wholly unwarranted remark, and was ordered to resume his seat forthwith.

Ms Gallaher resumed her questioning of the expert witness: was there any established behavioural link between molesting fifteen-year-olds and molesting babies? The witness stated that the two types of fixation usually went hand in hand. She had never heard of Wagner and Steiglitz, or Campanella and Losurdo, whose articles to the contrary Ms Gallaher cited at some length. Ms Gallaher promised to call a distinguished criminologist from the University of Dundee, who would rebut Ms Nic Fhinneadha's evidence in every relevant detail. Ms Nic Fhinneadha tearfully declared that she had devoted her life to the children of Ireland.

The judge intervened to halt this unseemly browbeating of a witness, and adjourned the court for the day.

{{{{{o}}}}}

Early on Friday morning Mr Matt Wellan, known as the Snowman, materialized in front of the Four Courts and spoke to Peter Simons at the main entrance on the quays.

He trusted Simons, and thought all other reporters were swabs. He had served time for armed robbery as a young man, but had no convictions for the past fifteen years. His nickname, the Snowman, had nothing to do with supplying cocaine, but came from his albino complexion. He claimed to have evidence that the late John F. Hughes had conspired with members of what he termed the anti-drugs establishment to blacken his name and frame Mr Fennessy, and vowed that he would give evidence for the defence in the Fennessy case. He was going to talk to Fiachra Ó Neachtain the moment the day's proceedings were over.

{{{{{{o}}}}}}

Mr Morrison Cox, fresh-faced under his wig, took Séamus quickly through his appointment and responsibilities as Acting Director of the iDEA, before leading him through the brief statement that he had made. Billy O'Rourke had received a tip-off. Séamus did not know Billy's source. He had known of Billy's plan to arrest a courier working for one of the Dublin drug barons. He had spoken to the defendant in the iDEA building late on Sunday night, and had established a rapport with him. The defendant had agreed to write out a statement, having previously refused to give a verbal statement to Mr O'Rourke and Mr Woulfe. Séamus had made no suggestions as to the content of the statement. The defendant had commenced writing shortly after midnight and had been finished at approximately eight-fifteen.

The vague nausea in Séamus's stomach sprang not

from the tedium and tension of the courtroom, nor from any doubts about his evidence, but from Bridie Morgan's side-of-the-mouth remark that John Florio, who had just bought Theresa's house for much more than it was worth, was a shyster lawyer who specialized in bribe-takers and political twisters.

When Mr Morrison Cox concluded his questions and sat down, the defence launched their broadside. The senior man, Roche, a blustering scarecrow, started off with a windy question impugning the iDEA as nothing more than a cynical waste of money by a publicity-mad Minister. Séamus shook his head wisely and conceded that Mr Roche was entitled to his point of view, while he himself as a public servant was precluded from answering him on a political level. However, he could at least assure the court that the iDEA was an efficient administrative unit.

Mr Roche returned to the charge: 'Is it not the case that the ten-year mandatory sentence for drug couriers is merely a cynical ploy to dicky up the statistics and sustain the burgeoning prison industry with its bloated overtime payments to Guards and prison officers?'

Séamus replied courteously that he thought not.

Challenged on the constitutionality of the recent Criminal Justice Act, Séamus assured the court that the Department had taken competent legal advice. He refused to speculate on the European ambitions of Richard Frye, merely giving his personal opinion that Mr Frye was an exceptionally able Minister who devoted his energies fully to his current job, and raised a muffled titter by adding, 'I would say that, wouldn't I?'

On the structure, staffing, funding and administration of the iDEA, he was on secure ground and spat back his answers like a schoolboy, without needing to refer to notes.

Mr Roche changed tack: 'Would it surprise you, Mr Joyce, to learn that Mr Fennessy was gift-wrapped as a sacrificial offering by one of Dublin's drug barons, so that you and your cohorts would leave the said drug baron to carry on his trade undisturbed?'

Séamus considered this for a moment. 'It would surprise me, indeed. But it would make no difference to the case. Say Mr Fennessy was set up by a drug dealer who subsequently turned him in; the fact remains that he was carrying prohibited drugs when he walked through Dublin Airport. That, as I understand it, is the charge.'

'Kindly confine your answers to my questions, Mr Joyce. Why did you promise to reduce the estimated value of the haul if Mr Fennessy falsely gave the name of a man who had had nothing whatsoever to do with sending him to Amsterdam?'

'I gave no such promise. I made it perfectly clear that no deals were possible.'

'When you arrived, your Mr O'Rourke was dangling the prospect of such a deal before the prisoner, if he would implicate a certain named individual who is not before the court.'

'My Mr O'Rourke must answer for himself. I heard no such offer.'

'How did he manage to add in the second consignment of heroin to bump up the value? Do you keep supplies on tap?'

'That is an absurd question.'

'Nonetheless,' sighed Mr Justice McQueen, 'you must answer it.'

'My answer is no. I resent the question.'

'Resent away, Mr Joyce. Now. When your creature O'Rourke placed that filthy pornographic magazine on the table in front of Mr Fennessy, was it your impression that Mr Fennessy was already familar with its contents?'

Involuntarily, Séamus caught the defendant's eye. He remembered the look of surprise and revulsion on his face that night in the iDEA building.

'You hesitate, Mr Joyce?'

'My honest impression,' he admitted, 'is that he was not.'

'Ah. So that too was planted on him?'

Séamus regained his composure. '*Non sequitur.*'

'Leave aside the Latin, Mr Joyce. What is it that "does not follow", in your estimation?'

'That it was planted on him. He might have been asked to bring home a magazine for a friend. I've done the same myself. Not pornography, of course. My wife is interested in interior decoration, and I used to bring home Continental magazines on the subject.'

'This was when you were working as some sort of Eurocrat?'

'It was.'

'You enjoyed being a Eurocrat, didn't you?'

'I have always enjoyed my work.'

'And aspire, do you not, to creep back to the fleshpots of Brussels, on the coat-tails of your patron, Richard Frye, when he lands the European drugs control job.'

Séamus tried to smile. 'My aspirations are neither here nor there.'

'And, Mr Joyce,' roared Mr Roche in an access of fury, 'in furtherance of that ambition you are prepared to countenance corruption in the organization that you now head, you are happy to have your subordinates collude with drug barons to frame a gullible citizen, so that they can ply their trade in peace.' Mr McAnnespie began to cough politely. Mr Roche plunged on: 'You are happy to come in here, Mr Joyce, and perjure yourself as to what you personally saw and heard on the night of Sunday the third of October and the early morning of Monday the fourth of October, not two weeks ago. Isn't that the truth, Mr Joyce?'

'It is not.' But his heart missed a beat. The prosecution counsel was standing up, clearing his throat.

'Do you have an objection, Mr McAnnespie?' The judge enquired.

'My learned friend has accused the witness of corruption and perjury, my Lord, and I must question the propriety of his tactics.'

Mr Justice McQueen nodded. 'Counsel will kindly bear in mind that casting unsupported aspersions on a witness's character is not an acceptable ploy in this court. Please continue carefully, Mr Roche.'

As if he could read Séamus's thoughts, Mr Roche spoke softly: 'You may kid yourself, Mr Joyce, that you have answered my questions fairly. You may think of yourself as a decent individual. You may imagine that your responsible post in the public service dispenses you from the requirement of complete candour. But the devil is in the detail, and your small sly concealments – or those of your colleagues – may leave an innocent man to rot in jail. That is why you had to swear to tell us the whole truth, Mr Joyce. Not the economical version.'

The judge harrumphed. 'What is your question, Mr Roche? The witness can hardly be expected to conceal what he hasn't been asked about.' The courtroom tittered.

Mr Roche flapped his gown like a bullfighter. 'At what time,' he demanded, 'did Mr Fennessy first write the confession that has been placed before this court as Exhibit D?'

'On Sunday night and Monday morning, the third and fourth of October.'

'I repeat –'

'He started writing shortly after midnight and stopped at about eight-fifteen.'

'Did you see him write the statement?'

'I was in the same room. I fell asleep several times. He added the last few sentences when I returned to the office after going to visit my wife.'

'Billy O'Rourke's report states that the final draft was written while you were out of the office, between seven in the morning and twenty past eight.'

'I can't confirm that. What difference would it make?'

'It brings us to the heart of the conspiracy to frame my unfortunate client. O'Rourke's report claims that a pocket radio was switched on, and that Mr Fennessy wrote about being recruited by Mr Paul Blake only after Mr Bosco Woulfe mentioned, in his hearing, that Mr Blake was dead.'

Séamus raised his palms in a gesture of surrender. 'What's the problem?'

'Mr Fennessy had written the name of his friend, Paul Blake' – Mr Roche jabbed a finger like a man summoning an elevator – 'no later than twenty minutes past midnight!'

'How do you know?'

Instead of answering, Mr Roche retorted with another question: 'Is this court to believe that Mr Fennessy wrote out his entire statement in one hour and twenty minutes? The youthful members of our jury will recall how hard it is to write ten pages in a three-hour school examination. According to your agency's report, Mr Fennessy wrote fourteen pages in less than half the time. Come on, Mr Joyce!'

'But in an examination, you have to think before you write. The prisoner was working from his own notes.'

'Where are those notes?'

'In the file.'

'No, Mr Joyce. They are not.'

Séamus shook his head. This was new, and slightly disturbing. 'First I've heard of it.'

'Your minions' – again the jabbing forefinger – 'deliberately concealed those papers, in order to hide the fact that my client had named Mr Blake in the earliest draft of his written statement.'

'Why do you blame my staff, Mr Roche? The draft could have gone missing somewhere else along the way.'

'You can at least confirm that the draft sheets existed?'

'Certainly. When Mr Fennessy finally signed the statement, I saw a number of sheets of paper on the table, crossed out.'

'And what were you doing all the time the prisoner was working on his statement, in your office, in your presence, before your very eyes?'

'What was I doing? Resting, partly. Surfing the Internet, partly.'

'Really?' Mr Roche feigned amusement. 'And what sort of sites caught your fancy?'

'Oncology, if you want to know. My wife is ill.'

That stopped Mr Roche in his tracks, for just long enough to let Mr Justice McQueen intervene sweetly: 'What is the relevance of this line of questioning, Mr Roche? It is your client's contention, I believe, that the late Mr Blake did not knowingly send him off to commit a crime.'

'That is so, my lord.'

'Having seen the book of evidence, do you anticipate that the prosecution will be denying that the defendant met Mr Blake before going to Amsterdam?'

'I believe not, my lord.'

'Then why labour to establish that the prosecution is denying the defendant's link to Mr Blake? Everyone agrees he met Mr Blake. That is common ground.'

Mr Roche tried to recover his footing. 'What I am showing here is the iDEA's initial attempt to suppress the link with Mr Blake, and their concealment of evidence that my client openly stated that link from the outset. They were later forced to change their tune, when other evidence emerged. But their manifest dishonesty in this matter of timing, at the very start of the case, vitiates and poisons the entire web of prosecution evidence. And their initial attempt at a cover-up subsequently led them into making further blunders which I will use to blow this tawdry case out of the water.'

Mr Justice McQueen smiled, like a simple man unconvinced by a clever trick. 'That remains to be seen, Mr Roche. I think we have devoted sufficient time to this matter of timing, at least for the time being. Kindly resume your questioning. Unless, God forbid, you have come to a full stop.'

Roche snorted and turned slowly back to Séamus, his momentum lost.

'Your deputy's written report states that Mr Fennessy's statement was written after seven o'clock on Monday morning. He makes no mention of earlier drafts.'

'If you say so.'

The judge, flicking through a sheaf of papers, intervened once more. 'Perhaps I could clarify the issue once for all, Mr Roche, and move us on from this backwater. Does your client suffer from arthritis?'

Jerome helpfully shook his arthritic head.

'Good,' said Mr Justice McQueen. 'Now, I've taken a shufti through my photocopy of this exhibit – the defendant's confession, if we may call it that – and as the jury can see for themselves, Mr Blake's name occurs on the ninth, the eleventh and ah, the fourteenth pages of the handwritten statement. The last five pages, in short. As five pages can undoubtedly be penned in an hour by a man with your client's fluid handwriting style, is there any reason at all why he should not have introduced Mr Blake's name during his final hour of handwriting, after Mr Blake's death had been announced on the radio?'

Mr Roche cast his eyes slowly, sadly, around the courtroom, dwelling significantly on the jurors, and dropped his voice to a hoarse whisper. 'My Lord, Mr Joyce's agency falsely stated that my client added the name of Paul Blake after hearing of his death on the radio. My client will deny that with every fibre of his being. That radio was never switched on in his hearing. He was told of his friend's murder in the police car, on his way to the District Court, long after his statement had been handed over. The iDEA itself now accepts the evidence of two later witnesses, Davnet O'Reilly and Jenny McGlinchey, confirming his meeting with Paul Blake, a meeting which they still hoped to disprove when they conspired to fake the time that the defendant came to know of Mr Blake's death. As it happens, yes, their deception was pointless. But it shows how they go about their work. My client will tell of the scurvy trick by which Mr Joyce's deputy led him to add the time to the confession he had largely written out the night before. We now know that his earlier notes and drafts have been spirited away.' Mr Roche fixed his gaze on Séamus. 'If this pattern of concealment and deception is true, then you, Mr Joyce, are an unprincipled time-server and, whether you like it or not – whether you admit it or not – you are associated with a sinister conspiracy which may extend even to the murder of Mr Paul Blake, horrible though that prospect may be to contemplate. My Lord, I have finished.' He sank to his seat, defeated. He had gone too far.

Mr Justice McQueen leaned over his bench, emitted a dry cough, and said with heavy levity, 'That's it, Mr Joyce. You're free to go off about your business, lawful or otherwise.' A titter of relief spread around the court.

But as Séamus was moving gratefully to leave the witness box, old Gerald McAnnespie SC struggled to his feet. 'My Lord,' he quavered, 'my learned adversary Mr Roche has raised certain moral questions and adumbrated certain vague accusations, without perhaps giving my witness an adequate opportunity to deal with them. Although we may all feel that this particular topic has been, so to say, done to death, I wonder if it might be permissible, in order to set the jury's mind at rest, and for the avoidance of doubt, to proceed with a very short supplementary direct examination.'

Coming from his own side, this was a stab in the back.

The judge's bonhomie had evaporated. 'Very well, Mr McAnnespie, but I do have a luncheon appointment, so make it snappy, would you be so kind?'

Gerald McAnnespie faced Séamus. 'As prosecution counsel,' he enunciated, 'it is my unpleasant duty to present the case against Mr Fennessy. However, I am not entitled to adduce as true any evidence about which legitimate doubt subsists.'

Séamus nodded, mystified.

Mr McAnnespie continued: 'The defence is hinting at what might be termed, to use Lord Justice Denning's memorable phrase, an "appalling vista" of corruption in your organization, an overarching conspiracy between policemen and civil servants to pervert the course of justice, to the detriment of one Jerome Fennessy, a citizen of this Republic who has no criminal record and is entitled to just and fair treatment from the public servants whom our taxes support. Are you aware of any such conspiracy, Mr Joyce?'

The answer was self-evident: 'No.'

'And do you have any doubts in your mind as to the evidence that you have given here?'

Séamus thought for a moment. 'Apart from my doubt as to the defendant being aware of the contents of the magazine that we confiscated – no, no doubts.'

He caught the defendant's gaze again. Like a spaniel's on its last journey to the vet. He glanced away, only to find the mild blue eyes of Gerald McAnnespie burrowing gently into his brain. And then he noticed, in the public gallery, staring straight at him, the lumpy face of Decko Dowd. How long had Decko been in the room? Why had he not noticed him earlier?

'Are you a corrupt individual?' the lawyer was asking.

'No, I don't think I am.' Where had Decko sprung from? Why on earth had he come?

'To countenance the falsification of evidence,' the lawyer quavered, 'would be a grave dereliction of duty for a person in your position. Have you done that?'

Before Séamus could reply, the judge cut in acidly:

'Mr McAnnespie, you are lobbing very soft shots to your witness. He's hardly going to claim to be an unprincipled perverter of the course of justice. Do you expect to carry on much further with this line of enquiry?'

'No indeed, my Lord. Now, Mr Joyce, may I have your answer to my last question: have you falsified evidence?'

'Yes. I mean you may. No. I mean I have not.' Again a suppressed titter spread around the courtroom. What was funny, for God's sake?

'Would you be prepared, as Mr Roche has alleged, to see an innocent man rot in jail?'

Séamus looked directly at Mr Roche, who was staring contemptuously at a spot on the ceiling. Decko, on the other hand, was waiting earnestly for Séamus's answer. 'No,' he said, a little too loudly.

'One final question.' The mild blue eyes fixed on him again. 'Suppose you were to discover wrongdoing by trusted subordinates or superiors, such that unmasking that wrongdoing would cause you personal disadvantage. What then?'

Séamus knew the answer at once. He aimed it straight at Decko's soulful face: 'I would not be afraid to act. Painful though it might be, I would do what is right, and hope to be granted the strength to bear the consequences.'

'No further questions,' said Mr McAnnespie.

'Thank goodness for that,' said the judge tartly. 'Adjourned for lunch.'

{{{{{{o}}}}}}

The regulars were hugely entertained. McAnnespie was always pulling stunts like that (known in the trade as his 'Johnny Gielgud impressions'). Peter Simons, who had studied at King's Inns, recalled a case when the wily old barrister had suddenly rubbished his own first witness, an obvious perjurer, and still managed to have the defendant jailed on a charge of embezzlement. It afterwards transpired that the man was entirely innocent. McAnnespie's high-minded jettisoning of a vulnerable witness, before the defence could get at him, had the jury eating out of his hand. This jury would fall for it too.

It was generally agreed that Senan Roche had lost the run of himself. As a young barrister, he had been sure-footed. In his dotage, he was too fond of the savage indignation vibe. He was trying to wrestle in boxing gloves.

Admiration too for the way Mr Justice McQueen was stamping his authority on the proceedings. If Jerome Fennessy were convicted, that would help to remedy the harm done by his libertarian fellow-judges, Donncha 'Dumbo' Devin and Her Courtship Miss Maura Wade, whose dismissal of two pukka cases launched by the iDEA was seen as a direct affront to the Department of Justice. Queenie would enjoy skewing the trial anyway, being a vindictive bitch like his father before him.

Friday afternoon's proceedings were tedious in the extreme. Trixie sat beside Peter Simons as an Aer Lingus supervisor was grilled by Senan Roche as to who might have had access to Fennessy's bag on the aeroplane. Simons scribbled a series of limericks rhyming on Roche, Joyce, McQueen and Lingus. A customs official was put through his elephantine paces on the question of who might have had access to Fennessy's bag in Dublin Airport. Peter drew a rude caricature of Mr Justice McQueen and his trademark tweed hat, captioned 'The Man Who Mistook His Hat For A Wife'. Queenie, a bachelor, was known to be short-sighted when not sporting his judicial half-spectacles.

At four o'clock, Senan Roche launched a passionate plea to have the case struck out forthwith, as the prosecution had made no attempt whatsoever to prove the defendant's criminal intentions. The judge turned him down like a gas flame, and enquired when the prosecution might be in a position to introduce their remaining witness, Mr Billy O'Rourke. On learning that Mr O'Rourke hoped to be well enough to appear on Monday, Mr Justice McQueen adjourned the sitting for the weekend, with much stern admonition of the jury to avoid discussing the case or looking at media coverage of it.

As the reporters trooped out for a pint in the Wig and Pizzle, the Snowman reappeared, whiter than ever. He would not after all be giving evidence for the defence. He was moving abroad, would not say where. He begged them not to print a word about him, as he didn't want to fetch up like the Robin, in the city morgue with a cardboard label tied to his big toe. Or poor Leo Jordan who didn't know what was good for him. He was off to Dublin Airport.

'God speed,' said Peter Simons.

{{{{{o}}}}}

Emotionally shattered by his court appearance, Séamus Joyce had come to Theresa for comfort. She lay back and let him talk his fill.

Although it seemed unfair, he went over his worries about the high price for the house in Bluebell. Bridie Morgan had signed the contract on Theresa's behalf in the auctioneer's office, so Séamus's name appeared nowhere on the documentation. Still, he didn't like it.

'Séamus' – Theresa opened her eyes – 'we had this last night.' A touch of the old resentment, the anger that had soured their last years, was creeping into her voice. But it was muffled by her illness, the mildness of creeping mortality.

He forced himself to be cruel, and pressed on: 'Suppose they wanted to compromise me in my job, how would they know the house was being sold by my wife?'

'Who said they knew?' Theresa breathed in exasperation. 'Can't you take your luck?'

'We must not accept the money.'

'Don't be ridiculous. It's a fine house. Worth every cent.' And she closed her eyes and played dead. The nurses ejected him, politely. It was mid-afternoon.

He had time for a quick visit to the office, then homeward. A bath and a bottle of Mosel wine. And a long sleep. But it was not to be. The office was in crisis. The Secretary of the Department of Justice, Sal O'Sullivan, urgently required all financial details on the advertising contract for next year's drugs awareness campaign. The European Court of Auditors were tightening on transparency in the tendering process. Could Séamus kindly dig out the relevant tender documents, and drop them around personally? In the Friday bloody evening bloody rush hour?

He could have replied that he was not answerable to the Department, as the iDEA was required to report directly to the Dáil, but financial procedures were a grey area, and would not make a healthy battleground for a war against Sal O'Sullivan.

Thoughtful Eileen McTeague had already prepared an archive box containing the relevant files. 'Sorry to land this on you,' she said, as though it were her fault. 'And you won't see me at all next week. I'm using up some of my annual leave and going to Paris with my niece. She booked on Ryanair.'

He wished her a pleasant break. Eileen blushed as though he had done her some singular favour.

Driving into the city, he cursed Brussels, Luxembourg, advertising agencies, and auditors. On the car radio, an adenoidal man gave a brief sketch of the day's non-events in the Fennessy trial. Almost as tedious as the reality.

Sal O'Sullivan, in a boyish haircut and maroon trouser-suit, showed no signs of Friday fatigue. She emanated freshness and vigour from every squeaky-clean pore. She had captained the university tennis team during her brilliant undergraduate career, he remembered, while he himself was immersed in the Jazz Society. Sal had gone on to take diplomas in business and accountancy. She was married to some sort of food critic. She ushered Séamus into her office, used the telephone to summon young Damien Thornton from the accounts section, opened the archive box, began to range the documents on the conference table like a card-player laying out a hand of patience.

Séamus coughed. 'What's going on? May one ask?'

'We're being extra sensitive because of the whiff of gunpowder.'

'Sorry?'

'Election rumours.'

'Really?'

'Maybe. Which to timorous beasties is almost as good as really.' Sal raised one eyebrow to signify that a joke had taken place.

Séamus did not admit to being amused. 'I had full authority to assign that contract, you know.'

'Of course you had, Séamus, and what's more, you ran it past Bob O'Leary in the legal department. Everything in order according to Bobbo. We don't deny it. This is just an additional check. Nothing personal.'

Young Thornton came clucking in. He would not catch Séamus's eye. He was wearing a black dandruff-disclosing blazer.

Sal had a long thin neck, suitable for guillotining. The pair of them hunched together over the table. Séamus stood watching them, speechless.

After much flipping through files and quick jotting of figures, Thornton's shoulders began to relax. Sal O'Sullivan emitted a long low whistle, not unmusical. 'Yep. Just as I thought.' She looked up. 'Clear as day. Copper-fastened. We can stand it.'

'Stand what?'

'Someone's been sniping in Luxembourg. We don't know who.'

'Why wasn't I told?'

'Only heard today, while you were in court. Predictable stuff. You threw the contract to a preferred bidder, on the basis of a pitch that didn't meet published criteria. But these documents prove that Klinger underestimated the media costs, while Barron Wilde were fifteen per cent over the quote you accepted. These are the original documents, I take it.'

'You take it.' His voice was strangled.

She winced. 'Sorry to be a pain, Séamus. You've been leaked against. Rumours were fed to Mr Comerford, who to his credit has been entirely sceptical. Radio Free Dublin may run the story, but nobody cares what they say. *Sunday Business Post* are also interested. They're due to phone me for a soundbite tomorrow morning. I always take calls from journalists, as a matter of principle, and I'm terribly bad at faking. That's why I had to see the papers myself. Once I've spoken to them they'll have to print the story, if at all, as an example of dirty tricks against the iDEA, and Comerford will be left explaining that he has nothing to do with it. Damien, could you ever be a dear and run this, and this, and this, through the Xerox? Just so they're to hand, in case I have to brief the Minister?'

Thornton picked his way out. Sal smiled brightly at Séamus. 'Is Decko behind this?' he asked.

'Not sure. Possible. The problems with the Robin's arrest have left him tetchy and suspicious.'

'As opposed to what?'

'You remember how he questioned Billy O'Rourke's version of the Maher shootings last year? He said nobody gets that lucky with a pistol. Not even Billy the Kid. Now he has to swallow the proposition that you, a career civil servant, took down Raymond Kinnear with a single shot to the back of the neck.'

'It was my second shot, actually.'

'Decko's theory is that Billy shot Mr Kinnear as well as the Robin. He's rather obsessing about this. Been to see me twice.'

'It's a non-starter. It defies the laws of physics. Ray Kinnear had come through the hedge and was about to shoot him. Obviously, he was facing him. Does Decko think Billy can shoot in circles?'

'He says the bullet came from a gun that wasn't offici-ally issued to Billy. Billy has a licence to carry a private handgun. He was carrying it as well as his service revolver, on the night of the shooting, but it's not the weapon that fired the fatal shot. Ireland being Ireland, Dowd has seen a sneak preview of the incident report, which contains the interesting statement that the bullet that killed Raymond Kinnear and the bullet that killed the Robin came from the same weapon. If that's true, the gun that the Robin was holding to your back can't have been the same gun he had taken from you after you shot Kinnear.'

Séamus's mind was racing. He was already groping towards the obvious explanation: Tom Stringer, who had certainly shot the Robin, had also shot Ray Kinnear, and therefore Séamus himself must have missed when he fired on Kinnear. Therefore he himself hadn't killed anybody. He felt a creeping sense of relief mingled with deflation. Innocence regained.

'It's only a matter of time,' Sal went on, 'before Mr

Dowd launches a full-blown conspiracy theory involving third parties who opened fire on the men he was arresting, then shot Mr Kinnear when he drove up your laneway. This would shift the blame away from himself. But it would blacken the iDEA more than somewhat.'

'What am I supposed to do? Challenge Decko to a duel in the Iveagh Gardens?'

'He's doubly suspicious because he can't believe how lucky the iDEA has been with all the horse that Billy's been snaffling.'

Coming from Sal, 'horse' struck a false note. Sal was not a slangy person.

'Horse, meaning heroin,' Sal said, as if answering his unspoken question. 'Couldn't find it in Partridge's *Dictionary of Slang*, which is my constant insomnia cure. How do you feel your court appearance went? You'll get your conviction, you know.' Her brisk friendliness was wearing.

Damien Thornton came twittering back with the files.

'Let's keep in touch,' Sal O'Sullivan said. 'I'm always here should you feel the need to consult. It's lonely at the top.' She gave him a folded sheet of pink notepaper. 'That's my new mobile number,' she told him. 'Very few people know that. Not even Damien.' Damien squirmed. Séamus hesitated for a moment. Would he tell them what he felt about their arrogance in summoning him here? Protest at her tricky little interrogation?

No. He was a civil servant. His private feelings were irrelevant. Besides, she had done him a favour by forewarning him of Decko's suspicions. How long before all that would come into the public eye? A month, a week, a couple of days? It depended on how desperately Decko needed to cover his ass.

Back at iDEA headquarters, everyone had gone. He walked up through the empty building, dumped the box of files in Mary Rice's office, scribbled a note explaining that with Eileen away in Paris he had no idea where these papers were kept.

He drove home. It was late, and he was hollow with hunger and exhaustion. On the mat was an aerogramme with a German postmark. He tore it open. 'Dear S., I have just heard that your wife is once again ill. Please know that you have my greatest sympathy, and I wish that she may very soon recover. Sincerely. Ad.Ph. Novacek.'

Just what he needed. Heidi's sympathy.

No sympathy from Sal. Yet Sal also knew about Theresa's illness. Sal was afraid of being effusive, so she was cold. He would be the same. Idiot. He unlocked himself from this echo chamber of useless thoughts by lighting a small fire in the cold grate and burning Heidi's letter in it, before opening a tin of beef Stroganoff and boiling up water for basmati rice.

The bottle of Sylvaner from the cellar was cool and sweet. It reminded him even more of Heidi. Her garden, in the spreading shadow of the hills at evening. Her slow smile as she watched him. The quivering strength of her grip as she held him to her. The scent of roses.

All his life he had done his public duty, at the cost of his private existence. What good was that? He was damned. On his tomb would be carved: *Here lies one who had no faith. He cauterized his soul and did without hope. He wondered why love escaped him.*

The more he drank, the worse it looked. Sal was right: it was lonely. And always had been. The person he missed was himself. Could Sal be trusted? Why had she said horse? Why had she said snaffling?

Horse. Meaning heroin. From 'horse-shit'. 'Smack' was the more usual word in Dublin, but Billy sometimes joked about 'horse'. And he had talked last week about 'snaffling' some 'horse', in Séamus's private office, with nobody else present. In Séamus's mind, 'snaffle' was a Billy word. Billy's phrase had stuck in Séamus's mind. Why was that?

He drained the glass. The sweetness seeped through his system. 'Snaffle' and 'horse'. An entirely irrelevant image leaped into his mind: a grubby postcard pinned above the writing-desk of Jeremy Quaid, back in his student days at King's College Dublin. Quaid was a tutor in English, had read all the books, and was carving out a reputation as a caustic critic in small-circulation magazines. He loved literature but hated living writers, especially respectable novelists of a certain age. Against these, he conducted regular vendettas. Over his desk the grey card displayed an epigram by the South African poet Roy Campbell, transcribed on Quaid's bockety typewriter:

On Some South African Novelists

You praise the firm restraint with which they write –
I'm with you there, of course:
They use the snaffle and the curb all right,
But where's the bloody horse?

Snaffle and horse. Pure coincidence. Billy was not a poetry reader. But Sal, this afternoon, had said the same words Billy had used in Séamus's office. Hence, the office was bugged. Either by Decko or by Sal. Or both. Impossible. Yet even more impossible that it should not be so. Prefer the lesser miracle. Hence, possible. Neigh, probable.

He was surprised to feel a whinny of laughter bubbling in his chest. The laughter of recognition: like a tedious baby finding its mother. Not funny at all. Snaffle and horse. Had Sal meant him to pick it up? Did Partridge exist, or was he just a joke, another bird like the Robin?

He capped the half-full wine bottle, replaced it in the cellar, filled himself a brimming glass of chlorinated Dublin water from the kitchen tap.

{{{{{{○}}}}}}

Billy O'Rourke strode to the witness stand, gamely concealing his limp.

Mr Morrison Cox, junior counsel for the prosecution, took the wounded hero on a slow waltz through his statement: the defendant's preliminary admission, the first search of his overnight bag, the second search revealing the additional stash of heroin and pornographic magazines. Billy was deadpan; the defence team sat in torpor.

In response to questions, Billy told how he had checked the defendant's story of being recruited by Paul Blake. Interviews with Mr Blake's widow and two employees of Blackwood's Club on Merrion Square showed that the defendant had undoubtedly called to see Mr Blake on the day he flew to Amsterdam. Mr Morrison Cox asked if he had ascertained the purpose of the defendant's visit. Had the defendant in fact been recruited as a runner by Paul Blake? Billy shook his head. Mr Blake was never known as a drug dealer. He was not here to defend himself. The defendant could say whatever he liked about a dead man.

This provoked an eruption. Senan Roche SC rose like a rocket, incandescent with ill-controlled rage. This was a most scandalous abuse of direct examination: inviting a police witness to indulge in unwarranted speculation.

Mr Justice McQueen gave a dry cough and suggested that Mr Roche might try to contain himself.

Mr Morrison Cox asked whether Fennessy might be clutching at straws and naming a dead man whom he had known slightly, in the hope of diverting attention from himself.

Billy looked at the judge, hesitated, grinned. 'I couldn't possibly comment.'

'No further questions,' said Mr Morrison Cox and sat down.

'Do you wish to cross-examine the witness?' the judge enquired.

'If I might, yes, then I will raise just a couple of points' – Roche was all geniality and honeyed tones – 'if the witness doesn't mind.'

'Fire ahead,' Billy said.

'Tell me, Mr O'Rourke, how well did you know the late Mr Blake?'

'Never met him in my life.'

'Why then did you and he share a connection with Mowbray's Bank in the Cayman Islands?'

'Run that by me again?' Billy shook his head in astonishment.

Senan Roche raised his voice. 'Mr Blake's investments were held in Mowbray's Bank, and we have a witness who will testify that she saw you in Mr Blake's club, Blackwood's, writing with a gold ballpoint pen on which the word Mowbray's was clearly engraved. Those pens are not for sale. The bank gives them only to its favoured customers.'

'Haven't the foggiest what you're on about. And even if I did own a pen saying Mulberry's, what would that prove?'

'It's Mowbray's, Mr O'Rourke. What it would show is that you have a connection to Mr Blake's bank.'

'Nonsense, Mr Roche. It could be sheer coincidence. Suppose I did own a Mulberry's pen, I could have found it on a park bench, or bought it from an Oxfam shop. Anyway, I have no such pen. Though, mind you,' Billy said, with disarming frankness. 'I do own a nice ballpoint pen, come to think of it.' He plucked a metallic pen from inside his jacket, held it up to the light. 'It's goldy all right, I grant you that.'

'Pass it over,' snapped Senan Roche.

An usher took the pen from Billy's hand, brought it to the defence counsel. Senan Roche peered at it for a moment, shook his head, handed it back. The usher returned it to Billy. Billy held it up again, began to chuckle. 'Ah, yes, Mr Roche, I see how the little girl went wrong. The clip on this one says Waterbury. Supposed to be a modelled on a Waterman. I bought it in Tenerife on my holliers, a few years back. I suppose the word *Mowbray* and the word *Waterbury* could look a bit alike, if you had a romantic imagination.'

'That is not the pen,' Roche insisted. 'My witness is certain of her facts.' But everyone knew the defence had lost the clash.

That Waterbury pen was the result of a brilliant piece of organization by Gloria Mennon, after Billy told her about what little Davnet had told Trixie Gill. Worldwide searches had turned up a range of gold ballpoint pens, and the Spanish-made Waterbury was picked as the most plausible candidate. The duel between Roche and O'Rourke was featured in Trixie's witty court sketch in the following day's *Gazette*, under the headline 'Defence Screws Up Ball Point'.

There was now no question of Davnet turning up to give evidence. Boyle, the arresting officer, had called to the house and interviewed her parents in the kitchen. After his visit, her father had shouted at her, her mother had drunk a pint of gin, her sister Maureen had accused her, through her tears, of setting out to wreck the whole family and lose Daddy (as Maureen preferred to call Pa) his disability pension and have Mammy sent to jail. When Fiachra Ó Neachtain, solicitor to Jerome Fennessy, telephoned on the afternoon of Billy's evidence, to confirm her willingness to testify in court, Pa grabbed the receiver and bellowed, 'No! No! Go away! No! We're not having her mixed up with crime. We're not! That paedophile tried to corrupt her. I don't care what you say. No! They abuse their position of trust. He sent her a postcard saying he loved her. I don't care. I'll take the stand against him. It's time for parents to fight back against this kind of exploitation. I'll go to the *Herald*. Is that what you want? I'm holding you responsible. That child is doing her Leaving Cert. I won't have her interfered with, by you nor anyone else. No, No, No!' He slammed down the receiver with sweating palms. According to Maureen, citing Doctor McEniff himself, sudden stress could cause a fatal coronary in Daddy's delicate state of health.

{{{{{{○}}}}}}

Séamus was deep in administration. The iDEA was to move to new headquarters in Sandyford. Paddy Goldborough had leased the shell of a warehouse, and the Board of Works were fitting it out in style. Séamus, flanked by Mary Rice, went through the floor plan with the senior architect: reception area, offices, interview rooms, conference rooms, communications centre, satellite dishes, canteen, toilets, showers, smokers' roof garden, security fence, landscaping, sentry boxes, underground storage. Outside windows would be clad in reflective bullet-proof glass. The costs of conversion were high, but the Minister had secured the budget. The spacious Director's office would be next to the administrative services on the top floor, lit by a conical skylight and far removed from the underground bunker of the Investigation Unit which would be occupied by Billy and his sidekicks. Heating, air and lighting quality met European standards, and a provisional fire certificate had already been obtained. Statisticians and computer programmers would be housed in an additional circular building, done in the style of a Martello Tower. There would be a small pond, a helicopter landing area, and parking for seventy cars. The whole place could be ready by Easter, if approval was given immediately. Séamus signed the front page of the dossier and handed it back to the Board of Works architect. She stood up to go.

'I want weekly updates from your project manager,' he said. 'Starting next week.'

Next into his office was the sexy thirty-something presenter from JMKP's London office, with an armful of designs for the drug awareness campaign. The advertisements were to run on posters, television, radio, internet and direct mail shots. There was a subsidiary slogan – '*That's* the *i*DEA' – which was to run in small type at the bottom of every advertisement, subliminally reinforcing the corporate image of the Irish Drugs Enforcement Agency without detracting from the main warning message. The main message featured a slogan reading DRUGS: REAL FUN? The letters of the last two words then merged and blended, rearranging themselves to form FUNERAL. She showed him this effect in a streamed video sequence on her multimedia notebook computer, on a set of rotating outdoor posters, on a concertina-folded brochure, on a flip-through booklet for younger children. She wore a little black dress and a small but perfectly-formed cleavage. She watched his reactions like a cat stalking a canary.

Séamus had engaged an independent consultant to vet JMKP's campaign. Someone in Brussels had recommended a sociologist named Jeff Murdoch, attached to the media studies department of an English university. Murdoch was a bearded chain-smoking Scot with the figure of an overweight gorilla in a safari suit. He arrived slightly late, sprawled in Séamus's swivel chair, lit a cigarette uninvited, watched the presentation unblinking, and finally demanded: 'At whom exactly are these messages targeted?'

'The general public?' smiled the presenter, swinging the straight fringe of her oil-black hair in front of her eyes.

'And the drug-taking public?' Murdoch quizzed her through clouds of smoke.

'Most of us don't.'

'And you hope to hit both of these groups with one message?'

'That's the brief.'

'Fag?'

'Beg pardon?'

'I'm offering you a cigarette, Miss.'

'Oh. Not for me.'

'I saw you at the airport, Miss. If I'd known who you were, we could have shared a taxi and I'd have been here on time. Now, Miss, if you run with this slogan, the druggies will know you're lying, because they take drugs and they're still alive. The others will also know you're lying, because their friends, or their children, or their friends' children, or their children's friends, take drugs every bloody weekend and they're still alive. Not all of them, I grant you, but more than those who dabble in motorcycles or suicide, which are statistically the big killers. Run this slogan, Miss, and you'll wipe out your credibility.'

'What are you suggesting, Jeff?' She stood against the window, displaying her Cleopatra profile.

'I'm here to consult, Miss. You're here to suggest. Actually, I admire what you've done. The campaign is fallacious to the core, so you might as well make that clear straight away. Illegal drugs don't lead to funerals, unless they're abused in ridiculous quantities. This fag I'm smoking now, and the one you had at the airport, are more lethal and more addictive than heroin. The biggest drug-pushers on the planet have names like Philip Morris, R. J. Reynolds and BAT. We both know that. Everyone here knows that.'

Séamus cut in: 'What is your recommendation, Mr Murdoch?'

'My honest recommendation would be simple enough. Tell the bloody truth. Say that most illegal drugs will do you little harm, apart from bringing you into contact with a criminal class entirely created and sustained by a politically expedient ban on the drugs in question. You might mention that ecstasy, almost alone among recreational drugs, carries an unpredictable risk of sudden death to a small but significant number of users, and is therefore best avoided. You might warn them that LSD can also produce unpredictable reactions. Tell them not to use dirty needles. Suggest they refrain from posing as so-called "drug addicts", because apart from anti-drug campaigners and vigilantes, "drug addicts" are possibly the most ballbreaking poseurs on God's earth. Advise them to demand clean and safe production of recreational drugs, applying the same standards of safety and quality control that already apply in the fast-food sector. Tell them to give up smoking and alcohol. But if they must, advise them to try low-tar Silk Cut and Talisker whisky, which is a lot better than the bloody Jameson I was given on the plane.'

'More than one,' Mary Rice muttered.

The presenter was indignant. 'You expect us to promote these views?'

'Of course not, Miss. You've given these chaps what they want.' He turned to face Séamus: 'This agency was created to advance the career of a political opportunist, Mr Frye, inventor of the immortal phrase "Let's Give the Dealers Dublin Justice". So don't be half-hearted. Go the whole hog. Tell the people that drugs kill. They know it's a lie, but they like to hear it. Continue to promote the ban on drugs, thereby feeding the petty crime that goes to pay for them and the criminal industry that supplies them, which in turn justifies your agency's existence. That is your clear and present duty.'

Mary Rice stopped scribbling in her notepad and broke in contemptuously: 'Who are you, Mr Murdoch, to tell us our duty?'

'I'm a consultant. Tear up those notes, dearie. My official opinion is quite the opposite. It will cost you eighteen hundred pounds sterling. For that you get a typed report broadly endorsing your strategy. We independent consultants only get contracts if we independently tell people what they independently want to hear. That's the university serving the community. Along with transparency and quality assurance and value for money and relevance and the other Thatcherite crap. Your campaign is marvellous. It will go down splendidly with all market segments. My report will suggest a few little tweaks to typefaces and background colours, based on the latest British research, and propose a follow-up study to be undertaken in one year's time, at public expense, by an independent consultant in the field of media sociology, such as myself. I will add in free of charge four pages of erudite comparisons with similar campaigns from around Europe, all of which have been abject failures apart from boosting the ratings of the crooked politicians who backed them. My subsequent academic article documenting your campaign will offer judicious but not uncritical praise, citing a number of equally worthless studies published by my friends and acquaintances, who need the citations, God knows, in order to hang on to their miserable jobs.'

The buffet lunch was a tense affair. Everyone was glad to see the back of Dr Murdoch. The presenter declined to share a taxi with him, and stalked off on foot towards Booterstown DART station.

{{{{{{o}}}}}}

Billy was still on leave. He was resting, staying with friends. (Could Billy have friends?) He was running a slight fever. But his mind was as active as ever. He had risen from his sickbed on Tuesday and called around by taxi to deliver a micro cassette tape making the case for recruiting more operational staff. Séamus promised to edit his ideas into a suitable memo to the Minister. Mary Rice gave the cassette to the new secretary, to type into a draft for Séamus to edit. The new secretary, whose first day at work this was, blinked her dark eyes and confessed that she had never worked a dictation machine before, whereupon Billy, always willing to oblige a beautiful young woman, wrote the whole thing out for her on the Agency's headed paper, using the now-famous Waterbury ballpoint pen with which he had confounded Mr Senan Roche. The doe-eyed beauty flung herself into the task with two-fingered enthusiasm, and produced a two-page word-processed version which she then proceeded to delete whilst attempting to save it. Mary Rice was not amused. Still fuming from Dr Murdoch's visit, she curtly relegated the silly girl to receptionist duties and retyped Billy's document herself.

It emerged that Billy was also continuing to co-operate with a weakened and embarrassed Decko Dowd, generously sending him an intelligence tip-off which resulted in the seizure of a substantial consignment of marijuana at Dublin port.

Gilbert Covey breezed in at lunchtime on Wednesday, straight from a media strategy meeting with his counter-parts in Health, Education and Justice. He turned on the television news in Séamus's office. This morning, a small-time heroin distributor in the South City had been found stabbed to death beside the Grand Canal. According to the television reporter, recent successes by the iDEA and the Drug Squad had prompted several drug barons to move their stocks out of the Dublin area, or stash them away for the time being. Heroin supplies were drying up, and that was hurting small dealers and causing internecine conflict. With no reserves to be traded, everyone was down to just-in-time supplies and any shortfall could lead to mayhem on the streets.

Gilbert made a phone call to the television newsroom from Séamus's desk, berating them for putting such a negative slant on a good news story. 'Why don't you tell them how we're squeezing drugs out of the local communities,' he urged. 'Tell the women of Dublin they can walk today on streets they had to avoid five years ago.'

Séamus avoided all discussion of operational matters, for fear of leaking information through Decko Dowd's hidden microphones.

The Minister telephoned. He was happy with the way things were going, and wanted everyone in the iDEA to know that. Credit where credit was due. And Séamus should have been happy too, because the rollercoaster of Theresa's health had taken another upward turn: the doctors were now speculating that the growths on her oesophagus might not be malignant after all. If their present findings were correct, she could hope to make a full recovery, though from what disease they could not or would not say.

{{{{{o}}}}}

On Wednesday afternoon Séamus received a ballistics report on the operation in which Ray Kinnear and the Robin had met their deaths. Fourteen of the bullets fired at the church had been recovered. Six came from an AK47 assault rifle. The Guards, needless to say, did not own an AK47, nor had any such weapon been recovered from the Robin's people.

Sal O'Sullivan sent another report by confidential courier. Matt Wellan, the Snowman, had left Ireland for Heathrow late on Monday night. He had told one of Declan Dowd's informants that things were getting too dangerous for local drug wholesalers. A new multi-national group was narrowing down the franchises in Dublin. In future, only three local men would be invited to tender for distribution networks in the city. North-side, Southside, Westside. They would have to buy their supplies from one source, and elements within the police were alleged to be protecting that source. The Snowman was going to lie low in England for the foreseeable future. His operators were running scared.

A more disturbing item to Séamus personally was the missing surveillance videos from Hyperbulk, but this only came to light on Wednesday evening. When the midget nun failed to contact him again, he assumed that her accusations had blown over. All the more sinister, then, to find her squatting in his garden when he drove home from the hospital. His headlamps caught her crouching in the bushes, dressed in clerical black.

'Obviously I couldn't phone,' she said. 'How's your wife?'

'What are you doing here?'

'Acting prudently. Did you know that prudence is an active virtue? Not the avoidance of peril at all costs. Now I'm going to tell you what happened on Thursday evening, when I went down to Hyperbulk. The head of security at first refused to see me. He denied that I had spoken to him on the phone. He also denied that they had recorded any cassettes in their video cameras, said the cameras were just for show and didn't actually film anything. I got to see the manager, who assured me that they always keep videos for two days. They are in a city-centre consortium for tracking shoplifters. He told the security manager to produce the videos, but the wretch said that he had given them to the Guards. I asked him whether the Guards in question included a spotty fellow called Boyle. The manager let slip that the same Boyle had been trying to wheedle free drink from the shop. He promised to recover the videotapes by Friday noon. When I called back on Friday, the head of security and the manager had both gone on leave, and nobody knew when they would be back.'

'Why did you wait before telling me this?' Séamus asked.

Mother Polycarp sighed: 'I tried to get Davnet to go into court and give her evidence. She was torn between a desire to do the right thing, and fear of retaliation against her family. Her father drinks his disability pension every month. Her mother works in the black economy, keeping accounts for a businessman with whom she may be committing adultery. Davnet doesn't want this sordid situation made public, as Mr Boyle threatened to do. She finally decided to speak out, only to find that Mr Fennessy's defence team thought it would be counterproductive. They floated part of her evidence on Monday –'

'The ballpoint pen –'

'– and they're afraid to put her to the test. Their sole defence witness was Mr Fennessy himself. The poor man went through his ordeal today.'

'An unimpressive performance, according to my informants.' Sal had sent a junior official from Justice, who sat in court every day and reported by telephone in the late afternoons.

'A complete flop.' Mother Polycarp confirmed. 'Jerome was meek and self-deprecating. Lacking in anger, which has now deserted the ranks of the seven deadly sins and repositioned itself as one of the moral virtues. I want you to come and see Davnet.'

'I can't interfere while the case is before the courts. Besides, Mr Fennessy may get off.'

'Mr Joyce, you are falling prey to wishful thinking. Presumption, we used to call it. Presumption looks like hope, but destroys hope. It would be nice if your victim escaped. But we cannot rely on Providence to pull our chestnuts out of the fire while we fail to do our duty.'

He started to reply, then stopped as the absurdity of the situation struck him. 'I cannot believe that I am having a conversation about official business in my shrubbery at ten o'clock at night with a woman in black.'

'Camouflage. I have spoken to you outdoors because

your house will have been bugged, probably using a microphone inserted in the telephone receiver. Same with your office.'

'What on earth makes you think that?'

'We know what others will do by thinking what we ourselves would do. I read about these things late at night. Old people suffer from insomnia. Very well, Mr Joyce, I will leave you to your rest, with one proviso. If the verdict is wrong, you must set it right, within three days. If you don't, I'll do it myself. I will continue to pray for your wife's recovery. And yours.'

'I'm not sick.'

'Sick to the core, Mr Joyce.'

{{{{{{o}}}}}}

He nursed a brandy by the empty hearth, listening to Joe Pass threading guitar melodies. No good tonight. He switched the music off. His mind was choked with loss. Accusing voices clustered around: Senan Roche, Mother Polycarp, Richard Frye, his dead mother. All found him wanting, in different ways.

That ridiculous attack in the courtroom. It had been no more than a theatrical stunt, the defence counsel ranting abuse to obscure the sad truth that Jerome Fennessy was guilty as charged.

One day Theresa would die. Then he would have to ask himself what he had done with his life, and hers.

{{{{{{o}}}}}}

On Thursday morning Mr Gerald McAnnespie SC rose to make his final submission to the jury. In dry, level tones he reminded them of the uncontroverted facts of the case, urged them to set all distractions aside and simply return a verdict in accordance with the evidence, painful as it might be. We all suffer vicariously when we see a fellow-citizen down on his luck. We want to help. To be merciful. But we must remember that the man we see before us as the victim of his own foolishness is also the perpetrator of deeds that may have created other victims whom we do not see. They too deserve our protection.

The entire speech took less than ten minutes. Senan Roche blustered on for half an hour, impugning the good character of the police, the iDEA Director, the Minister for Justice and certain elements within the media. He reserved particular venom for the planting of child pornography to blacken the defendant's character. That absurd act of overkill showed the iDEA's utter contempt for the intelligence of the jury. 'If you convict,' he roared, 'you will be endorsing that contempt. Members of the jury, you saw my client in the witness box. He humbly admitted the indiscretions of his past life, those flaws in his character that made it easy for the cynical men behind this pantomime prosecution to seize upon him as an easy victim. Jerome Fennessy is not a saint. He has not always been a wise man. But his nature is harmless. He has fallen among predators. They've caught him, they've trapped him, they've trussed him up like a chicken. You must not let them destroy him.'

Mr Justice McQueen advised the jury to consider

dispassionately the credibility of the various witnesses that had come before the court. How likely was it that they had invented their evidence? How mutually consistent was that evidence? If the police had dreamed up a conspiracy to scupper the defendant, how likely was it that a senior civil servant such as Mr Séamus Joyce would lend his support to this perversion of justice? The jury's responsibility was solely to decide the facts of the case. The question of the defendant's moral responsibility for what had happened would only come up in the event of his being found guilty on the facts, and was a question for the judge to settle.

The jury filed out, and were back within an hour. Guilty on both counts: importing drugs and importing pornography.

Mr Justice McQueen thanked them profusely for their patience in sitting through more than a week of this distasteful case. It had been prolonged far beyond what was necessary by the tactics of wild accusation and unreasonable cross-examination adopted by the defence. He had allowed Mr Roche a broad level of flexibility in running those tactics, lest it be thought that an already weak defence brief might be further cramped by heavy-handed umpiring. Now that the verdict was in, however, he could safely say that the defence line had been grossly irresponsible and injurious to a number of dedicated public servants. Mr Fennessy had not merely degraded himself by working for pedlars of drugs and pornography, but had sought, through his counsel, to besmirch the reputations of the men, and women, who strive, on behalf of all of us, to stem those twin tides of filth. He had also attempted to drag in the name of a respected businessman, the late Mr Paul Blake, on the basis of a slight acquaintance. Mr Fennessy had been caught red-handed on this occasion. How often in the past had he escaped scot-free? There was a minimum sentence of ten years' imprisonment to be imposed for the crimes of which Mr Fennessy stood convicted. Normally, judges tend to be restive about statutory minimum sentences, feeling – perhaps rightly – that they cut across the discretionary consideration of individual circumstances which ought to inform an enlightened sentencing policy. On this occasion, however, he was happy to impose the statutory sentence in the knowledge that it fitted the depravity of the crimes committed.

The judge then indulged in a dramatic pause, which Jerome misinterpreted. 'I would like to thank –' he began . . .

'Silence!' Blushing tomato-red, Mr Justice McQueen thumped his desk like a toddler clamouring for food. 'Jerome Patrick Fennessy,' he intoned, 'I sentence you to ten years' penal servitude on the charge of importing illegal narcotic substances contrary to the provisions of the Criminal Justice Amendment Act 1999, and to eighteen months' penal servitude on the charge of importing prohibited indecent and licentious materials contrary to the provisions of the Censorship of Publications Act 1965. The sentences to run consecutively.'

As the prisoner was led downstairs, Mr Senan Roche SC applied for leave to appeal on the grounds of prejudicial pre-trial publicity, misdirection of the jury, infringement of the defendant's constitutional rights and excessive severity of sentence. This ritual application was refused.

The journalists decamped. Friday's papers would be full of the case, including juicy details of the defendant's background as sedulously planted by Gilbert Covey's public relations wallahs. Naturally, they had also done their own thoroughgoing research and arrived independently at various distinctive points of view. The *Irish Independent* had prepared a major exposé of the connections between drugs, pornography and organized crime. The *Irish Times* would be concentrating on Jerome's troubled relationship with his mother. The *Star* was covering Jerome's alleged links with the Snowman. The *Sunday Tribune* was planning a piece on the power-struggle between the Minister for Justice, the Garda Síochána, the iDEA and the judiciary. Trixie Gill filed a particularly vivid account for the *Gazette* of how Jerome Fennessy had preyed on young girls during his time as a teacher. She herself had some first-hand knowledge of these things, having had a highly satisfactory affair with the deputy headmaster of her trendy day-school.

The *Evening Herald* led with the conviction, headlining it THIRD TIME LUCKY FOR DRUG CHIEFS. Gilbert Covey considered this treatment mealy-mouthed and begrudging, and voiced the hope that later coverage might be more generous to the iDEA.

Before the following morning's papers hit the streets, however, other political developments had intervened to push Jerome off the front pages, and much of Gilbert's carefully planted material was dropped due to pressure of space. As Peter Simons was heard to remark, the best-laid plans of poxy spin-doctors gang aft agley.

Part Three

Séamus Joyce missed the verdict, being tied up with a German visitor. Guido Schneider, one of Europe's leading anti-narcos, was touring EU capitals to canvass support for a new initiative, EuropaRein. This would supersede the Europe Without Drugs programme which Ireland had proposed. Séamus had been briefed by a curt phone message from Máire Benedict: withdraw the Irish plan, back the Germans. They in return would favour a prominent Irish presence in the permanent Narcotics Directorate that would oversee EuropaRein and all other such initiatives. After mid-morning coffee and sandwiches at the Shelbourne Hotel with officials from Justice and Foreign Affairs, Guido and Séamus had walked down to Leinster House, dogged by Guido's minders, to pay a courtesy call on Richard Frye.

They had barely entered the conference room when Máire Benedict burst in with news of the Fennessy verdict. She gave the news like an announcement of military victory.

So it was all over, then. The Minister patted Séamus's arm, his half-smile radiating quiet satisfaction. Séamus felt his options narrowing like arteries. He would have to head off that turbulent nun, convince her that the verdict was fair, get her to keep her mouth shut.

Meanwhile, Richard Frye was outlining the urgency of

establishing the European Union Narcotics Directorate without further delay. He was brisk, decisive, upbeat. He described the unprecedented success that Ireland was having in cutting supplies of drugs on the street. He outlined the ground-up approach of the Neighbourhood Concern movement, which had reined in the worst excesses of vigilantism and sidelined the paramilitaries. He presented Guido with a morocco-bound copy of *The Drugs Problem: An Irish Solution*, and suggested that the Irish formula could be replicated across Europe. He pointed out that none of the really influential bodies at the heart of the European Union had ever been headed by an Irishman. Guido Schneider smiled, and listened, and smiled, and stroked his close-cropped greying beard.

'My plane awaits,' Guido said at last. 'I shall convey your highly persuasive arguments to my political masters. We greatly appreciate your enlightened support for the EuropaRein project.'

Máire Benedict cut in: 'The Boston TV crew have to leave in twenty minutes, Minister. They've been interviewing Mr Comerford.'

'Ouch,' smiled Richard Frye.

'I shan't detain you, then,' Guido Schneider said. 'Perhaps my old friend Séamus could conduct me out to my car.'

'You know each other?' The Ministerial eyes registered Séamus's enhanced standing, as an entomologist might notice an interesting variant of insect life.

'Indeed so,' said Guido. 'I too was briefly at Aachen in the Pleistocene Era.'

Séamus escorted him downstairs, out into the weak sunshine, towards his car in the visitors' lot. It was true that Guido had briefly flitted across the horizon in Aachen, as a temporary member of the German delegation to the Permanent Liaison Committee on Security Affairs. But he had never been a regular fixture, and until now had made no allusion to their shared posting. As they went downstairs he took time to rehearse his warm recollections of a communal evening in a beer garden, when Séamus had sung 'The Rose of Tralee'. This was just within the bounds of possibility. He linked Séamus's arm and nudged him in the ribs and coyly hinted that he knew all about his fling with Heidi Novacek. 'You are quite the heartbreaker, I think, Séamus,' he murmured. 'Frau Novacek was not the only German lady with a soft spot for the Irish representative. You remember dark Lieselotte in the firearms secretariat?'

'Mata Hari? Never noticed my existence.'

'On the contrary, dear Séamus. When you were recalled to Dublin, Lieselotte went around with an expression of thunder for weeks. And the taxation problems with your auditing section, Séamus, these were settled?'

Séamus was appalled: firstly that Guido had heard of the row with the departmental auditors, and secondly that he would mention such a thing. He made no answer. But there was more. 'If you should need assistance,' Guido Schneider was breathing into his ear, 'this can be effectively arranged. We have a budget. It's all perfectly legal.'

Séamus stood still. 'I'm sorry, Guido,' he said carefully. 'I don't need assistance. The state pays me a salary.' He could feel himself blushing ridiculously.

Guido was not in the least embarrassed. 'This salary,' he said with great seriousness, 'is transferred electronically into your personal bank account?'

'Yes.'

'And you have no requirement for further funding? For example, I have heard that Mrs Joyce is not quite well.'

'No indeed. Thank you. I'm afraid you may miss your plane, Guido. Dublin traffic can be quite sticky.'

Guido nodded. His car was a silver BMW with opaque dark window-glass. The driver was a soldierly young man with straw hair and blank eyes. He held the door while Guido got in. Guido waved. 'Do you have any message for your old acquaintances? I shall again be in Aachen next week.'

'No message, thanks.' The bodyguard slammed the door and the car swept off.

Baffled and angry, Séamus set off for Grafton Street to buy a sandwich before catching a taxi. In the Royal Hibernian Way, a little semi-enclosed shopping arcade watched over by office windows, he stopped to look at the headlines outside Tuthill's newsagents. Somebody hailed him from behind. 'Great stuff, Séamus.' Decko Dowd's military moustache and gruff manner made him seem like an older, squatter version of Billy O'Rourke, except that his accent was Dublin and there was an irredeemable heaviness about him, as of a man who knows he is going to die. He was escorted by a bull-necked bruiser whom he introduced as his cousin Gary, visiting for the weekend.

'Screwed Fennessy good and proper,' Decko went on. 'Fair play to you. Heard about my dawn raid?' He was being matey. Séamus had dreaded meeting him.

Séamus nodded. 'You got quite a batch.'

'Seventy-five grand. Tip of the iceberg.' Decko's eyes kept swivelling, as though he were expecting to greet a friend at a party. His cousin Gary, lagging against the window of Monaghan's menswear shop, scanned the horizon more slowly. 'I don't like it, Séamus,' Decko said.

'Why not?'

'I should be grateful,' Decko said. 'Billy keeps giving me tip-offs. Decent man. Guy we bagged this morning once worked for the Robin. He talked. He said the Robin used to be protected by Billy. In those days only the Snowman's consignments got busted. But now the Robin's dead and his former henchmen are being picked up, apart from the ones that work for the Crow, like Pat O'Hara who used to run Blackwood's Club for the Robin. Now he does South Inner City heroin for the Crow, and nobody can touch him. I'm telling you this, by the way, because I think you're probably an honest man, deep down. And I'm not asking you to do anything, yet.' Decko's eyes were weighing Séamus like a hangman.

'Tell me, Decko, why are we having this conversation in the Royal Hibernian Way?'

'Casual encounter, Séamus. I'm on my way up to Harcourt Street, and popped in here to buy a real Irish gansey for my cousin Gary. I had no idea you'd be here, apart from having two retired Guards shadowing you all morning. I don't want to call you in the office, you see, because you never know who's listening.'

'So tell me everything.'

'Can't do that. But here's the gist. Things are changing, Séamus. Old maps being torn up. The shortage is ending, but only for some. Certain boyos in the inner city have been let buy fresh stocks, just enough for two days, and they have to buy it from the Crow. Price is high, but demand on the street means a nice profit.'

'Who's the Crow?'

'Worked as an engineer in Atlanta. Came home to Ireland, set up an electronics firm. Supplies equipment to South American paramilitary groups. No previous involvement with the drugs trade, but he's won the distribution contract for the syndicate that's replacing the Robin and the Snowman.'

'Why haven't I heard of him? Who's protecting him?'

'Can't say. Not yet. You should check your bank accounts.'

'I go through them once a month. There's nothing irregular.'

'Check some more, Séamus. Word is you're getting money from Vaduz. Better you tell Sal than she hears it from someone else. You're a decent guy. Excuse us.' They turned away into Monaghan's. Séamus bought a box of Leonidas chocolates at the boutique opposite, and walked off without looking back. If Theresa didn't want them, the nurses might.

{{{{{(o)}}}}}

That afternoon in the office, the mood was upbeat. Everyone knew the two recent acquittals had been bad news, and the conviction of Jerome Fennessy was a turnaround. Mary Rice prepared a document requesting an extra ninety square metres for administration in the new building. Gilbert Covey wanted to hire an apprentice spin-doctor to be stationed in Sandyford. Bosco Woulfe produced an unofficial list, naming disaffected souls among Declan Dowd's lot who might be enticed into joining an enlarged iDEA. Séamus, munching his lunchtime sandwich, turned down five telephone requests for comments and interviews, referring all journalists to the Minister's office. One of the callers was that slithy tove, Peter Simons of Radio Free Dublin. Still bellyaching about Billy's pen. Séamus asked him how the hell he was supposed to monitor the personal writing instruments of his staff. Neither was it his business to comment on the conduct of a court case. He suggested to Mr Simons that he might devote some of his talents to investigating the effects of drug addiction on Dublin's poor. Simons laughed and told him about a two-hour documentary on that subject, planned for late October. The Minister had refused to take part. Perhaps Séamus could persuade him?

Billy phoned in to congratulate all and sundry on the conviction. He was lying at home in bed, he said, with a sore leg and a bottle of Bushmills to rub on it.

Séamus found it impossible to concentrate. Theresa had been better last night, and worse again today, but that was nothing new. The doctors were trying different drugs, and proposed to start a new course of treatment on Sunday, when Dr Maguire Gibson got back from an oncology junket in Hawaii. Then there was Guido's extraordinary effort to bribe him, and Decko's dark hints about money from Vaduz. He had checked his printed bank statement last week, just as he always did. But if the rumours started, he would be vulnerable, because of the auditors' investigation into his German expenses, and because his wife had sold her house in Bluebell for too much money. Everyone would assume he was corrupt. The Minister would withdraw his protection. Theresa would be hurt. And then there was that damnable nun.

He forced himself to think rationally about these frightening things. He made a mental list. He would check his account tonight. See Sal tomorrow. Visit Mother Polycarp on Saturday. Talk to Dr Maguire Gibson on Monday. Discuss the house price again with Theresa when she was stronger.

Had Theresa bought a grave? She always planned ahead. Perhaps she would recover. And he would look after her. He sometimes wished that he could pray. But he had not prayed since boarding school. Prayers had not worked there.

There was a call on his direct line. A familiar voice: Eileen McTeague. He was surprised that Eileen should call in from her holiday break in Paris, but she was already back at home in Dublin. It had only been a three-day break. She apologized for intruding. She had heard the outcome of Mr Fennessy's case.

'Did you have a nice time?'

Wonderful, said Eileen. They had taken a riverboat

cruise, and gone halfway up the Eiffel Tower. She was worried about something connected with Mr Fennessy's case.

Of course gentle Eileen had no idea that his telephone might be bugged. He quickly suggested they could discuss it on Monday morning. He urged her to enjoy her weekend. But Eileen kept talking. She had been so upset to read Tuesday's *Gazette* in her sister's house, after coming home. She had checked the *Irish Times* as well, just to make sure. 'It's Mr O'Rourke's pen, you see.'

'Yes?'

'Is it true that he denied having a pen with Mowbray's engraved on it?'

'Yes.'

'But he does have a nice pen saying Mowbray's. Not Waterbury, Mowbray's. I noticed the name because my aunt used to send me Christian books from Mowbray's bookshop on King's Parade in Cambridge.'

'But besides the bank and the bookshop, there could be another company called Mowbray's that manufactures pens. It's nothing to worry about.'

'There could be twenty companies called Mowbray's, but why would Mr O'Rourke deny that he owned the pen, and under oath?'

'Perhaps you misread the name on Billy's pen.'

'No, I particularly noticed it. Billy has such nice handwriting, although he uses a ballpoint pen. I bring him letters to sign. How could he deny it?'

Séamus sighed. 'I'll ask him about it. If there's something wrong, we'll put it right. Later, though, because now I've got to go and see my wife in hospital.'

A sharp intake of breath. 'I'm sorry, Mr Joyce, I never even asked you how Mrs Joyce is.'

'Not very well. Goodbye for now, Eileen.'

'I'm terribly sorry, Mr Joyce.'

He put down the phone and left the office briskly, without explanation. Nobody asked him where he was going.

{{{{{{o}}}}}}

Theresa was asleep, huge dark circles around her eyes. The nurses said that she had not been able to finish her lunch, had complained of new abdominal pains. Probably the new drugs. The house doctor had prescribed heavy painkillers.

He sat by her bedside as the light began to fade. Her breathing was regular, her features strained but motionless. No chance to talk things over. Theresa was out of it.

'Forgive me,' he said.

The house doctor was unavailable, dealing with an emergency. Dying is not an emergency, if you do it slowly. It was starting to rain.

Back home in Glenageary, he switched on the burglar alarm, went into his study, found his leather slippers (the ones Heidi had given him), took out the statements for his joint bank account with Theresa, laid them on his desk and read them backwards, line by line, covering a period of nine months. He could recognize every single payment. No secret cash from Liechtenstein. And that was his only current account. He had closed down everything in his German bank before leaving Aachen.

He was yawning with hunger. It was only six o'clock, but he needed some fuel. On the radio news programme, the Fennessy trial made a fleeting appearance, with the child pornography conviction taking precedence over the drugs conviction. Séamus microwaved a frozen chicken korma, drank the end of a bottle of Gigondas, started to flick through his Visa, MasterCard and American Express statements, in search of unexplained lodgments or refunds.

Nothing. Nothing. Nothing. The same with Theresa's credit cards.

There was another route by which a windfall could have reached him from Vaduz. Theresa kept two business accounts, current and deposit, and her bank would not be surprised by payments from abroad. Her files were stored in an old oak cupboard in the boiler-room, neatly ranged in Peerless file boxes, ready for the annual visit of her tax accountant. Once a month she clipped all her receipts and bank statements together, placed them in a plastic folder and filled in the accountant's summary sheet. Séamus had bought the plastic folders in Germany, on her instructions: five dozen, enough for five years. Not even her illness had stopped that routine.

He descended the spiral staircase into the dark boiler-room, groped for the switch. The light was not working. In the darkness, he found the torch behind the boiler. Its battery was run down, and it cast more shadow than light.

The cupboard door stood slightly ajar. He had carried

her September folder down here the day after she had gone back into hospital. He had laid it on the top shelf, separate from the rest, as she had not quite finished writing up the summary sheet. He had then closed the cupboard door, as he always did. Now he shone the weak torchlight into the cupboard. The top shelf was empty. After a split-second of empty dismay, he probed further with the torchlight. The September folder was repositioned on the middle shelf, in sequence with the other folders going back to the start of the tax year. Not where he had left it.

He changed the lightbulb, lifted the folder from the cupboard, went through its contents. Theresa's current account had been over eighteen hundred euros in credit by the end of August. During September, three and a half thousand had come into the account, and five thousand had been transferred to her savings account. The balance then stood at slightly over three hundred euros. She had sold no houses in September. Where had the three and a half thousand come from? He compared the incoming payments to the summary from August. Two were identical: 'Ranelagh rent' and 'Harold's X rent'. Those were houses she had purchased in March but had not yet started to renovate. Then her design fee from MB Hotels, a tax refund, her commission from Mogador Fabrics, and other small payments, all neatly annotated, entirely unremarkable, and amounting to three and a half thousand euros. Problem solved.

Turning to her savings account, he traced the credit transfer of five thousand euros from her current account. No other new payments. The savings account now stood at three hundred and ninety-six thousand euros, which he knew would shortly be augmented by the money from the Bluebell house sale, to be used as a war chest for the purchase, renovation and resale of yet another house. If she ever rose from her hospital bed.

The premium price on the Bluebell sale, paid over by John Florio, might conceivably be regarded as money from Vaduz, presuming that Florio maintained a Liechtenstein bank account.

Probing Theresa's papers made him feel as if she were already dead and he were her pathologist, not her loyal husband. But there was no escape. Had she been well, he would have asked her about it. If outsiders were interfering with her business, then he had to protect her. Replacing the August and September folders, he checked back through solicitors' letters and press cuttings relating to her house sales over the past year. Three sales had been made in the springtime selling season, long before the Bluebell house; all were for amounts roughly in line with the market. But then, they would be, wouldn't they? He had taken over at the iDEA only four months ago, so nobody would have been interested in trying to compromise him back then, when he was becalmed.

He closed the cupboard, switched off the light and came back upstairs to fetch some brandy from the drinks cabinet. He switched on the side lamp, which cast a slanted light across the carpet. The footprints told him to keep looking.

Theresa had bought this white sitting-room carpet last year, and although she had had it treated with

ScotchGuard Séamus always worried about staining it, which was why he usually wore his indoor slipppers when venturing into this room. But somebody else had come in through the French doors from the garden, in tennis shoes, leaving the faintest of grassy imprints. The steps led to the fireplace, which Theresa had had blocked up when the gas fire was installed.

The mirror above the mantelpiece was crooked. Theresa did not leave things crooked.

He moved the mirror to one side, half expecting to find a safe set into the chimney breast.

Of course not. Stupid.

The faint footprints led to the dining-room, became invisible on the parquet floor. They must have had some electronic means of disabling the alarm. Whoever they were. Representatives of Declan Dowd? Sal O'Sullivan? The Robin? The Crow? Some other bird? And what, if anything, had they found? He wandered through the house, an illegal alien, shining his torch on door handles, on shelves, on drawers, on cupboards, on anything that might have been touched or opened. No sign of anything.

Theresa was a hoarder of documents. She had a rosewood writing-desk, with a secret compartment. Her favourite piece. She kept it in her bedroom. He knocked before entering. Force of habit.

Had other eyes scanned the documents that he now extracted and unfolded and read? Nothing financial, just her old British passport, that put her date of birth eight years earlier than his, and her marriage certificate to Albertus Kowalski of Leeds, and her divorce papers dated just before her marriage to Séamus Joyce, and her two sets of wedding photographs. Also three letters from the agency to which she had given up her little girl for adoption, thirty-six years ago in Sligo. A poorly focused snapshot of Theresa and Mucky Smith, standing stiffly side by side on a promenade, with a quintessentially British seaside pier behind them. Obviously purchased from the sort of sad photographer who used to hang around windswept resorts in the days before disposable cameras. And a bundle of love-letters on sky-blue paper, in copperplate handwriting, from a man named Ernst. First name or surname? Old postmarks. Pre-Mucky?

None of this was unexpected. Theresa's real age had flashed before him once, on an insurance payout. He had soon realized that her fiancé Thomas Rawlings was a convenient fiction. The obstetrician had let slip that his stillborn son was not her first pregnancy. Her cultivation of Mucky Smith had bothered him not from fear of being cuckolded but only because he suspected that this was the only reason he had been sent to Europe. He had guessed there were other affairs. Not now, not any more, but when she was in her prime.

All he had ever wanted was peace. Or so he had believed. He didn't care about any of this. He'd worked it out once before, sitting alone in his apartment in Aachen, after being confronted by chance with slight but unmistakable evidence of Theresa's other life. He was not a fool if she betrayed him. He was only a fool if he betrayed her. And then, of course, he had been a fool. But not this kind of fool.

He could have read these papers at any time. Now they choked him with blind anger, like white smoke filling the room. Not against Theresa, but against those who had come into his house. What right had they to read of her divorce, granted on the grounds of Kowalski's cruelty? Who were they to spy on a woman's search for happiness? Theresa was entitled to her secrets, although their life together might have been so different had she chosen to confide in him.

Here was a handwritten note from Daniel's wife, his own former sister-in-law.

Terresa you theeving cow was one of them not enough for you I made Daniel tell me all about you now I'm going to leive him and go back to my Mum how could you carry on even after we was married. I don't care about you or your tick Irish husband who probly knew all about you and your incest – I hope you suffer for it I hope you burn in Hell Go to Hell Rose.

He was dead on his feet. So much more to do. Keep going, don't think. He lifted the telephone by Theresa's bed, to call the twenty-four-hour service of his bank. It was more than a week since his last statement. But he replaced the receiver without making the call. The old bat, Mother Polycarp, had said that his house would be bugged. She was probably off her chump, but safer to assume that she was right. The Guards had done security checks when he had first been nominated to the Drugs Enforcement Agency, but that was weeks ago and things could have changed. The same could apply to his mobile telephone. Any call could be monitored.

Even his mobile could give away his location. He switched it off.

He fetched a miniature DAT cassette recorder and sleeve microphone from his bedroom, fitted new batteries, tested it by muttering the days of the week, played it back. Perfect quality. He had picked up ninety minutes of Jean-Louis Kremtz at the Olympia last summer, with this same digital equipment, and captured every note. He clipped the sleeve mike on his shirt, set the alarm, walked out the front door and drove to a public telephone box in Dalkey. Nobody was following, so far as he could judge. Feeling faintly ridiculous, he punched in the number of his bank's twenty-four-hour telephone service, recited his code, and questioned a young woman called Aoibheann about the present state of his joint account. In the ten days since his last printed statement there had been no credits. He could not check Theresa's accounts, as she did not believe in telephone banking and had never set up her passwords. He asked whether the bank had any other accounts in his own name. She asked for the passwords for those other accounts. He explained that he did not have the password, did not even know whether such accounts existed. He told her that he had been a customer of the bank for thirty-two years, and explained that his wife, who was a businesswoman and looked after their finances, had promised to set up a savings account for him to make certain payments on her behalf while she was in hospital, but now she was poorly after her operation and he did not feel able to question her about it. After informing him that Séamus Joyce was quite a common name,

Aoibheann reluctantly agreed to look through the various account-holders of that name and try to match his home address. No, no, no, ah yes, no sorry, that was another Glenageary Joyce. No, no, no. Yes! In fact there was a new savings account, giving his home address, opened in the Blackrock branch just ten days ago, with a cash deposit of six hundred euros, though she shouldn't really be telling him that. The person had produced a driving licence by way of identification. The account had subsequently received three giro lodgments, each for three hundred euros, through Berwald & Company in Vaduz. Where was that? There was no certain way of identifying the party making this particular kind of lodgment, as the originating bank would have received the amount in cash. Did Mrs Joyce have business in Vaduz?

He thanked Aoibheann politely and rang off. Fifteen hundred. That was his price. He had been holding the sleeve mike close to the earpiece as he talked, and now he played back the tape. Perfect.

He started on Sal O'Sullivan's number, then stopped. If his phone was bugged, so might hers be. He would make an excuse, call on Sal tomorrow.

He found Mother Polycarp's card, called her number. She picked up at once. He apologized for telephoning a convent so late in the evening, and she snorted with amusement. 'Convent? Haven't lived in one of those for yonks. We're based in the community nowadays. Come on over, Mr Joyce.'

She gave him the address, and directions to find her house. He drove through town, thinking of Jerome Fennessy spending his first night in jail.

It was a nondescript house, in a drab suburban side-road. The evening was dark now, and because he was tired the street lamps hardly seemed to pierce the darkness. It was almost ten o'clock.

There was no answer to his ring, but a car pulled up behind him. The old nun climbed out of the car, and a little red-haired girl popped out on the far side.

'I'll make some tea,' Mother Polycarp said. 'You can talk. Séamus Joyce. Davnet O'Reilly. About time you met.' She led them into a modern kitchen. 'We're on our own,' she said. 'Sister Mary Michael is out on her soup run. Pull up a chair. Biscuits in the tin, Davnet.'

The girl was white-faced, with puffy eyelids. 'I can't believe I let him down,' she said in a squeaky doll's voice. 'I should have gone into the court and demanded to be heard, even if the defence refused to call me.'

Mother Polycarp cracked an egg and scrambled it at great speed, simultaneously toasting two slices of wholegrain bread. 'You'll have this,' she said.

'No, thanks.'

'It's rude to refuse my cooking, young Davnet. I'll report you to Miss Power.'

The little girl tried a wan smile. 'It's my first food since Wednesday,' she said.

'Conscience is the enemy of appetite,' said the old nun. 'For those who happen to have a conscience.'

Davnet nibbled at the food, sipped her tea, and began to talk in a low voice, so quiet that Séamus could hardly hear. She told how she had seen Billy O'Rourke with his Mowbray's pen, and then seen the same name on Gloria's papers. She told of her visit to the lawyers and her false arrest by 'Pimple' Boyle, and the intimidation that had made her father cave in. She had missed a week's school, and could not concentrate on her work, or sleep, or hold down her food. Her father no longer spoke to her. Today's verdict had filled her with despair. She wanted to kill herself.

Séamus listened without comment.

'Do you believe me?' Davnet asked. Mother Polycarp froze.

'I'm sure you're trying to tell the truth,' he began. 'But when you suggest that a conspiracy involving –'

'Do you think I'm telling lies?'

'I didn't say that.'

'There isn't a whole lot of middle ground on this one,' Davnet pointed out. 'If I'm not telling lies, then I'm telling the truth. And I'm not suggesting anything. I'm saying it straight fucking out. I'm telling you there is a conspiracy. Even if it means you're going to come after my father and mother.' She was on the brink of hysteria.

'Don't be unfair, Davnet,' Mother Polycarp interrupted. 'Mr Joyce isn't going to come after your family.'

'You're a very articulate young woman,' Séamus began.

'That's what your deputy thought too,' Davnet cut in. 'Except he wasn't trying to flatter me. He resented me and Jenny for being of normal intelligence. What have you got against people who try to think?'

'You're being unfair again,' Mother Polycarp said. 'It's not people, just girls. Tell Mr Joyce about the three-legged rottweiler and the tap. He may know what it means.'

'It's probably got nothing to do with anything,' Davnet said, 'though Mother Polycarp thinks it has. When Jenny and I came into Blackwood's Club to be interviewed by Mr O'Rourke, he was talking on his mobile. He said the Jesuit was behaving himself, and there would be no need to let the three-legged rottweiler out of her kennel. He said the tap had been turned on, just in case, drippy drippy. He said the Jesuit was in love with him.'

'The Jesuit?'

Mother Polycarp cut in: 'Your initials are SJ. Society of Jesus. Jesuit. You should be flattered. Who's the three-legged rottweiler?'

Séamus could not speak.

Heidi was slightly lame. Her left leg had been shattered in a traffic accident, when she was a child in East Germany. It had healed well, but remained imperceptibly shorter than her right leg. Her front teeth were small and sharp and slightly gapped. She sometimes carried a cane. All of which made her a three-legged rottweiler.

How long had they been watching him? Drippy drippy? Fifteen hundred euros? Was his life to be poisoned? Were his sins to contaminate everyone he loved? How meanly he had treated Heidi!

'I see you understand,' Mother Polycarp said. 'I don't want you to tell me. Just so long as you know. It's important, because the responsibility is yours. You are the one who has to set things right. Starting with what lies nearest to you.'

'What do you expect me to do?'

'Start by setting Jerome free, Mr Joyce. Tear down the pillars. If it's unholy, it's not a temple. If it's unjust, it's not a court. *Fiat justitia, ruat caelum*. Let the heavens fall, so long as justice is done.'

'I did Latin,' Séamus protested. 'No need to gloss it. Do I look like Samson to you?'

Davnet smiled, a lovely smile. The old woman chuckled. 'Not exactly, Mr Joyce. But we must make do with what we are.'

{{{{{{o}}}}}}

He sat in the kitchen, listening to the girl. Her red hair reminded him of Sarah Clancy, his first love. This was the second time lately that he had thought about Sarah. Who was a respectable matron now in some English town. Or dead.

He hardly heard what Davnet was saying, about people who came to Paul Blake's club, although he nodded from time to time. He forced himself to concentrate, and asked: 'Did you think Mr Blake was a friend of Billy O'Rourke?'

'No. Why?'

'Was Mr Blake homosexual, by any chance?'

'No way. Ask Jenny.'

'Davnet,' growled Mother Polycarp, 'is this necessary?'

'I'm sorry,' Davnet said. 'I'm sure he meant no harm, but lots of people find Jenny attractive. For some reason.'

'And you never said,' Séamus nerved himself to say,

'that Mr Blake had some sort of liaison with Billy O'Rourke?'

'Of course not!' She giggled. 'Is that what he told you?'

He left at last, promising to look into what he had heard. 'I'll get a message to Jerome,' Mother Polycarp said as he climbed into his car, 'to keep his hopes up. Sister Leonard does prison visiting.'

'Please don't mention my name.'

'Three days, remember. And I should warn you, and your criminal associates, that I have deposited a full account of this affair in a safe spot.'

He drove home to his empty house, got ready for bed. The place was his no longer. Nor his life.

One day he would be ready to think about Theresa and Daniel. Not now. Even the Fennessy case was less unthinkable. Tomorrow he would tackle it: talk to Billy, and Sal, and 'Pimple' Boyle. Or start with Sal, tell her about the mystery payments from Liechtenstein. Drippy drippy. Would he also have to tell her about Heidi? If necessary, that too. What was left to lose?

He could not sleep. Music was out of the question. On his bedroom radio he heard the first cannonades of a political row. The leader of the opposition was braying about scandals at the heart of government.

That in itself was nothing new. A slight stink of corruption had for some decades been discernible in Ireland, fouling the air like an old familiar drain. A self-righteous native kleptocracy had swollen on the proceeds of small favours done, modest sums diverted, decisions reversed, grants obtained, investments announced, land deals sweetened, planning laws flouted, political donations siphoned into private fobs. Conscientious public servants had abetted this process by performing their duties with such bloody-minded earwigging obtuseness that normal business could not be transacted, while venal colleagues dismantled the artificial barriers they had erected. Recently, some of the smell had started to leak, and even the dear old Revenue Commissioners, who for years had snoozed like poodles on Prozac, were beginning to wake up and nip delicately at the sinners' heels. This did not mean that the kleptocrats would be punished, as a layer of less spectacular fraud had been carefully fostered over the years, to provide a cushion. A couple of honest judges, however, and a handful of journalists worthy of the name, had been raising a stink.

Tonight's story was more of the same, but had potential. An Irish statesman had raised money in America to promote an international news magazine, produced in London, which would project an authentic Irish viewpoint into every corner of the English-speaking world. The magazine had failed after seven unreadable issues. Its overpaid staff of opinionators and gossipists were thrown on the streets, and the American backers lost their money. The statesman who had launched the idea emerged, however, as joint owner of a valuable office building in the heart of London.

One furious Philadelphian matron resolved to challenge this outcome in the High Court in London, and had garnered support from a member of the Irish Dáil, a supporter of the government party, who had himself lost ten thousand pounds on the venture. This gentleman had discovered that two Cabinet minsters, shareholders of the survivor company, were also showing a handsome profit on their investment. He wanted the heads of the two ministers (neither of them Richard Frye), and had refused to be bought off with the usual inducements. Moreover, he spitefully published details of another controversy, concerning a toxic dump.

As a result of this furore, the morning's conviction of Jerome Fennessy did not rate so much as a mention on the midnight news.

Séamus woke from a nightmare, just after five o'clock in the morning. He could remember nothing of his dream, but lay cold and stiff listening to the noises of the house, its creaks and settlings. He thought of Daniel asleep in Málaga.

If Theresa was going to die, why should he expect to live? And for what? 'What's he saving himself for?' had been Auntie Mary's cruel remark about her hypochondriac neighbour, Father Griffin, who had sniffed his way around the town with a dirty white handkerchief covering his nose, and had died of old age forty years ago, while Séamus was still singing in the parish choir. It was a great funeral. *Ave verum*, *Salve Regina*, *O salutaris hostia*, *Sacerdos et pontifex*. Way to go.

At seven he rose and breakfasted, while the corruption debate snarled on the radio. There was talk now of a snap election. If that happened, it would freeze the Fennessy case. Issues of justice and crime always become contentious during political campaigns. Could he persuade the little nun to button her lip until after the vote? The Minister would certainly block any attempt to review a successful drugs conviction.

He got dressed and selected his audio cassette for the day. Sidney Bechet's 'Petite Fleur' would rebuild his shattered head.

In the office there was hubbub. Mary Rice had arrived early and was busily assembling and printing out files of legislative proposals for Gilbert Covey, who was composing press releases with the aid of his new assistant, a self-assured young man whose name Séamus did not catch. Máire Benedict had left a telephone message, and when he phoned her back she told him that the Minister was considering a change of tack. Could the Europe Without Drugs campaign be announced publicly after all, and could the Germans subsequently take it over into their new initiative, EuropaRein? Would Séamus please square this with Guido Schneider and the Scandinavians? They would understand the political pressures. And would he draft a document outlining the Irish proposal and the favourable preliminary responses that had already come from Scandinavia? The Minister would like to be able to show how Ireland was leading international opinion on the drugs menace. Could he please seek an immediate endorsement from the French and southern Europeans? They had been sitting on the Irish proposals. The Minister wanted a response by mid-morning.

He promised to do his best. She was not interested in promises. He asked Mary Rice for the files. One of the girls brought them in. He started telephoning. As he had suspected, it was impossible. Guido Schneider laughed long and heartily, and enquired why ever, in the name of all that was holy, we Teutons should assist to make our dear buddies in the Irish government look good, at the cost of scotching the imminent launch of our own initiative? Such a *volte-face* would be nothing short of ridiculous. Not even discussable with his Ministry. More than his job was worth. Apart from that unfeasible request, however, was there any other little favour at all that he could do for Séamus?

'Thank you for asking,' Séamus said. 'There is nothing that I want.'

'That is fine. Goodbye, Séamus.'

When he got back to the Scandinavians, they were no longer prepared to endorse the Irish plan in any way. His contacts in France, Italy, Portugal, Spain and Greece were unavailable when he called. His Austrian and Dutch counterparts telephoned spontaneously to say that, following mature consideration, they had independently decided not to endorse the Irish proposal.

In short, disaster. It was eleven o'clock. Gilbert Covey strutted into Séamus's office, and showed him three draft press releases covering the Fennessy case, new drug tests for public employees, and changes to the regulations on early release for prisoners.

'What do you want me to do with these?'

'Nothing. Just be aware. The Minister may release them today or tomorrow, depending on developments.'

'You don't need me to make any statement?'

'Not a sausage. Anyone contacts you, refer them to me.' Gilbert's contempt was palpable. He called a taxi from Séamus's phone.

Séamus left a cryptic message on Máire Benedict's voicemail, confessing his comprehensive failure on the European front. Then he contacted Sal O'Sullivan's private office. Her private secretary stalled him. Sal would be in after lunch. What was it about? He could not say. Where was Sal now? At a meeting in Government Buildings.

He put down the telephone.

The Minister was entitled to know the facts.

Suppose for a moment that the paranoid fantasies of the midget nun and the dumpling schoolgirl were true. Suppose Billy was in league with 'Pimple' Boyle to nobble a witness. Suppose he really was protecting a rival drug supplier? Would anyone care? Could Mother Polycarp be silenced? Short of strangling her?

He decided to see Sal first, and clear the lines about his finances. But first, feeling more than usually absurd, he took a thick pad of notepaper and wrote on it heavily with a ballpoint pen: first the words '*The Man – Saturday 6pm – Sunday noon????*', and then the address of a pub one mile west of Theresa's holiday cottage in the depths of County Kerry.

He silently tore off the top sheet, held the pad obliquely to the light. Too obvious. He tore off a second sheet, then a third. Now, the outline of the words was barely visible on the top remaining sheet. He folded and pocketed the spare sheets of paper.

All of which would work if his office was merely bugged for sound. On video, he would look a proper charlie. He placed the pad on his empty desk, summoned a taxi. It came quickly. He sat in the back, took the DAT recorder from his briefcase and clipped it to his trouser belt at the back. The little microphone clipped to the inside of his wrist cuff, with its wire going up the sleeve, over his shoulder, and down to the cassette recorder. Silly, but if he were to be accused of taking bribes, with an election in the offing, he would need proof that he had disclosed the payments to Sal O'Sullivan at the earliest possible opportunity. Once he had spoken to her, he would send her a written memo confirming their conversation. The files would vindicate him in future years. Séamus was a civil servant through and through. He had given his all to the State, and there was nothing left.

{{{{{{o}}}}}}}

Jerome had expected to be taken to the Victorian prison at Mountjoy. Instead he was housed in a new assessment and orientation unit on the outskirts of Naas. The place was secure but spacious, a cross between a kindergarten and a hospital. Concrete block walls were decorated in rubbery white paint. Floors were covered in restful green carpet tiles. Ramps ran alongside shallow flights of stairs. Wheelchair-bound criminals would feel quite at home.

His room was oppressively warm. They had left him a Bible and he read the story of Jacob, how he served seven years as farm labourer to his uncle Laban, on the promise of marrying Laban's beautiful daughter Rachel, and instead was fobbed off with her older sister Leah. And then he got Rachel as well after working another seven years. A long sentence. Being married to two sisters, your own first cousins, sounded kinkier than anything Jerome himself had yet done. Yet it was in the Good Book, so it must be all right. He closed his eyes and thought of Rachel, the younger daughter, shaking out her hair on the sheep-scattered hillside.

They brought him chicken for lunch. A vegetarian option was also available. Outside, there were fields, with big deciduous trees and white picket fences. Friendly staff watched his every move. The psychologist would see him after the weekend.

{{{{{{o}}}}}}

Just because you're paranoid doesn't mean they aren't out to get you.

On reaching Government Buildings, Séamus learned that Sal had been there an hour ago, but had gone straight through to Leinster House. In the parliament building some of the attendants had seen her talking to the Minister for Justice, before he had left the building with a group of advisers. She had probably accompanied him to Buswell's Hotel, where there was talk of a press conference.

Máire Benedict was waiting for Séamus at the entrance to the hotel. 'Where have you been? Where's your mobile?'

'Not working.'

'Get it fixed.' Always edgy, today Máire was honed like a slash-hook.

'You got my message?' he asked. 'About Guido Schneider stonewalling –?'

'The Minister wants to see you straight away.'

'That's why I came in. Is the election on, then?'

'The posters are at the printers. Come on. Upstairs. Hurry.' His early childhood had been ruled by such sharp venomous creatures. Máire bounded ahead. She was bony as a goat. From the slant of her shoulders, he realized how tired she was, under all that surface energy. Her fury came largely from chronic exhaustion. He lumbered after her, scratching his back. After some fumbling, he managed to switch on the DAT recorder.

They came to a bedroom on the second floor, upholstered in buttercup chintz. The door was ajar. 'My hero,' Richard Frye drawled. He stood alone, a pencil-thin slice of blue suiting against the yellow décor. No sign of Sal.

'I'm sorry, Minister. Guido wouldn't yield an inch, and he whipped the other countries into line.'

'I would have expected your old friend to be a push-over, Mr Joyce. Still, some other areas of your steward-ship have been less unfortunate. You may accompany me to my opening press conference. I will be referring to the Fennessy conviction. I may compliment you on that. Even toss you a question or two.'

'I'd prefer not, if you don't mind.'

'Why not, pray?' Richard Frye eyed him with dislike. 'Answering relevant questions is part of your brief. I like to hear a polyphony of voices from my esteemed collaborators. One does not wish to sound like a one-man band.'

'I have to tell you, Minister, that certain doubts have

arisen about our conduct of the Fennessy case. It would be wiser for me to keep my mouth shut until I have looked into it. And I have to speak to Ms O'Sullivan on another matter.'

A moment's chilly silence. 'The Fennessy case has been tried in a court of law, has it not? The defence's objections were swept aside, were they not? That's good enough for me, Mr Joyce.'

'There is evidence of the possible intimidation of witnesses, Minister.'

'Who is making these complaints?'

'I am not at liberty to say.'

'You must. I am your Minister.'

'Only when I have completed my review of the case. With respect.'

'My dear Séamus.' The Minister honeyed his voice to a conciliatory hum. 'One meets these cranks and busybodies. We cannot have government held up to ransom.'

'There may be nothing in it,' Séamus said. 'But if something was done wrong, I'll have to put it right. That's why I'd prefer to keep quiet for the moment.'

'Please,' Máire Benedict interrupted, 'the Taoiseach is waiting.'

The Minister ignored her. '*You?*' he said to Séamus. '*You? You* will have to put it right? We have a court system in this great little island. Perhaps you would prefer some other system? Let the defendant appeal if he thinks he was hard done by. It is not for *you*, Mr Joyce, to undo the work of our judiciary.'

'His legal team was entitled to be informed –'

'Your position,' Richard Frye hissed, 'will become untenable if you start to unpick the work of the agency which you nominally lead.'

'I'm not unpicking anything. I will investigate the matter carefully and discreetly. And I will keep you informed.'

'Mr Joyce, you will be out on your cauliflower ear if you even start down this road. I will not tolerate it. Do you understand what I am saying to you?'

'The legislation establishing the iDEA gives me a statutory responsibility, which I cannot legally evade, and for which I am answerable to Dáil Éireann.'

'How are the feeble risen! How he clambers up on his legalistic horse! I took pity on you. I rescued your so-called career from the doldrums. I am still protecting you against allegations of impropriety from your earlier incarnation. Do not be a complete idiot.'

'Please,' said Máire Benedict, 'they're about to start.'

Séamus continued evenly: 'Among the matters which have come to light, Minister, is an attempt to compromise me by paying money into a bank account in my name, from an unknown source. And one of my wife's houses recently fetched a suspiciously high price at auction. This too has to be investigated.'

Richard Frye whinnied. 'You don't mean to say, Mr Joyce, that you have been accepting bribes. In your exalted position?'

'I have accepted nothing. Funds were paid in without my knowledge. These funds may be coming from a source in the drug importation business.'

'And why would anyone want to do that? Are you

such a kingpin? A mover and shaker, a dreamer of dreams?'

'It has been alleged to me, Minister, that somebody within the police or within my own organization is working to shut down certain drug dealers, while building up others, especially one large importer who is poised to take over the Dublin heroin market.'

The Minister drew a deep breath. 'Leave us, Miss Benedict. Tell my great leader that I will join him in a minute, when I have disposed of this matter.' She slammed the door. The Minister turned to Séamus. 'It is amusing, Mr Joyce, to hear a deskbound bureaucrat such as yourself pronounce with such confidence on the ins and outs of crime. You might be better off leaving such operational matters in a safe pair of hands such as those of your capable lieutenant, Mr O'Rourke. Without giving too much credence to the fantasies being put about by Mr Declan Dowd, who has been improperly using the resources of my police to spy on the iDEA and seek to destroy it. Let us suppose for a moment, Mr Joyce, that there were some tittle of truth in your absurd theory about the iDEA favouring one big drug supplier.' The Minister moved back, stood beside the window. Light played on his left temple. A vein throbbed. 'Let us suppose for a moment that you are not speaking complete gibbering nonsense. Now. Which is better, Mr Joyce? One large importer or a dozen small competing ones, importing material of dubious or even dangerous quality, flooding the market with cheap and unreliable supplies, killing each other in unseemly disputes?'

'The tolerable number of drug importers is zero, I would have thought.'

Richard Frye chuckled. 'In the fairy-tale world of Hans Christian Andersen inhabited by many of my benighted countrymen, yes, in that world, perhaps, zero drug importers would indeed be the optimum quantity. But not in the real world. Think it through for a moment, Mr Joyce. Tell me, do you regard your task as one of prevention or one of containment?'

'Prevention, of course.'

'Reflect for a moment, Mr Joyce. The object of your agency is to channel the supply of drugs, not to dam it. A certain Secretary of the Florentine Republic once said that we must build dykes and barrages to contain the fury of the river in flood. We cannot stop the flood, any more than we can halt the vicissitudes of fortune.'

'Machiavelli,' Séamus said.

'Correct, Mr Joyce. You are an educated man. Machiavelli, a tragic and much-maligned figure, states a modest aim – an honourable aim – to preserve normality in an abnormal world. A certain Elizabethan dramatist puts it more poetically, and more adventurously. He refers to a tide in the affairs of men which must be taken at the flood. He too does not suggest that the flood can be prevented. Indeed Mr Shakespeare suggests that we throw ourselves onto the flood. Think of it as navigation, Mr Joyce. We spread our sails on the flood tide of reality. We cast our bread upon the waters.' He took Séamus's arm in a gesture of friendly condescension. Séamus had preferred him in hostile mode.

'We are trying to change the reality, Minister.'

'No. We are merely making it acceptable. That i politics, Mr Joyce. That is democracy. That is what th people want and cannot say.' He released Séamus' arm, but his voice now was purring, intimate, seeking understanding and complicity. Still he had not noticed the microphone, which in Séamus's mind was burning like a beacon. Séamus ventured a comment: 'A pessimistic view –'

'No, Mr Joyce. Realistic, I'm afraid. But by accepting that reality, I will reduce this plague of drug addiction There will be fewer junkies on the streets of Dublin because of the dykes and barrages we have built. The river will go on flooding, but it will flood harmlessly, in our designated channels. It will pass through. You mus remember the difference between aspiration and reality Mr Joyce. Come back to our drug supplies. What are you going to do with our miserable drug addicts if their supplies disappear?'

'The supplies will never disappear, Minister. But we must keep trying.'

'That is not sensible, Séamus. We are men of the world. We must not be childish. Keep trying what we know to be impossible? Far better to accept human nature and work with it, in the way least disruptive of the public good. We do not live in the Garden of Eden. In a democracy, the politician is a mediator, shuttling between fallen man's aspirations and his frailties, between conscience and original sin. Jesus himself said in the Gospels that if we give scandal to these little ones, it would be better that a millstone should be tied around our neck and we should be cast into the deepest sea.

Another image of water, you see. Not the domesticated mill-race, but the insatiable sea. That threat of drowning, with a millstone around your neck, is Jesus's version of the cement waistcoat.'

'An unusual way of putting it, Minister.'

'But you take the point. Far better to avoid scandal. Speaking of which' – he dropped his voice like a handkerchief – 'I have indeed become aware of certain transfers from Liechtenstein to you and your lady wife.'

'Why did you not tell me about the transfers?' Séamus allowed his anger to show.

'I was waiting for the penny to drop, if you will forgive the pun. Now, Séamus, I have absolutely no desire to cast you into the deepest sea. You are a valuable and talented colleague. If you play your cards correctly, you will be confirmed as full Director of the iDEA, and in about a year's time, when I move on to higher things, you may also be offered further openings at a European level. In the meantime, if you promise me your discretion for the duration of this unfortunate election campaign, I give you my word that your Mr Fennessy will be given the benefit of any doubt which may be found to exist. Assuming that the election is called next week, it will be over inside one calendar month. Do you think Mr Fennessy will last that long as a guest of the Irish taxpayer? He wouldn't do anything foolish, do you suppose? No danger of apoptosis?'

Sharp knocking on the door announced a new irruption by Máire Benedict, followed by the rotund, fluffy figure of Wee Willy Green, personal spin-doctor to the Taoiseach, Gussie Hand. Wee Willy cooed at Richard

257

Frye like a pigeon. 'Ah! Oh! Now! All present and correct, *a Risteáird a chara*? The clans are gathering downstairs. First we'll have education from Sandy, then taxation from the bould Pat, then your good self, and lastly roads and potholes and shiny new buses from Freddy. Slogan of the day: A Bird in the Hand is worth Two in the Bush. Hand, you see? Then tomorrow it's the Northern dimension: Hand's Across the Border. On Monday, the posters will be up: Strengthen the Hand of Government. The Taoiseach doesn't like the cult of personality, but I keep telling him he's the government's best asset. What you do think, *a Risteáird a chroí?*'

'Willie, I concur absolutely. Gussie, as far as I am concerned, is the Hand of God. May I introduce Mr Séamus Joyce, one of the leading lights of my Department?'

'Ah, Joyce,' said Wee Willy. 'Are you related to the Joyces of Bettysford?'

Máire Benedict interrupted, exasperated: 'We are running late!'

'So we are, Máire, so we are. Or the Joyces of Cashlawn? Florrie Joyce is one of my great friends. No? Well, Séamus, we must converse at our leisure on a future occasion. Until we meet again, *slán agus beannacht.*'

'And my best to your wife,' Richard Frye called as they left.

{{{{{{o}}}}}}

Séamus walked slowly downstairs, switching off his recording machine.

Peering into the crimson-coloured Slaney Suite,

where the Government press conference was about to start, he spotted Sal O'Sullivan up near the stage, with the Secretary General of Finance. Her own Minister was already seated on the podium. There was no point in trying to talk to her now. And no need. The DAT recording contained proof that Richard Frye himself had known about the payments.

First things first. To clear his name he had to deposit copies of the tape. If he posted a copy to Sal, would it reach her? What would she do with it?

Could he trust Mother Polycarp to hold it for him? No, she would be too impatient. Eileen? He could not put her at risk. Decko Dowd? Decko had his own agenda. Mary Rice? Probably in with Decko.

He had already laid the beginnings of a false trail. Best to continue in the same vein. Nobody was following, as far as he could see. He hurried along narrow laneways and withdrew three hundred euros from an automatic teller machine. In The Sound Man he bought a small Panasonic radio cassette recorder – the cheapest one with a suitable input jack – as well as a cable to connect it with the DAT machine, some batteries, and a three-pack of C90 cassettes. He paid cash. The sound of a distant car alarm, like a seagull on the wind, struck sorrow through his heart. Why so poignant? He knew at once: because of the Robin's wailing voice, the night he'd died. No going back. No going back.

On Dame Street he hailed a taxi and was driven out along the quays towards Kingsbridge. In stop-go traffic, he fitted the batteries to his new Panasonic and listened to the lunchtime news on the headphones from the

DAT recorder. They were already playing a clip from the press conference in Buswell's Hotel: the Taoiseach stating his unequivocal support for each and every minister in his government, and rejecting all rumours of a planned reshuffle. Ministers were then given their own soundbites: Alexander Leamy promised a hundred new buildings for primary schools; Patrick Corr promised to remove half a million workers from the tax net; Richard Frye announced fast-track trials for all serious crimes and claimed that Ireland was emerging as Europe's leader in the war on drugs. Freddy Murnaghan promised to connect Ireland's towns and villages with a network of smooth superhighways that would be the envy of the civilized world.

In the crowded booking hall of the railway station Séamus bought a ticket to Killarney, paying with his Visa card. The next train was due to leave in fifteen minutes. He found a public telephone and called the clinic. A nurse took the call, but he did not recognize her voice. Theresa was asleep. He left a message: he was busy today but would phone her tomorrow from the cottage. The nurse mentioned that a Garda had called by, looking for him.

He waited for ten minutes, then telephoned the iDEA and spoke to Eileen. Speaking above the background noise of a station announcement, he explained that he was tied up this afternoon. She said that a Mr Boyle was very anxious to contact him.

He walked towards the platform, sauntered into Easons, bought a music magazine, returned to the concourse and mingled with the crowd arriving from another train. On the far side of the concourse a bus was about to leave and he shuffled aboard.

He was stepping into a new life. Having given up his hopes of peace, he felt peaceful at last. Rest can only be found in motion: the seagull asleep on the waves.

The bus pulled away from the station, crossed the Liffey, sped along the quays, passed the Four Courts and Capel Street Bridge. Séamus hopped off at Bachelor's Walk and hurried up to Arnotts in Middle Abbey Street, where he paid cash in the bargain basement for three pairs of underpants, a vest, a shirt and an overnight bag, He hailed another taxi on O'Connell Street and got out at Rathmines. He waited until the taxi had gone, then walked for three hundred yards as far as Fenwick's Dublin Inn. He told them he was in town for a funeral, asked for a single room for one night. The receptionist wanted an imprint from his credit card, but he explained that he had had his pocket picked two days ago in Cork, and was waiting for his cards to be reissued. He paid for the room in cash, and signed in as P. J. O'Brien, giving his address as Independent Estates, Western Road, Cork. He promised to pay cash for all his incidentals, and ordered a sandwich and coffee in the lounge.

He had not realized how hungry he was.

He had changed. Negative to positive. As simple as that. The real catalyst was almost getting killed on the night they'd shot the Robin. A new perspective. If he risked everything now – cast his bread upon the waters – what could he lose? He would have done one good, clean thing in his comfortable life of repressed pain.

He rigged up his tape recorders, transferred the DAT recording to an ordinary C90 cassette. He listened to the tape as it ran. Marvellously sinister. He imagined Mother Polycarp and little Davnet, murdered. He wondered when Theresa would hear of his disappearance. He pictured Gilbert Covey at work, concocting some foul story to discredit him. He reached for the telephone directory, tapped in the number of Radio Free Dublin. Peter Simons was just back from lunch.

'Who's this?'

'I've got something I'd like you to hear.'

'What is it?'

'A tape. About the Fennessy case.'

'Do I recognize your voice?'

'Possibly.'

'When and where?'

'Now. Fenwick's Dublin Inn.'

'Give me twenty minutes.'

Séamus made a second copy of the tape.

He realized he would have to go down to the lobby to meet Simons. He hadn't given him a room number. But only fifteen minutes had passed when the telephone rang on the coffee table beside the television set. The receptionist sounded suspicious. 'Mr O'Brien? There's a Mr Simons here to meet you. He says you're called Joyce. I told him we have no Joyce staying, but he described you. He's on his way up.'

'That's quite all right. Thanks.'

'Why does he call you Joyce?'

'It's a double-barrelled name. O'Brien-Joyce.'

She rang off. He sat feeling stupid. Why had he not

remembered to tell Simons to ask for Mr O'Brien? Stress. It must be stress. He was not up to this sort of thing. Not cut out to be a spy.

Hearing a knock, he stood up to answer the door. He was still undecided as to how much background information he should reveal to the radio reporter. How much discretion could he demand? All to be negotiated. He disliked Simons as a scandalmonger and destroyer of good order. Still, any port in a storm. Misfortune makes strange bedfellows.

He opened the door a crack. A huge burly figure stood there. Black woollen ski-mask, black leather jacket, bulging blue jeans. Séamus tried to slam the door. The huge shape shoved it fully open, rushed in, pushed Séamus across the room, grabbed him by the arms and lifted him bodily off the ground before flinging him onto the bed. 'Hand 'em over!' it roared.

'What?'

'Tapes!'

'Who are you?'

'Tapes!'

The balaclava was obstructing the man's vision. He pulled at the eyepieces, saw the two little tape-recorders on the coffee-table. 'Gotcha!' He scooped them up.

Séamus made a dash for the door. Nearly made it. The monster had him by the collar. He was choking. He drove his head and elbows sharply back. A howl of anguish, and he was free. He reached again for the door handle and was flung to the ground and dragged backwards across the carpet. 'I'll be friggin' dug out of you!' The voice was muffled. Séamus managed to raise himself to a kneeling position, but received a sharp kick in the ribs, then a dizzying slap across the head knocked him prone on the light grey carpet. Thick black shoes prodded him. He rolled sideways, caught at an ankle and pulled sharply. The other man toppled, landing awkwardly on the floor between the beds, then sprang to his feet, once again adjusting the balaclava over his face. Now he was swinging a flexible cosh in his huge fist with its two ruby rings. His black shoes were sensible black leather lace-up affairs with thick rubber soles. Not many gangsters favour that style of footwear.

'You can have a taste of this lad if you like,' he hissed at Séamus, waggling the cosh. 'This lad will break your fingers. Or your friggin' face.'

Séamus made no move, just crouched on one knee beside the coffee-table.

'Are you going to come quietly?' the big man demanded. 'Are you going to do what you're friggin' told?'

The telephone rang.

'Ah, Mr Boyle. I think it must be for you,' Séamus said conversationally.

'What the fuck?' Amazement.

'You've walked into the trap. And please don't use bad language. You're being recorded.'

'Who's that on the phone?' Pimple demanded.

'Why don't you see?'

Pimple Boyle reached tentatively for the telephone. Séamus caught the bottom hem of his black woollen mask, pulled it sharply down over his eyes, crunched his own head against the big man's chin. Pimple Boyle, off balance, tripped over the coffee-table, crashed to the floor beside the dressing-table. Without thinking, Séamus heaved the television set down on Boyle's head. It bounced across the carpet.

Pimple Boyle lay still. Séamus pulled the mask back a little. Pimple was still breathing, noisily. The telephone receiver was off the hook. Séamus held it to his ear. The receptionist was petulant. 'Hello? Hello? Room two five eight? There's a Mr Tandy to see you now, Mr O'Brien-Joyce. What was all that racket?'

'I tripped over your coffee-table. Don't worry. I won't be suing. Just ask Mr Tandy to step up.'

'Sir, we don't allow meetings in the bedrooms.'

'Ask him to wait, then. I'll be down.'

'Oh, he's gone upstairs. You'll have to bring him back down, Sir.' She rang off.

The real Peter Simons was standing at the door, toad-like and saturnine. 'Who's that?' He gestured at the recumbent masked figure.

'His name is Patrick Boyle. He's a Guard.'

Peter Simons winced. 'The man does not look one bit well,' he said. 'I'll phone an ambulance from the car. Let's be missing.'

Séamus retrieved his tapes, the Panasonic recorder and the DAT machine. Peter Simons bustled along the corridor and downstairs by the fire escape, Séamus trailing in his wake, and unlocked a battered green Punto in the hotel car park, its seats littered with papers and junk. As they drove around by the front of the building, two tall men were trotting in the main door.

Peter Simons drove rather too fast for a couple of

minutes, before flipping open the glove compartment. It contained three mobile phones.

'They can find your location through those,' Séamus warned him.

'No: these are registered in different names. Speakeasy accounts.' Simons tapped in 112, asked for the ambulance service. 'There's been a fight. Fenwick's Dublin Inn, Rathmines. Room 258. Man with serious head injuries.' He rang off. 'I'm taking you straight to my studios, Mr Joyce.'

'But they'll be watching!'

'Why?'

'I have evidence that Richard Frye is colluding with drug dealers.'

'On those tapes?'

'Yes.'

'Play it, Sam.'

Séamus extracted Barry Manilow from the car stereo and fed in one of his C90 tapes. Peter Simons listened with murmurs of appreciation. 'And how did you get this lovely recording?' he broke in.

'Miniature DAT machine on my belt, and a sleeve mike. I'm used to it. I like to record live jazz.'

'How come you were carrying this equipment?'

'I had to protect myself. Somebody had been making bank transfers into an account in my name. I had to get it on the record that I told my superiors once I found out. As you'll hear in a minute, the Minister already knew.'

'And you already have this stuff in digital form?'

'Of course. DAT. Digital Audio Tape.'

'Thank you, Mr Joyce! We don't have to go anywhere near my studio. We can leave it all to Julian the Apostate.'

He did a U-turn through a petrol station and headed out of town, started to weave through suburban side-streets, then drew up outside a small semi-detached house with peeling paintwork and an unkempt front garden. 'Follow me.' He plunged out of the car and hammered on the door of the house.

A well-upholstered woman flung open the door. 'Tweeter!' she cried. 'Who's this?'

'Mr Séamus Joyce. Where's my benighted nephew?'

'Dreamland. It's only half past three.'

'Lead us to him. We crave his unique endowments.'

She shrugged, led them upstairs, tapped on a bedroom door. 'Wakey wakey, Jewel! It's your rich uncle come to visit.'

No answer. She stood aside. Peter Simons breezed in, flung open the curtains and began to pummel the hump under the bedclothes. 'Wake up, you waster. This is your chance to save the world. Twenty euros if you get it done inside the next five minutes.'

'Forty,' said a muffled voice. 'And tell your sister to fetch some French Roast.'

'Fetch it yourself,' his mother said. 'You've missed another day. They keep attendances, you know.' She turned to her brother, who was already flicking the switches on a Heath Robinson computer system, all dangling wires and components. 'Up half the night, surfing the net. He hacks into computer systems from here to California. I have no notion what harm he's doing.' She spoke with pride.

'Harmless, Prince of Denmark, thass me,' the boy said, sitting up in bed. His eyes were red and half-closed, his chin speckled with stubble. 'I'm inventing a game. Monsters of Deceit. We're going to be, like, rich. So what's the story, Uncle Tweeter?'

'Digital recording, requiring to be put about.'

'French Roast? Please, please?'

'In your dreams,' said his mother. 'Oh, all bloody right.' She flounced out of the room.

'We've got the tape here,' Peter said. 'And a DAT recorder.' Julian staggered out of bed. His pyjamas needed some repairs. 'Give,' he commanded. He connected the lead from the DAT recorder to the back of a dismembered computer. 'How long?'

'Under ten minutes.'

Julian listened for a moment, then rewound.

'No probs. Nice quality. Who's the old fart talks like a book?'

'That's Mr Richard Frye, outgoing Minister for Justice. Mr Joyce and I are about to deconstruct him.'

'Right on,' said Julian. He clicked his mouse around the main screen. Various icons and pictures of devices appeared and disappeared. 'Thar she blows,' Julian said. 'MP3. Takes a few megabytes, but I'll compress it for uploading.' He started the tape again, in fast mode. The voices squeaked like mice. Julian monitored a row of flickering bars on his screen. 'Perfecto,' he said. 'Where's that coffee?'

Twenty minutes later, Peter Simons composed an e-mail to nine news organizations, three in Ireland, three in Britain and three in America, with copies to ten individual journalists. 'Greetings from Dublin, Ireland. Your attachments folder contains audio file ireland.mp3. On this file you will hear Irish justice minister Richard Frye admit that he knew about secret payments being made to one of his officials. He offers the official promotion if he will keep quiet. He states that his aim is not to prevent the importation of drugs into the Irish Republic but to concentrate it in the hands of one reliable supplier. Minister Frye further admits that he knows the recent trial of a drug courier was fixed, and promises to release the prisoner after the election if the scandal can be hushed up in the meantime. We are distributing this recording free of charge on a non-exclusive basis, to stop it being suppressed and to protect our source from retaliation. Feel free to broadcast, duplicate, transcribe or otherwise publish the content of this sensational tape-recording in any way you like, with no payment of licensing or copyright fees. You may check out the authenticity of the recording with any reputable member of the Irish media. The minister's voice is well-known and easily identifiable. This tape is brought to you by Radio Free Dublin, which will broadcast it on its five o'clock news bulletin today, unless prevented. Please credit Radio Free Dublin in your own use of this material.' He signed it 'Peter Simons, investigative reporter.'

'And now, my fee?' Julian asked.

'Thirty days' credit,' his uncle said. But he paid up when throttled.

'Can they trace the message back to this house?' Séamus wanted to know.

'No way. I gave it the I.P. address of a public access computer in college. Easy peasy.'

Séamus was still puzzled. 'How are you going to broadcast it at five o'clock?' he asked Peter. 'Won't they stop you on your way to the radio station?

'The newsdesk can download it. They don't even need me to be there.'

'But won't they raid your offices?'

'So what? Story's out. If we'd tried to keep it as an exclusive, they could have blocked us. The thing is in so many hands now, it's going to leak no matter what they do. Ladies and Gentlemen, The Internet. Public service broadcasting at its scurrilous best.'

{{{{{{o}}}}}}

During the hours that followed, Séamus found it hard to believe that a semi-gutted computer in a teenager's bedroom could wreak such universal havoc.

Radio Free Dublin was raided by the police, and their downloaded files impounded. An injunction was instantly sought, on behalf of the Department of Justice, to prevent certain named broadcasters from playing the recording on air. The national radio news station blandly reported this fact and announced that they were running tests to determine the authenticity of the copy of the recording which they themselves had received. They mentioned the web address of an American site where the whole recording could be heard or downloaded, then took some minutes to look back over the career of the Minister for Justice, with ample extracts from his speeches denouncing drugs, drug users, drug culture, drug dealers, drug barons, drug importers, drug growers and several South American governments. They also let slip that edited highlights from the recording were now being played on Ulster Television and on Radio Belfast, against whom no injunctions had yet been sought. Séamus, still sitting in Julian's bedroom, asked if he could see the Ulster Television coverage, and was amazed to see an old clip of himself, filmed years ago at a meeting in Brussels, jerking across a small inset within the computer screen.

Julian's mother came upstairs and invited Séamus to join her husband in the downstairs lounge, where a television set and a portable radio yapped competitively. She gave him paracetamol for his headache, Dettol for his bruises.

The political reaction was instantaneous. Three independent Dáil members announced that they would vote with the opposition in a forthcoming confidence motion. Their decision stemmed partly from the current financial scandals and partly from their own thwarted ambitions and animosities, but the Frye revelations had been the final straw. Their announcement removed all doubt about the impending election. Once the campaign was on, the drugs issue would be heightened to a surreal pitch. The Three Musketeers, as the trio of independent deputies were instantly dubbed, had already jointly accused the government of sleeping while cannabis burned.

Séamus ate fish fingers and ketchup and yearned for Theresa's cooking. His ribs were aching where Pimple

Boyle had kicked him. That was how Adam felt, after Eve was haled from his side.

Decko Dowd arrived at the house, with four mean-looking men who sat in the kitchen. Decko prowled around the house and garden, pronounced it safe. Julian's father retired to his study. Séamus asked if someone was guarding Theresa. Decko told him that two men had been stationed at the clinic.

That night, the Taoiseach drove to the Phoenix Park and requested a dissolution of the Dáil, which the President granted at ten o'clock. The election would take place in four weeks' time.

Meanwhile, the injunction hearing on the Radio Free Dublin tape had begun in judge's chambers. According to later reports, Mr Rodney O'Keeffe SC, for the Department of Justice, alleged improper and unauthorized behaviour by a public servant, and possible technical interference with the tape. Mrs Justice De Barra listened politely for twenty minutes before inviting counter-comments. Ms Lorraine West, Counsel for Radio Free Dublin, briefly likened the Minister for Justice to an emperor who not only wears no clothes but objects to being caught with his pants down. Continuing the metaphor, she opined that the truth would come out in the wash. She left it at that.

The injunction was refused, and soon afterwards Peter Simons introduced the entire recording on Radio Free Dublin, with a personal introduction describing Pimple Boyle's attack on Séamus Joyce, and Pimple's injuries, which had not yet been reported.

At nine o'clock, the recording was featured on the

main RTÉ television news, and Mr Comerford, the opposition spokesman on Justice, called for the Minister's resignation. Pimple Boyle had regained consciousness in St Vincent's Hospital, but his condition was still precarious. RTÉ played a clip of the Government Press Secretary, fulminating about dirty tricks and categorically denying that the Minister had spoken to Séamus Joyce that day. This was followed by a hasty retraction, at the behest of the Taoiseach. Yes, said Gussie Hand, Richard Frye and Séamus Joyce had certainly had a conversation in Buswell's Hotel this morning, and his adviser Mr Green had himself come in at the end of it, and had said exactly what was recorded on the tape. Of course he had no way of knowing whether the earlier part of the tape recording was authentic. It might have been altered or edited.

Decko Dowd appeared again in the living-room, took Séamus aside: 'You led them a merry dance, boyo. Frye's driver saw you going into The Sound Man after you left Buswell's. Billy found out you'd bought the tapes, and the transfer cable. They guessed what had happened, more or less. If you hadn't left the false trail leading to Killarney, you'd have met Billy instead of poor old Boyle, we'd have no tape, and you'd be dead. Billy's disappeared.'

'Did he set off for Killarney?'

'Gilbert Covey saw the outline of the writing on your desk pad, and assumed you were off to Kerry. He phoned Billy, who had a friend in the Branch run a check on credit card transactions. You used Visa for the train ticket. Nice one, actually. Billy boarded the

Killarney train at Portarlington, searched it end to end. He only realized you'd tricked them when he got a call from Pimple's backup team. We have the intercepts. He got out at Templemore, stole a car from the Garda college, and vanished.'

The news story rolled on. Peter Simons appeared on PrimeTime, accompanied by Fiachra Ó Neachtain, and filled in some of the background to the Fennessy trial.

The Minister for Justice issued a brief statement, denouncing the secret tape-recording as a breach of statutory duty. Séamus Joyce would be dismissed forthwith. The national newspapers, having obtained copies of the audio files, seized on the story. Trixie Gill finally returned Mother Polycarp's call, and wrote a passionate piece about the injustice done to Jerome Fennessy.

At three o'clock on Saturday morning, Richard Frye was sacked from his ministerial post, and informed that he would not be nominated as a Government candidate in the forthcoming election. The Taoiseach assumed temporary control of the Justice and Law Reform portfolio, and promised a full investigation.

At four o'clock, Decko Dowd escorted Séamus to a hotel where, under heavy guard, he got some hours of fitful sleep despite the soreness of his ribs and head.

In the morning they drove him to the clinic, to see Theresa.

{{{{{o}}}}}

She looked much better than he had seen her for months.

'Now!' exclaimed the cheerful nurse. 'Here's your husband for you.'

Theresa had that glint in her eye again. 'What a dreadful bruise.' She fingered his forehead lightly.

'I'll leave the two of you together,' said the nurse, 'and make a cup of tea for the men.' The door closed.

Theresa withdrew her fingers from his face, and whispered:

'I was such a fool.'

'Don't worry about anything, Theresa.'

'I should never have married you.'

She surveyed him with dismay. Not the resentment, the menopausal anger of the last few years before her illness, but something close to despair.

'I'll look after you,' he said. 'No matter what.'

'My first husband was a man,' she went on quietly. 'Your brother was a man. You're an empty shell. You've been going through my things, haven't you?'

He said nothing.

'You knew about Daniel, of course.'

'Not until now.'

'I knew about your German Frau. That I could have put up with. But the one thing you had was your job, and now you've spoiled it. You've hurt everyone who tried to help. You produce nothing. You wreck what's there.'

'I produce justice. That's my job. Who told you about her?'

'The wife of the British delegate. As soon as it started. Girl power. Mucky used to worry about leaving you in Germany. An occasion of sin, he called it.'

'Mucky Smith wasn't your type, I would have thought, Theresa.'

She glanced at him with perfect indifference. 'What would you know?'

'You didn't like alcoholics.'

'I married you for safety, and paid for it with every waking moment. Yes, Mucky was a drinker. So was Kowalski. But those were men.'

He looked at her and saw a stranger. 'It's over, isn't it?' he asked softly.

She nodded.

'They're going to discharge you?'

'Any day now. New drugs, new woman.'

'You'll need somebody to look after you.'

'They've promised me a Filipino.'

'I'll move my things,' he said.

No reaction. She closed her eyes. The interview was over. He left the room, spent, hollowed and free.

{{{{{o}}}}}

Decko drove him to Sal O'Sullivan's home in Dartry. There was a sentry box at the gate, and thick green glass in the lower windows. Inside, the decoration was twenty years out of date, but every surface gleamed with polish. In the kitchen Sal's bearded foodie husband made them an omelette and tossed a large green salad in almond oil and balsamic vinegar. Sitar music was playing in the background.

'You've been in the wars,' Sal said. But of course she knew nothing about Theresa. She meant the events of the past few weeks. He forced himself to concentrate.

'Which of you bugged my office?'

Sal grimaced. 'Decko arranged it, on my behalf. And Miss Rice was working for us as well. I hope you won't consider me ungrateful, Séamus, but after all that we put you through, I'm afraid I'll be advising the Minister to close the iDEA.'

He nodded. 'You're right. We were worse than useless. But you'll have to look after my people.' He was a thousand miles from what he was saying. Emptiness underfoot.

'The present Taoiseach also concurs,' Sal said, 'though it may no longer be his responsibility after the election. He hopes you will remain involved in the area.'

'I'm going to resign.' His voice was dead in his ears.

Sal's expression gave nothing away. 'Why would you do that?' she enquired.

'Because I don't want to be what I've become.'

Sal paused. 'It's your decision, of course, but perhaps it would be more discreet to wait until after the election.'

'I don't care about discretion.'

'To put it another way: if you resign now, it will strengthen Mr Frye's position.'

Séamus nodded. 'I'll wait.'

Sal gave a quick lopsided smile: 'Not that such political considerations would ever cross our technocratic minds.'

Decko put in: 'Gloria Mennon, Billy's associate, has vanished. Her secretary was told to shred all files on offshore funds, but we grabbed most of them before she got going.'

'Did Billy have money there?'

'We can't tell. Only a few of the accounts have names. The Fraud Squad took the files to decode them. Mr Hand is trying to hold things up until the election is over.'

Sal switched on the lunchtime radio news. Because of the election, all issues were foreshortened. The iDEA story had ballooned to a grotesque scale. The opposition parties were scathing, and the government piously endorsed their concern. Richard Frye phoned in, protesting at the violation of his rights. Political parties could nominate spokesmen, while he had to sit on the sidelines and hear his character impugned. Invited to put his case, Frye told how he had developed certain suspicions about Joyce. He was aware that Joyce was carrying a tape-recorder on Friday afternoon. What he had said was merely intended to test Joyce's integrity. Which had proved signally lacking.

Peter Simons, phoning in on another line, alleged that a numbered account in Mowbray's Bank, Cayman Islands, belonged to Richard Frye. He asked if the former Minister would care to comment on the source of the funds in that account, which had been set up during the previous election campaign. Frye called him an unprincipled liar. Peter Simons invited him to sue, and promised further revelations.

In Sal's kitchen, Decko Dowd punched the air. 'Those fuckers blackened Leo Jordan's name.'

{{{{{{o}}}}}}

On Sunday Jerome Fennessy was released pending an appeal, and housed in the Oscar Hotel at the expense of the *Courier*, the Irish edition of which had bought his story. He spent a whole day answering impertinent questions. Then he went out for a little walk along the Liffey and bumped into Trixie Gill. She took him to tea in Wynn's Hotel, and told him how much she had admired his dignified bearing during his trial. She also revealed that Miss T had confessed to another student that her accusations against Jerome during her school-days had been false. 'You should never have been put out of your teaching post,' Trixie said. 'That's how things started to go wrong for you.' She was so sympath-etic, so genuinely interested in his experiences. He tried to pay for the tea, but she wouldn't hear of it. Nor would she give him her telephone number. On Monday morning the *Gazette* carried a half-page article, cast as an exclusive interview: 'Jerome Fennessy Talks to Trixie Gill.' The *Courier* was not pleased. They stopped their cheque and informed the Oscar management that they would not after all be paying Jerome's hotel bill. Peter Simons splashed that story on his radio news pro-gramme, and the *Gazette* agreed to keep Jerome in the hotel at their expense for one more week. Trixie wrote a series of articles that were syndicated in several news-papers abroad. The US news programme, *Eyes Wide*, came to look in at the Irish elections and naturally touched on the Fennessy case. Trixie was cast as their local expert, and with her gamine effervescence became a coast-to-coast star for fifteen minutes. Davnet O'Reilly, standing against the background of Joyce's Tower in

Sandycove, told how she had noticed the Mowbray's link between Billy and Gloria. Flattered by the falling light, red-haired Davnet looked like a goddess on a good day.

There was a consensus that Richard Frye's counter-attack lacked credibility. The fact that Séamus had himself raised the troubling payments weighed strongly in his favour. Yet political commentators were far from writing Frye's obituary. He announced that he would be standing as an independent candidate in the election, to vindicate his good name.

Séamus again called to visit Theresa in hospital, motivated by a sort of bewildered pity. What had led her to this? But she refused to receive him. The nurses had turned hostile.

Wednesday afternoon was spent moving out of the house. Even in his catatonic state of shock, he was dismayed at how much gear he had accumulated. No furniture, but hundreds of tapes, CDs, old vinyl records, hi-fi equipment, books, clothes. The men from the removal firm worked with practised speed, packing his things expertly into cardboard boxes for storage, leaving Theresa's effects untouched. They probably split households every day of the week.

The separation was picked up by the newspapers, as was Theresa's former liaison with Minister Mucky Smith. The *Sunday Dispatch* alluded to rumours of Séamus's affairs in Germany – they made him sound like Casanova – and mentioned Theresa's relationship with Ernst Gottlieb. Gottlieb was dead now. He had been an overseas director of MB Quality Hotels. The

Gazette made a damaging item out of this, suggesting that her income as a design consultant had been little more than payment for sexual favours. Theresa issued libel proceedings. Séamus was doorstepped by a television reporter. To his amazement, he found himself smiling at the camera, as he said not a word.

Richard Frye announced that those who are dishonest in their private dealings cannot be trusted in the public arena. He was founding a new party, to be called Justice.

Billy O'Rourke was recognized by some late-season holidaymakers in Dingle, County Kerry. There was a sighting in Cork, another in Lanzarote. All were mistaken.

{{{{{{o}}}}}}

Public attention slipped to other matters as the election campaign picked up. Lobby groups auctioned their support to the various parties. The usual promises were made. The iDEA story began to fade.

Sal O'Sullivan announced the findings of her investigation into Séamus's finances during his years in Germany. A set of memos had been discovered which showed that the Minister's office, including Máire Benedict, had been fully aware of how his expenses were calculated. Mucky Smith had personally approved the procedures. The Taoiseach stated that in his opinion, Mr Joyce was vindicated with a vengeance. Máire Benedict resigned her post.

Davnet O'Reilly went to see Jerome Fennessy in his hotel. He thanked her for prising open, as he phrased it, the oyster-shell of his case. Now they could go to London together.

'That was not the point,' she told him.

Next day she called again, bringing her sister Maureen as a chaperone. Jerome promptly fell in love with Maureen, who was wearing a faded yellow dress of her mother's. Maureen and Jerome went to dinner together, escorted by a bodyguard from the Special Branch. Maureen drank too much and they parted acrimoniously. Jerome then sprang his aged mother from her nursing home, and they set out for the Costa Blanca, where the mother had bought an apartment some years previously in a moment of madness. She had wanted to die in Spain, ever since the Civil War.

{{{{{{o}}}}}}

Richard Frye tipped Trixie a list of offshore bank accounts held by Mr Gussie Hand. Between the Isle of Man, the Channel Islands and the Dominican Republic, the Taoiseach had amassed a modest nest egg. His protestations might have been more effective had the Government advertising campaign not recently moved to a new slogan: 'Hand's Up for Financial Security!'

Séamus had nowhere to stay. Declan Dowd offered to rent him a spare room. Mrs Dowd made him welcome, stuffed him with hearty food. He could feel his waistband getting tighter. She herself was barrel-shaped, and favoured flowery housecoats. No wonder Decko had proved so susceptible to the charms of Miss Bentley of Rotherhithe, the gangland vamp.

Four young Special Branch men took turns to sit in Decko's kitchen, night and day, twelve hours on, twelve hours off. Mrs Dowd fed them too. They had placed monitors and microphones and panic buttons all over the house. Mrs Dowd showed little sign of panic. Her son was in his late teens, studying business in Birmingham. The walls of Séamus's room were covered in the insignia of Aston Villa.

These days, he was driven to work by an armed policeman. There was plenty to be done. The iDEA was to be merged into Decko's squad, with the administrative offices and archives for the combined operation to be housed in the iDEA's new office block in Sandyford. The merged force would be given a fresh title: *Cosc*, from the Irish, meaning 'veto' or 'hindrance'.

Billy's sidekicks had been redeployed to other duties, and most were under active investigation by a special Garda unit.

The merger meant that elements of two offices would have to be moved to different locations. The internal layout of the Sandyford building had to be renegotiated. Séamus, whose official title had now shrunk to Acting Director (Administration), tried to preserve his policy sections more or less intact, while leaving Decko's operational staff housed as far as possible in their city-centre office. But Séamus's star was waning. The Department scented blood, and Sal O'Sullivan let them rip. Tons of dead files that had clogged Department storerooms and police stations across the country for decades were to be shipped out to Sandyford. Séamus's protests were unavailing. The place would become a general dump.

Mary Rice grew bad-tempered as she fought for shrinking floor space and computer facilities. Séamus had failed, yet again.

Heidi telephoned one evening. He had no time to think before Decko's wife put the telephone receiver in his hand. He had forgotten the silvery thrill of Heidi's clear voice. She had procured Decko's telephone number from the secretary general of the Permanent Liaison Committee, who knew a man in the Department of Justice who knew where Séamus was staying. She asked him if he would come now and visit her. Séamus said he would love to do that, but at present he was tied up with urgent business. She was thinking of taking a short break in Ireland. He asked her to wait. As he put down the telephone there was a fluttering in his chest, like life trying to kick in. Or it might be the sign of an incipient heart attack, brought on by Mrs Dowd's killer cuisine.

He was summoned to a meeting with Theresa's solicitor, Mr Pendler, to discuss the details of the separation. His offers of a fresh start were dismissed. Mr Pendler was not empowered to discuss that possibility, but wished to suggest instead that Séamus might like to make over half of his salary to his wife. Séamus agreed at once, but Mr Pendler advised him that in order to avoid future legal challenges to the separation agreement, he would have to take independent legal advice before signing any documents.

He went through the motions of engaging the services of Bridie Morgan who, apart from Mr Pendler, was the only solicitor who had ever dealt with his and Theresa's financial affairs. At least Bridie would not be contentious. But to his surprise, she took a hard line. 'Half your salary? Bollocks! She's the one with the assets. You're only a poor shaggin' underpaid civil servant. I'll sort Cathal Pendler out. He had no right to ask you that. I'll soften his cough.'

And despite his protestations, Bridie Morgan brought back a very different deal: Theresa now claimed none of his salary, and indeed offered to make over a small house in Donnybrook to him if he would agree to forgo any claims against the rest of her property. 'The woman is getting away with murder, Séamus. If you sign this, you're letting her off the hook.' Séamus signed.

{{{{{{o}}}}}}

Walking back from Bridie Morgan's office, he stopped to sit in a public park and take the winter sun. It was years since he had done such a thing. He chose a bench under tall rustling trees.

Fifty metres away, a man in an anorak stopped to tie his shoelaces. Decko's minders were on the job.

People began to walk by. A teenage boy and girl stopped to argue, standing close to Seamus's bench but unaware of his presence. 'You had to bleedin' do it, didn't you?' the boy accused her. 'So what?' she spat back. 'She had it coming.' The boy began to laugh, and they moved on, arm in arm.

Three young women hurried past. Behind the laurel bushes on the far side of the lawn, two heavy-set men intersected briefly and stood close together. One handed the other a small paper bag. They separated and the man with the bag sauntered over towards Séamus. As he passed, he reached into the bag and pulled out a hamburger.

A park employee shuffled along, spiking litter with a long spear. For a while there was nobody. Then there came an extended procession of characters, each one miming his or her allotted personality with variations of posture, aspect, body language, speed. There was the tired but responsible family man, the short-sighted woman who expects to be struck for no good reason, the faded beauty, the honest frump, the blameless trickster on whom nothing will ever be pinned. Two African men, strolling like princes. Then a frail old white-haired man, quivering with repressed rage, or perhaps just Parkinson's disease. Séamus thought about his own father, and a familiar thought that had lurked in the sluggish waters of his mind for years floated to the top with crystal clarity: When a man dies, what is lost is not only what he has been, what he has made of himself, but also what he could have been, what he could have done, all his possibilities that have come to nothing. So we mourn those shadow beings, for we too are trapped in our lost potential. In life, we are our social roles, in death, we are what we have never been.

What might his father have been, had he not married such a viper? And Séamus himself? Would a different match have made a man of him? He was now his father's age at death. Or close. Would children have reflected a different self? Like that gaggle of small boys coming galloping over the sward, inexpertly kicking a football.

He needed to talk to Billy.

{{{{{{o}}}}}}

Theresa's health had improved spectacularly. He got this information under false pretences from Dr Alphonse Maguire Gibson, who had been out of the country and was unaware of their falling-out. The consultant was gratified by how well Mrs Joyce appeared to be responding to his latest course of treatment. The truth was nothing like that, according to Bridie Morgan, who cited as her source a senior house officer who worked under Dr Maguire Gibson. Realizing, while the great man was away in Hawaii, that the cocktail he had prescribed was damaging and potentially lethal, the house officer had silently altered the prescription to a more beneficial combination of drugs. The great man had distractedly approved the change on his return. Theresa was now simply recovering from the consultant's earlier mistakes. She had never had oesophageal cancer. 'Just a brass neck,' was Bridie's comment. Séamus had no idea how reliable her source of information might be.

Tom Stringer called by Séamus's office one afternoon, unannounced. He was going home to America, wanted to bid farewell to his Irish friends. Séamus said not a word about the bullet that had killed Raymond Kinnear.

'Still worried about Billy?' Tom asked Decko.

'Only as long as he's alive,' Decko said.

'That nurse, in Kildare,' Tom said. 'He talked about her once or twice.'

'Funny, I wouldn't have called him the confiding type,' Decko said. Séamus was surprised to feel a pang of jealousy: Billy had never even accepted a drink from him, never opened up personally in any way, except for those defensive remarks about family life, that night they had sat waiting for the Robin.

'Could be he's gone back to her,' Tom said. 'Wouldn't say what her name was.'

'There was something about a nurse in the files,' Séamus said. 'Ten years ago.'

'Where would you start looking?' Tom wondered, 'Anyhow, I got a plane to catch. Heathrow tonight, Washington tomorrow, suitcases in New Orleans.'

After he had gone, Decko gave a laugh. 'I've got my own ways of flushing Billy out. Never mind the nurses' register. I'm going after his Yank fancy-woman.'

Next day, Decko's people arrested John Florio, the crooked solicitor who had bid for Theresa's house. They collared him in a bank where he was depositing a briefcase full of dollars, and charged him with money-laundering. Among the documents found in Florio's house were the deeds of ownership of three apartments in Bloomfield Wharf, a complex of residential and office buildings which had belonged to a British–American property group, one of whose silent partners had been Gloria Mennon's late husband, Sonny Mennon. After Sonny's fatal speedboat accident in the Florida Keys, Gloria had come into ownership of apartments number 323, 356 and 458 Bloomfield Wharf. These were now seized by the Criminal Assets Bureau. Gloria had lived in number 458, the penthouse apartment. But she had vanished, leaving everything exactly as it stood, down to dirty coffee-cups and a washing-machine full of damp synthetic clothes.

{{{{{{o}}}}}}

Séamus, having nothing to lose, was taking his own line in the hunt for Billy O'Rourke, using his dubious authority as Acting Director (Administration) of the iDEA to monitor the money trail investigation.

Garda code-breakers had identified Billy O'Rourke's personal offshore account with Mowbray's. Fourteen thousand euros had been withdrawn in the previous week, leaving marginally under three hundred in the account. Billy had lived in a bedsitter, with a cardboard-partitioned kitchen and bathroom in a corner. Decko's people took the place apart. It was like an animal's den, dirty and bare. One saucepan, one crumpled frying pan, one mug, two knives, one fork, two teaspoons. A single secondhand paperback book: *The Adventures of Huckleberry Finn*. No hi-fi. Worn sheets, no pillow. Teabags, stale bread and tins the only provisions. An empty gun-case. A bottle of cheap whiskey. The neighbours knew nothing.

In Covey's former office, two young detectives tapped all day on a portable computer, assembling a list of registered nurses in County Kildare aged between twenty-three and forty-eight. Their sources were local-authority and hospital records, as well as files from the nursing registration board. The age range was considered wide enough even for Billy, allowing that the liaison suggested by Tom Stringer might have dated back some years. Of course the whole thing might have been sheer fantasy on Tom's part.

Billy's local account with the Provincial Bank had a balance of four euros and thirty-two cents. The manager cagily allowed that there had been more in the account up to quite recently. He promised to print out the records as quickly as possible. It might take a week or two.

With Decko's approval, Séamus co-opted Alan J. Lennox from the Fraud Office in this part of the investigation. Lennox knew how to put pressure on the Provincial Bank. The records of Billy's account were produced within six hours.

Lennox sat in Séamus's office with a sheaf of printouts and a school copy-book which he covered in hieroglyphics. He didn't like computers, preferred to scribble everything in blue biro.

Most of the history was simple. Over the nine years since the Provincial account had been opened, there had been no lodgments other than Billy's regular monthly salary, paid by electronic transfer. Except once, when compensation had been paid for his injury in the Maher shootout. That had come to two hundred thousand pounds in old money.

Payments from the account fell into two categories. Lennox listed the frequent small cash machine withdrawals by which Billy must have met his day-to-day needs. No receipts were kept, and the small withdrawals usually amounted to less than half of Billy's monthly salary. There was no supermarket loyalty card to track his expenditure. However, when one of Lennox's associates called around with photographs, staff in the non-stop shop near his favourite cash machine remembered Billy as a frequent visitor, usually late at night, never spending more than fifteen or twenty euros. Once he had detained a drug addict who was threatening the cashier with a syringe. That was when they had found out what he did for a living.

He had two credit card accounts, but rarely used them. Balances were paid off promptly, by giro.

The other category of payment was more interesting. Apart from Billy's frugal living expenses, there had been regular monthly withdrawals of large cash amounts directly from the Provincial Bank. Round figures. In the beginning, these had been for amounts like two hundred and fifty, four hundred, three hundred pounds. In recent years, the amounts had crept steadily higher. One month, a thousand. The next, fifteen hundred. The following month, twelve hundred. Then, when the compensation had come through after the Maher incident, a further jump to six thousand, then eight, then six thousand again, and so on until the value of the award was more than halved. Last week the whole remaining balance had been taken out: seventy-one thousand two hundred and ninety-four euros.

There was no savings account. Billy had always run a surplus on his current account, and never earned a penny's interest. In effect, he had lent his money to the bank free of charge.

Alan J. Lennox wrote in his copy-book: 'Beneficiary?' He totted up the large cash amounts. Over nine years, including the final liquidation of the account, they came to more than a third of a million euros.

Lennox showed the figures to Séamus. The beneficiary of the surplus funds could hardly be Billy himself, he explained. If Billy had been interested in money, he would not have run those surpluses on his current account. 'Man didn't give a damn,' Lennox marvelled.

The payments were too irregular for a mortgage. 'Keeping a woman,' Lennox said. 'Or even a small family if they didn't eat much.'

Billy's recruitment records, from almost ten years ago, listed his family members as his father, his stepmother, and one younger brother, David, resident in St Mogue's Hospital in Bray.

Séamus telephoned St Mogue's to enquire whether Billy might have been sending money to his brother, but the administrator of the hospital had no David O'Rourke on her books. She promised to enquire further, and called back to say that David O'Rourke had died six years earlier, well before her time. He had suffered from muscular dystrophy and various mental disabilities.

Had they ever employed nursing staff from County Kildare? The hospital administrator sighed. They were welcome to consult her records. She herself had no time or resources to conduct a search.

Billy's father, also called David O'Rourke, was proving hard to trace. There were many people of that name in the Irish and British telephone directories, and more still in the social security computer records. Decko assigned his two detectives to follow up every David

O'Rourke aged over forty-five, using both the Irish and English forms of the name.

Current security reports on Billy were patchy. The snoopers' records held no hint of the nurse from County Kildare. They reported only what Séamus already knew: it was believed that Billy had had two long-term relationships with women since joining the force. Neither woman had any criminal connections.

Séamus remembered Billy dismissing the idea of marriage. His life seemed set up to avoid the risk of entrapment. But was there another woman, perhaps Tom Stringer's fantasy nurse, who had soaked up his money in monthly instalments and was sheltering him now from the storm?

'Forget people's names,' Lennox said. 'Let's take a simple mathematical tack.'

Séamus tried to look intelligent.

'Seven-one-two-nine-four,' Lennox recited. 'That last withdrawal. Cash. Nice distinctive sum. Not even Mr O'Rourke would carry that around. Hardly used it for groceries, either. He'd taken out two hundred euros from the magic wall, just the day before, and the girls at Supashop remember him spending nine euros on food and paying with a fifty-euro note. If we're very lucky we might find a lodgement saying seven-one-two-nine-four in some account in Ireland, or a similar sum being put through currency exchange, in the days that followed the withdrawal.'

Under the anti-racketeering laws, Lennox's powers of investigation were extensive. Accompanied by a programmer, he called on the offices of the major banks and trawled their computer systems for recent transactions involving €71,294. Nothing. He tried again, adding the fourteen thousand euros withdrawn from Mowbray's. And this time he came up with one perfect match. A bank draft for €85,294 had been lodged to the account of Louisa Parlow of The Copse, Celbridge, Co. Kildare.

Séamus travelled with Lennox. Four Special Branch cars were already parked near the entrance of the estate. They identified the house and watched it for an hour. A grey-haired woman emerged, walked down the road and started up a blue Nissan Micra. They surrounded the car, out of sight of the estate.

She was Mrs Joan Broderick, aged sixty-three, a widow, by profession a nurse (retired), employed part-time by Miss Parlow to help look after her severely handicapped boy. Seán. He was ten years old, almost completely paralysed. He loved music. You could see it in his eyes. Such a shame. Miss Parlow was a lovely young woman, the child of refugees from Latvia, or Lithuania, or someplace. She had built a little world for the boy in that house. Music all day. Classical. It wasn't strictly a nursing job. Mrs Broderick did some household chores, gave the boy his massage and helped with his exercises. Miss Parlow played the cello. Beautiful. She couldn't take a job, because of the boy. It was just the two of them, alone in the house.

Mrs Broderick knew nothing of Billy O'Rourke. They showed her a photograph. Yes, she remembered. He had interviewed her for her job with Miss Parlow, in a Dublin hotel.

They checked her credentials, called in the local Garda sergeant to vouch for her good character. Mrs Broderick was widely respected in the parish.

She came back with them, knocked on the door. A thin young woman answered – bright squirrel eyes, sharp cheek bones, lank yellow hair, teddy-bear mouth – and six of them piled in, guns at the ready. The only other occupant of the house was a long helpless boy who lolled in a huge wheelchair, listening to symphonic music while coloured lights swirled slow psychedelic patterns over the sitting-room ceiling. His mother calmed him and left him with the nurse while she spoke to the men in the kitchen. Decko asked the questions, in a gentle, choking voice.

{{{{{{o}}}}}}}

Yes, it was Billy had got her pregnant. They had met in a youth hostel. She was sixteen then. He was home from America. They had quarrelled during the pregnancy. Billy had wanted her to move to Dublin with him. She had gone back to live with her parents. They had insisted on a home birth. When Seán was born disabled, Billy had blamed the midwife, but the doctors said Seán's problems were genetic. On the father's side.

Up to that moment, Billy had not known that his own brother was still alive. When he was very small, his father had told him that David had died in hospital. Now the father admitted that David was still alive, in St Mogue's Hospital, maintained by the Eastern Health Board.

He started sending her money, so that she could keep her child.

Her parents moved away to their dream cottage in Donegal, up the side of a hill. They were crazy. A handicapped child could not have survived there. Billy had rented this house in Celbridge for her, sending money month by month. She would not let him visit. She found him frightening. No, she never read newspapers. She knew nothing of his recent past. Five years previously, Billy had bought the house under the name of David O'Rourke, and made it over to her.

Decko explained to her that Billy's money was partly the proceeds of criminal activity, and as such would have to be confiscated. Her bank account would be frozen. Even the house might be forfeited.

'What about Seán?'

The nurse had reappeared. She put her hand on Miss Parlow's arm.

'You can apply to the Health Board for assistance,' Decko explained. 'The courts might give you back some money in the end.'

'Heartless. Heartless.' Her voice was clear as a church bell. Her intonation was not Irish, though her accent was pure middle-class Dublin. 'Heartless.' She sat down.

The nurse tightened her grip. 'Don't worry, Miss Parlow,' she said, 'we'll not let you down, no matter what they do to you.'

Séamus tried hard to think of all the young lives blighted by drugs. It was no use.

{{{{{{o}}}}}}

Guido Schneider was on a scrambled line. He apologized formally for presuming to probe Séamus's honesty by offering him a bribe. Then he offered some explanations. Richard Frye was, he said, a creature of the Junction, a multinational syndicate bringing together some of the world's leading criminal families, whose medium-term agenda was to control narcotics shipments within the European Union. They controlled three US Senators, thirteen Congressmen, dozens of politicians throughout Europe, and a conservative think tank for which Richard Frye had once worked. The politicians were kept in line by a judicious mixture of bribery, blackmail and intimidation. The Junction operated many legitimate businesses which they kept strictly separate from their drug-related activities. They had excellent contacts in law enforcement agencies.

Having funded Richard Frye's election in Ireland, the Junction hoped to get him into the top job in the European Union Narcotics Directorate. Hence their desire to enhance his reputation on the Irish stage. They saw him as a hugely promising figure. And Ireland was fashionable in Europe. Acting in concert with local suppliers and certain elements in the police, they had reduced the volume of drugs on the streets of Dublin, while simultaneously routing more drugs through Ireland to other European countries. This served two purposes: smooth supplies, and growing credibility for Richard Frye. Of course they could always find another front man.

One problem was getting reliable suppliers and handlers on the ground. These little people tended to fall out with each other, screw up big deals by pursuing personal profits. And yet one needed their local knowledge. It was to keep these people in order that one needed agents like Billy O'Rourke, administrators like the Crow, accountants like Gloria Mennon and troubleshooters like Tom Stringer.

He, Guido Schneider, was an entirely neutral observer in all of this. His government was slowly coming around to the view that it might be more beneficial, in the long run, to bring currently illegal drugs within the ambit of the pharmaceutical industry, and put an end to the drug wars for ever. Meanwhile, he tried to avoid useless heroics.

And again he expressed his regret at having offered money to an honest man like Séamus. It had been a crude ploy, one insisted upon by his superiors. He hoped that Séamus could forgive him in time.

{{{{{{o}}}}}}

Billy had gone to ground in a remote cottage in Wicklow. Off the beaten track, in need of renovation, unrentable even in boom times, it belonged to a woman he had known once. He arrived late one night with the stolen car full of groceries. The car was stashed in a shed in the woods. He had bought a fine brush and two small tins of black and white paint, with which he reassigned the car's number-plate from Donegal to Offaly.

The house was empty, cold. Some window panes were holed at the back where someone had broken in. Not that there was much to steal.

He showed no lights, burned no fire. He cooked by camping gas, slept in his car coat for warmth, let his beard grow.

Time to move on. He could do nothing for Louisa and the boy by staying here. He would send funds from abroad. No regrets.

His wounded leg still hurt, especially when he exercised it. Still, pain is a sign of life.

Gloria would contact him. She knew where to find him. They would go to the States. Louisa had cash enough for a year, eighteen months. In time he would make more. He had three passports, two Irish, one British. He would be useful to Gloria's family. He'd need some alterations to his face. The family would arrange that.

He followed the news on the radio. Gloria was officially missing. When the Criminal Assets Bureau moved to seize her apartments in Bloomfield Wharf, the High Court gave her two months to appeal.

An opinion poll in Richard Frye's backwoods constituency gave him a commanding lead. He had never lived in the constituency, but had recently signed contracts for the construction of a large prison, bringing highly paid employment to the area.

The radio carried news of Louisa's arrest, and the freezing of her bank accounts. She was released without charge, but her assets would be forfeited. The names of Séamus Joyce and Decko Dowd were mentioned. And Billy was listening.

{{{{{o}}}}}

He monitored police frequencies on his little radio. Not having a scanner, all he got was routine chat. Still, it gave him some idea of what Decko's people were doing.

His mind kept racing. He struggled to slow it down. He was caught in a daydream of revenge, so real he could smell it: smoke and blood and petrol.

Decko's house was positioned in a corner location in Leopardstown, not far from a dual carriageway. Billy had staked it out with Bosco Woulfe, during the ICRAD campaigns. He had watched Leo Jordan visiting the house. Leo was in cahoots with the Maher family. Leo was on the take, but Decko had bought this great Edwardian pile out of clean money. His roly-poly wife was loaded.

Decko had hurt Billy. He had condemned Seán to a life of institutions. He had burst Louisa's bubble. He deserved to die.

Billy knew every inch of Decko's place. It would burn like a Christmas pudding.

Evening came, and under cover of darkness and rain Billy made his only excursion from the cottage: a brief expedition to an arms dump on the edge of a pine forest near Glencree. Everything was there: an AK-47 assault rifle, three handguns, a rocket-launcher, six ready-to-go incendiary devices and a small stock of explosives and timers. All unattributable, all in perfect order under their thick plastic sheeting. He loaded the lot into the car and was back at the cottage within two hours. He was running a temperature.

Time to think clear. Could the thing be done? Decko was always armed and dangerous. He was fast, though not as fast as Billy. Timing would be important. He could use the incendiaries, starting a fire to draw Decko out of doors. If Decko stayed indoors, he could open the place up with the rocket-launcher. Even with guards on the house, the speed of the attack would blow them out of it. The advantage of total surprise. Ninety seconds for the whole thing. But one man, even Billy: could one man be that lucky?

And then the getaway. His leg was still weak, but he could move fast over short distances. He would park the stolen car about a mile from Decko's house, and take another car on the spot for the duration of the actual assault. After the hit he would switch cars, and there would be nothing to trace him. Midnight would be the best time to strike. There would be darkness, but also enough late traffic to clog up the pursuit.

He thought of his alternative escape routes: over the mountain, or out along the dual carriageway towards Shankill, or into the city or a combination of the dual carriageway and a small mountain road. They would block the obvious routes first.

It was madness to think of it. Madness too to think of Seán, his son, growing taller and weaker, sinking into the twilight of institutional care, cut off from the love of his birdbrained mother. That was unforgivable. He heard Seán's inarticulate voice calling for help.

His leg was becoming inflamed. He changed the bandages, poured disinfectant into the wound. If that poncy consultant had done his job properly, this would have healed perfectly by now. Another target for his hit-list? The thought of bursting into an operating theatre and wasting the men in green made him laugh out loud in the silent house. The sound brought him halfway back towards sanity. He was still running a fever. Nothing much, but disorienting.

The following night would be time enough to decide. They wouldn't be coming for him yet. He pulled the coat close around him, settled back to sleep on the broken sofa. He was hungry.

{{{{{{o}}}}}}

Séamus was working on telephone records.

When Billy had phoned the office after the Robin's death, he had been staying with friends. Where? Aided by Mary Rice, Séamus went through the telephone records for those days. The iDEA's internal exchange kept a record of all incoming calls, their numbers and duration. Mary checked the dates and probable times of Billy's calls. They listed the numbers and called them back. Most were official bodies whose telephonists knew nothing of Billy O'Rourke. Some were newspaper offices. Some were private individuals, and Mary, who knew the personal lives of iDEA staff members in some detail, could account for them all. Of six cellphone numbers, only one was unaccounted for. It rang without response.

Mary Rice procured printouts of the cells within the national network where that telephone had been located during the days of Billy's convalescence. It had been switched on sporadically during those days, in a string of towns and villages scattered around County Wicklow.

The iDEA was the only number it had called. Séamus got an Ordnance Survey map and plotted the locations with Post-it flags. They formed a ring, twenty miles in diameter, containing few roads but many woods and stretches of rough terrain.

Somewhere in there might be Billy's nest. No way of knowing, but an instinct like hunger was driving Séamus forward. He needed to walk all the way to Billy. To explain. To be forgiven.

{{{{{{o}}}}}}

Morning. Billy was stiff from the broken springs of the sofa, and also light-headed, but his mind was clear as mint.

He made a pot of strong tea, realizing that all night, through his dreams, his dull feverish brain had been running inner videos of the attack under different scenarios. Defended, undefended. Raining, clear. Asleep, awake. There was a conservatory at the back of Decko's house. In his dream, he had fallen through the glass.

Billy had been battling the odds since the age of five, when one day in desperation he had lashed out at the playground bully who was tormenting his four-year-old cousin, and had seen the bigger boy go down howling. Since then, Billy had never backed off. He could still remember the fear that had led him to that first fight, the moment of blank terror as he swung his fist, the sense of rightness restored once he had faced down his inner emptiness and acted like a hero.

Which was also why he had wanted to hit Decko. Not because it was in his interests, but because he needed that self-respect. And there has to be a price. Justice demands revenge. Justice is balance.

But he had no balance. Time to pull himself together. He was going nowhere today. Let Decko come and find him if he wanted a fight. He could stand a siege. He checked his weapons once again, laid them out in a line across the kitchen linoleum.

The mirror reflected a madman. He shook his head, combed his unruly hair, shaped the edges of his new beard with an old blunt disposable razor, which had probably last seen service on the slim legs of Slipper Barrett, owner of this cottage. Now residing in Memphis, Tennessee, under the protection of a decrepit sugar-daddy.

He heated some beans and corned beef from his tinned supplies, did more exercises for his leg. Still feverish, quivering like an old man. But the fever was beginning to lift, clearing from his brain like mist.

A car stopped on the main road, then drove off, fading away. Big engine, but quiet. He was out by the kitchen door in an instant, crawling through bushes, a pistol tucked in his belt, the AK-47 cradled on his arm, ready to wipe out the human race.

It was Gloria, walking down through the woods in an olive-green jacket, her clean gold hair shining, stepping through sunlight like a tiger.

She paced around the cottage, tapping at the windows. 'You there, Billy?'

He stood up slowly among the bushes. She turned,

came over, eyes widening. 'Wild frontiersman,' she mocked, stroking the crisp edges of his beard.

He lowered his gun. She was alone. She began to explain. She had been hiding out in County Cork. Her father had sent a minder, who would come back for them tomorrow morning at six thirty. She showed two airline tickets to Los Angeles in the names of Mr Joseph Santini and Ms Karen Santini. The minder was fixing passports. She had brought some chocolate, in case Billy was starving to death. 'You don't mind being called Santini?'

'Starring Billy O'Rourke as Joe Santini, the lovable hoodlum,' he grinned and stretched his arms in a show-biz crucifixion.

It struck him for the first time, now, that he could simply let go. No need to hit Decko. No need to do anything. If he was working in Los Angeles, a year from now, what difference would it make if some fool called Declan Dowd was walking around Dublin or lying in his grave?

Maybe he was growing up at last. Cutting his losses. His life had been spent trying to fix what could never be fixed.

Gloria looked him up and down with shining eyes. 'What do you use for coffee, wild man?' she asked. She took off her jacket, hunched up on the sofa with her shoes slipped off. As employers go, Gloria was not bad. She was obviously planning to take advantage of him. Which was all right so long as it didn't get serious. Gloria could be the clingy type.

He filled the kettle, lit the camping gas. When he

turned around, Tom Stringer was braced at the door. As Billy reached for his pistol, Tom silently shot him.

'Steady wrist.' But he could not quite speak the words. When the first shot hits the heart, there is less bleeding. Billy knelt and Tom shot him again. Billy died.

Gloria stood shivering at the cottage door until the body had been wrapped in black plastic for disposal. Her eyes were blurred with tears, but she knew Billy's restless soul could never be tamed. What was the alternative? Sure, they could have found Billy a job with the family, but he would never blend in back home. Besides, he was crazy. Those weapons! When the beam had been broken at the arms dump, they'd had to change their plans, because Billy meant trouble. Which the syndicate did not need. Not now they'd gone in with Tom's people, and committed to invest in a mainstream medicinal drug production company, ready for the distribution battles of five, ten years down the line, when recreational drugs would be sold through pharmacies. It was going to be a multi-billion-dollar trade, based on quality, sanctioned by governments, protected by armies, legal and taxed, policed, profitable and safe. Not yet, but soon. Which made good sense, if it worked out. Billy made no sense. Why the tears, then? Just shock. She was too raw.

Tom backed the Chrysler Voyager to the cottage door, hefted the body from the house, laid it gently in the back of the vehicle along with the arms cache in its separate plastic wrapping. Back inside the cottage he wiped away the blood with a rag soaked in disinfectant, while Gloria brushed the floor. They drove to Dublin

Airport. Gloria, head clamped in a tight brown wig matching the photograph in her Canadian passport, mingled with departing tourists on an Aer Lingus flight to Chicago. Sonny would meet her. As Father said, he had made a real good recovery from his recent death.

She wore dark glasses, fell asleep, dreamed of the heart being torn from her chest by a famished black dog.

Ireland was such a bunch of grief.

Billy's body made its onward journey to a farmyard by the Border. A man stood waiting, his head haloed in dirty white hair, eyes bloodshot. Tom Stringer pulled up near the cattle-shed, counted out the money, helped the old man heave the cold bundle from the Voyager. Billy went down to a dark chamber under the shed, to rest with other light forgotten bones.